"What are you th
he finally asked

"I'm thinking about you, David," Christie replied. "I'm thinking you're an exceptional man . . . a very special man. I only wish . . ."

"Yes," he pressed. She only wished what? Whatever it was, he just knew it was something awful.

"I wish, well, what I'm trying to say is that I want more than we can have."

"You want more than we can have? Christie, we can have it all! Christie, I love you."

She shook her head. "It's not good enough, David. I just can't convince myself that we have a future. But, David . . . I love you, too. No matter how sensible I try to be, I just can't get around that. It makes fighting the odds seem almost worthwhile."

ABOUT THE AUTHOR

Toronto author Dawn Stewardson was born and raised in Winnipeg, Manitoba, the setting for *Heartbeat*. "When I depicted Winnipeg in this book," she told us, "I tried not to look at it with nostalgia. Rather, I wanted to show it through the eyes of my heroine, a native New Yorker. And from that point of view, the city of Winnipeg would look like nothing but a quiet backwater town. I only hope," she added, laughing, "that none of my Winnipeg friends or relatives have lost their sense of humor. Otherwise, I might be in for a rough time on my next visit."

Books by Dawn Stewardson

HARLEQUIN SUPERROMANCE
355–DEEP SECRETS
383–BLUE MOON
405–PRIZE PASSAGE

HARLEQUIN INTRIGUE
80–PERIL IN PARADISE
90–NO RHYME OR REASON

Heartbeat

DAWN STEWARDSON

Harlequin Books

TORONTO • NEW YORK • LONDON
AMSTERDAM • PARIS • SYDNEY • HAMBURG
STOCKHOLM • ATHENS • TOKYO • MILAN

Published June 1990

ISBN 0-373-70409-7

Printed in U.S.A.

To the residents of Winnipeg, Manitoba
(including my parents),
who know it's a good place to live in
and that the forty-below spells
don't really last forever.
And to my husband, John,
who once made the mistake of wearing
a leather coat to Winnipeg at Christmas.
It froze stiff.

CHAPTER ONE

"THAT ONE'S red clover—with some Oregon grape root and a little figwort."

The man gave Christie another dim glance.

Wonderful. The sign on the wall might read Welcome to Canada, but if the entire population proved to be as welcoming as Mr. Canada Customs, she was going to have one terrific weekend.

She sneaked a peek at her watch and her anxiety level inched upward. The rate things were going, she might be spending her terrific weekend in the Toronto airport.

"And what have we got here?"

Christie glanced at the officer again. He'd removed most of the Baggies from the surface layer in her suitcase, uncovering the jar she'd wrapped her jeans around for safety.

"That's a mixture of Peruvian balsam powder, zinc stearate and slippery elm powder."

"What?"

"It's soothing. My father gets a recurring rash."

"Yeah? It's an awfully large quantity to soothe a rash, isn't it?"

Christie bit her tongue, certain that protesting her father was an awfully large man wouldn't go over well. If this fellow had a sense of humor, he apparently didn't bring it to work.

He lifted the jar from her case and held it up to the light, his expression suspicious. An uneasy feeling settled in Christie's stomach. The jar *was* awfully large. A giant-size peanut butter jar full of powder would last forever. But surely he wasn't wondering whether...surely just because the powder was white he wasn't thinking...well, maybe she'd better do a little explaining.

"I'm a naturopath. And I'm bringing all of these things with me because—" She paused. The officer was looking at her as if she'd told him she was an alien creature. "Naturopathy," she tried again. "You know? Alternative medicine? The healing power of nature? A degree takes four years of studies—subjects like nutrition, acupuncture—"

"Acupuncture? You mean you've got needles in here, too? As well as these drugs?"

She almost groaned out loud. Talk about foot-in-mouth disease. "No. No needles. And, as I said before, these aren't drugs. They're herbal remedies...all for my father. It's easy to get them in Manhattan, but I don't know how he'll make out in Winnipeg."

How will *he make out in Winnipeg?* she silently asked herself as the officer grunted and went back to rummaging in her case. But how well her father would make out in the city was only part of what was worrying her. There was also the question of how he'd make out with Kay Russell.

Based on Kay's brief visit to New York, she seemed like a perfectly lovely woman. But did a refined widow who'd been married to a doctor have any idea of what her life would be like with a not-so-refined retired homicide detective?

Not that Sid Lambert wasn't a wonderful man. But he was definitely a little rough around the edges. And the first time five-foot-tall Kay tried to drag Christie's six-foot-two father to a symphony... well...

"I think I'll just run a quick test on this powder."

Christie's attention riveted back to the man. "A test?"

"This looks as if it might contain a narcotic."

Oh, no! He *had* been wondering! A little voice inside her head began shouting about her being an idiot.

She stared at the jar, admitting to herself that she *was* an idiot. Well, maybe not exactly an idiot, but she certainly hadn't been thinking when she'd packed. She hadn't needed a passport to visit Canada, and the thought of a customs check hadn't even crossed her mind.

She glanced back at the man. He was watching her intently. Clearly, as far as he was concerned, she was only one drug test away from being arrested.

She smiled at him so broadly that her cheeks hurt. "Look, that really is a remedy for skin irritations. You can smell it. Or taste it. It won't hurt you a bit."

"We aren't allowed to smell or taste powdered substances. I'll just find a test kit and—"

"But my flight to Winnipeg leaves in ten minutes."

"Sorry. Your airline should have allowed sufficient connecting time to clear customs."

Oh, Lord! A weekend in the Toronto airport was seeming more likely by the second. And if she missed the plane, if Daddy's only child wasn't at his wedding, he'd have a fit.

"I . . . it's awfully important that I catch my flight. So maybe I'd better just leave the jar here. Would that be okay?"

"'Fraid not. I have to ascertain that this isn't a controlled substance. But the test doesn't take long." The man bent down and searched beneath his counter.

"Don't seem to have the right kit. Wait here while I find one." He sauntered off toward an office.

Christie checked her watch again and admitted defeat. Undoubtedly she'd already gone from catching her connecting flight to missing it. She felt a major pang of guilt. She should have booked an earlier departure from La Guardia. Or made the trip last night. Maybe, subconsciously, she'd actually wanted to miss the wedding.

But, consciously at least, she'd been determined to set aside her misgivings and put up a good front. Now she wouldn't even be putting in an appearance. Unless there was a seat on a later flight and she could phone ahead and explain and her father and Kay wouldn't mind delaying the ceremony a little and this custom officer's test kit didn't mistake herbs for narcotics. But what if it did?

Go directly to jail. Do not pass go. What? Why were Monopoly instructions suddenly racing around inside her head? Her powder was a perfectly innocuous mixture.

She spotted the officer heading back and anxiously watched him approach, unable to stop wondering whether Canadian jails were anything like the hell-holes Turkish prisons were purported to be.

He plunked a small white box down on the counter. Its navy blue print, proclaiming it was a Narcotics

Identification System, struck an extremely menacing chord in Christie's imagination.

"Those...those tests are fairly accurate, aren't they?"

"Absolutely accurate," he assured her, unscrewing the top from her peanut butter jar.

Absolutely? No way. Fairly accurate, she'd believe, but not absolutely. Her father might have been in Homicide rather than Narcotics, but she knew that "absolutely accurate" drug tests didn't exist. Even the dogs occasionally mis-sniffed oregano as marijuana.

The officer opened the box and pulled out a little plastic bag containing three tiny vials. "I simply put a sample of your powder in the bag...like so. Now I'll seal the top and, when I break the vials, we'll see if the liquid changes from pink to blue."

"And if it does?"

"Then what we'd have here is cocaine."

No. What they'd have here would be inaccurate test results. But what Christie Lambert would have here would be big trouble. She held her breath, praying the color remained pale pink.

He snapped the vials in half.

Still pink. Not a trace of blue. Well, of course not! She'd known everything would be fine. She smiled with relief.

The man almost smiled back and began rescrewing the top onto her jar. "Sorry for the delay. You're free to proceed now. Have a nice day."

Have a nice day. Sure. But maybe she still had enough time. She threw everything back into her case, then raced past a sign that read Connecting Passengers.

As she ran, she became conscious of a throaty roar. In some mysterious manner, despite the surrounding din, her ears had picked out that one particular noise.

She slowed to a walk, not a doubt in her mind that she was listening to her flight departing.

DAVID SIPPED his champagne, feeling marginally self-conscious about being on his own. He hadn't expected the noon wedding to be postponed until two o'clock and he'd run out of small talk an hour ago.

He surveyed the familiar living room, thinking about how much time he'd spent at Kay Russell's—initially as her late husband's intern, then as his colleague and, finally, as their daughter's fiancé.

It had been several months, though, since he'd been here—several months since he and Holly...

He glanced across at her. She was talking to her new husband, Mac McCloy.

Back in December, when Holly and Kay had left for their Christmas cruise, he certainly hadn't expected his fiancé to arrive back home in love with someone else.

Strange that when she had, he hadn't been more upset. Of course, by that point, both of them had realized there was something missing from their relationship. So even if Mac hadn't appeared in Holly's life...

As David gazed at them, Mac smiled down at Holly with apparent adoration. They seemed incredibly happy together. And they made a nice-looking couple—Mac tall and dark, Holly tiny and red-haired.

Ginger, David corrected himself, focusing on Holly's hair. She'd always said it was ginger-colored.

He continued watching her for another moment, feeling the same peculiar sense of sadness mixed with relief that he'd felt when they'd broken up. And then he looked away.

Their breakup might not have devastated him, but watching Holly with Mac was making him more certain than ever that the *something missing* from their relationship had been something missing within him.

He liked women. But he seemed immune to the insane strain of romantic love that attacked other people. And, if he hadn't been struck down by thirty-four, he was awfully unlikely to ever . . .

David silently laughed at his musings. What sort of man would wish insanity on himself?

"Hi."

He glanced down. Mac's son was grinning up. "Hi, yourself, Jason."

"Mr. Lambert asked me to be messenger."

"He did? What's the message?"

"I'm supposed to tell everyone that his daughter, Christie—his *errant* daughter, Christie, he called her— is on her way from the airport. That the wedding's going to start soon."

"Good. Thanks for letting me know."

David watched the boy move on to repeat his message. Holly had gotten a ready-made son. And Jason undoubtedly wouldn't remain an only child.

If love was actually giving David a permanent pass, not having children would be one of his major regrets. He tried to shrug off the thought. With four siblings, he'd probably end up having nieces and nephews galore.

Besides, there was a lot to be said for the single life. Sometimes it even offered pleasant opportunities. He doubted this was going to be one of those times, though.

Why not come to the wedding alone? Kay had suggested. *Sid's daughter is coming and she's really a darling.*

But the longer he watched Kay looking at Sid Lambert with visible stars in her eyes, the more obvious it seemed that she'd think anyone remotely related to him was "darling."

With Sid for a father, though, it was difficult to believe Christie could possibly have a "darling" appearance. A twenty-seven-year-old female version of the retired NYPD detective was difficult to even imagine.

When David had first heard about the man Kay had met on that cruise, Sid had been described as an oversized Kojak. And, except for the absence of a lollipop, the description fit perfectly.

If Christie Lambert took after her father in the appearance department, she certainly wouldn't have many problems with New York muggers. Of course, she probably wasn't bald, but David wouldn't bet against her resembling a Jets linebacker.

And, given some of the comments Sid had been dropping, she could be the epitome of overzealous flakiness. Herbal therapies might have their place, but she apparently had her father downing so many plant products that it was a wonder he wasn't sprouting leaves.

Outside, a car squealed to a stop, and Sid and Kay hurried to the front door.

David casually wandered a little closer to the hallway, wondering why he was so curious about Christie Lambert, telling himself it was simply because she'd be the only single woman under fifty at the wedding.

Of course, she'd also be the only woman who'd look like Kojak in drag, so...

A vision appeared in the living room doorway.

David blinked.

The vision was still there, firmly ensconced on Sid's arm. A vision in a pale yellow silk dress the precise color of her hair.

David stared in disbelief. This gorgeous, eminently unflaky-looking woman must be Christie.

Yes. Sid was introducing her as his daughter, leading her slowly from one guest to another.

David scrambled through every detail he could recall about genetics and decided Christie Lambert had to be adopted. That was the only logical explanation. Surely it was impossible for Sid to have fathered a woman who looked like a young Candice Bergen. Wasn't it?

Well... maybe not impossible. Christie *was* tall—five foot seven or eight. But she certainly didn't have Sid's build. She couldn't weigh more than a hundred and twenty pounds, and her long, slender legs definitely said, Cheerleader, not Football Player.

She did have blue eyes like Sid's, though. Well, no, that wasn't quite accurate. Their both being blue was all the two sets of eyes had in common. Christie's were enormous. And an incredible shade of cornflower blue.

She smiled at the man Sid was introducing her to and David noticed her lips. They were the most eminently kissable lips he'd ever seen. And she had a dimple! He couldn't remember seeing a dimple in years—thought they'd disappeared with back-combed hair.

But her long hair definitely wasn't back-combed. It hung loosely, like soft corn silk framing her face.

Sid and Christie stopped in front of David. "And this is David Lawrence. My daughter, Christie."

He took her hand. It was the softest hand in the world. And her face projected the most intriguing combination of sensuality and innocence. Where was the New York toughness he'd been expecting?

"It's nice to meet you, David."

Oh, God! She had the husky voice of a young Lauren Bacall. But why was he comparing her to Candice Bergen and Lauren Bacall? He'd been spending far too many nights alone, watching late movies. Christie Lambert wasn't a celluloid star on *Midnight Cinema*. She was live and here and now... and she was looking at him as if he were a simpleton....

Of course. He was supposed to say something appropriate. "Ah...yes. It's nice to meet you, too, Christie." He reluctantly released her hand.

Sid dragged her on to the next person, leaving David with only the lingering scent of her enticing perfume and a heart that was doing flip-flops.

Doing what? Hearts didn't do flip-flops. He was a cardiologist and he knew all about what hearts did and didn't do. But his was definitely doing something abnormal.

He stood staring at Christie, trying to figure out what had just happened to him. The only explanation he could come up with was that looking at Christie Lambert had triggered a hormonal release in his system—some strange heart hormones he'd never heard of.

But, no. What he was thinking made no sense. He was the guy who wasn't capable of love at all, let alone love at first sight. And the heart was a critical human organ—not a target for Cupid's arrows.

So why did he feel as if he'd just been hit by the proverbial ton of bricks?

CHRISTIE SMILED at the man her father was introducing her to, then glanced surreptitiously back at David Lawrence. He was still watching her.

And her initial impression had been accurate. He was the most gorgeous hunk she'd seen in...in...well, actually, she couldn't recall ever seeing a more gorgeous one. And dressed to kill—a navy blue pinstripe straight out of an ad for Giorgio Armani suits.

What was a man who looked as if he were about to take Madison Avenue by storm doing in a backwater Canadian town of half a million people?

Who was he? She'd recognized his name. Either her father or Kay had mentioned it. But where did he fit into the cast of characters she'd heard about but was only now meeting?

"And," her father said, "this is Holly, of course."

Christie smiled down at Holly. *Of course*—a younger version of Kay with the same large hazel eyes. And Holly was every inch as petite as her mother. They were the sort of women who made Christie feel like an Amazon. She wished she were wearing flats.

"It's good to finally meet you, Christie. And this is my husband, Mac McCloy...and my stepson, Jason."

Christie said "Hello" to the little boy, then focused on Mac. So this was the architect Holly had fallen head over heels for on that darn cruise. The same darn cruise Christie had practically twisted her father's arm to make him go on. The same darn cruise he'd met Kay on.

Someday Christie was going to learn to mind her own business. The way things had turned out, she might as well have twisted his arm to make him book himself onto the Love Boat for two weeks.

He'd gone on a Christmas cruise and now, barely into April, he was giving up his home and friends for Kay. And Holly had already broken her engagement, married Mac and moved to Colorado where he—

Holly's fiancé! That's who David Lawrence was. Or had been.

Christie eyed Mac McCloy again. Not bad. Not bad at all if your taste ran to tall, dark and handsome. And, actually, that was the direction hers generally ran. But, all of a sudden, tall, blond and blue-eyed seemed incredibly appealing.

Strange. She usually thought blond men looked wimpy. Out of the corner of her eye she checked David again.

Nope. Definitely not wimpy-looking. Must be his broad shoulders. Or maybe it was his rugged, square jaw that had made her pulse race. She was a sucker for a strong jaw, and his looked as if it had been carved from granite. And his nose was evenly chiseled out of rock, as well.

She followed her father along to the next person, wondering if Holly McCloy needed her head read.

With a fraction of her attention, Christie smiled appropriately at the final few people she was introduced to. There was something wrong with David Lawrence. She couldn't recall what it was, but she was sure Kay had mentioned something unfortunate about him.

Christie concentrated on remembering. She mustn't have been paying attention, but her brain wasn't a sieve. She tried to recall the conversation in detail.

He was a doctor! Damn! That was it. That hunk was a doctor. What a waste.

Of course, 99.9 percent of women surveyed wouldn't share her negative opinion of doctors—if the survey was limited to women who didn't work in the health care field, that is.

Those who did, though, knew what an egotistical bunch of know-it-alls doctors were. They seldom even got through pre-med before the Doctor-is-God syndrome struck.

So David Lawrence undoubtedly had a superiority complex the size of a hospital ward. And, if he was like the vast majority of physicians, he'd believe naturopaths were part of the lunatic fringe.

But what difference did either of those two negatives make to her? She wasn't in Winnipeg to play "three strikes and you're out." She was only here for the wedding.

The clergyman positioned himself before the fireplace and cleared his throat.

"This is it, baby," Sid whispered, bending to peck Christie's cheek. "I'm so glad you're here."

A giant lump suddenly formed in her throat. She tried to swallow it away. Impossible. She could barely even swallow past it. What was she going to do with her father living so far from New York?

She watched him walk across to stand in front of the minister, telling herself Kay would make him happy. But how could he be happy up here in the northern boonies? Winnipeg didn't even have major league baseball. As far as that went, Canada's national sport was probably snowshoeing. And, aside from Kay, he barely knew a soul.

The guests began arranging themselves in a semicircle, and Mac McCloy, her father's best man, joined him by the fireplace.

"Mind if I stand beside you, Christie? We seem to be the only two people here on our own."

Christie glanced to her left. David Lawrence was smiling down at her. Most men weren't tall enough to do that.

She managed to smile back. It would be rude not to. Especially when his smile looked genuinely friendly.

Music began drifting across the room—strains of Handel's *Water Music*—and Holly appeared in the living room doorway, carrying a small bouquet.

Moments later Kay followed her daughter into the room. She paused for a moment, gazing across at Sid.

Christie's eyes misted over. She clenched her fists, determined not to cry, and glanced back at her father. He was looking at Kay...smiling the way he used to smile at Christie's mother.

She felt her tears spilling and blinked rapidly, trying unsuccessfully to contain them. She didn't want to cry, didn't want to do anything to spoil the wedding. But she wished her father wasn't remarrying. No...what she desperately wished was that her mother wasn't dead.

The ceremony was beginning. Christie tried to concentrate on what the minister was saying, but all she could think about was her mother dying, about how awful those weeks in the hospital had been for her and—

Oh, no! She was sniffling so loudly that everyone in the room must be able to hear her. But she simply couldn't help it.

David reached across, took her hand and gently uncurled her fingers from the fist she'd made. "Hey," he whispered, squeezing her hand in his, "take it easy. Weddings are supposed to be happy."

FROM INSIDE, strains of the postceremony music drifted out to the deck behind Kay's house.

"You okay now?" David asked, looking closely at Christie. Her eyes were still luminous with tears.

She nodded. "Thanks for hustling me out here. Without you I'd probably still be standing in there making a complete fool of myself."

"You weren't making a fool of yourself, Christie. A lot of people cry at weddings."

"I know. But I was so determined to keep a smile on my face and then...well, I couldn't help thinking about my mother and..." A stray tear made good its escape.

Without thinking, David reached across and brushed it away.

She gave him a sad little smile. "It's so silly. My mother's been dead for over four years. But not a single day goes by without me thinking about her."

"I know. And it isn't silly. My father died three years ago. My mother hasn't remarried, but I can imagine what you're feeling. There are bad days—Christmas, their anniversary. I guess this must be one of the worst for you." He wished there was something more he could say. She looked so fragile, so vulnerable.

Christie gazed at David for a moment, grateful that an understanding someone had been on hand when she'd needed one. Then she turned to look out over the backyard, focusing on the surroundings, trying to compose herself. She'd only need a minute or two. At least, after all this time, sad thoughts about her mother rarely lingered for long.

The afternoon was surprisingly warm, but Kay's lawn was dull, lifeless brown. At home Central Park was already lushly green.

"It'll be beautiful in another month," David offered. "I guess spring arrives a little later here than it does in New York."

She glanced back at him, managing a smile. "You must be a mind reader."

"Not really. I'm just aware of the vicious rumors about Winnipeg being within shouting distance of the North Pole."

"And it isn't?" she teased, her smile feeling less forced.

"No. It's not even a hundred miles north of the Minnesota border."

"Ah. Practically in the banana belt, then. Dad's geography must be off. He told me he was expecting eight months of winter and four months of poor sledding."

"He's got it wrong. It's actually nine months of winter. That's why half the players in the National Hockey League come from Manitoba."

She laughed quietly. Only moments ago she wouldn't have believed she'd ever laugh again. David was amazing. How could a man she scarcely knew say the right things to help chase away her blues?

She glanced at the back door, knowing she couldn't stay outside much longer. "I guess," she murmured reluctantly, "I'd better go in and join the party. I don't want Dad and Kay to think I'm unhappy about their getting married."

"You shouldn't be, Christie. Kay's a terrific lady."

"I know she is. I only wish I could stop worrying about what Daddy's going to do with himself in a strange city. At home he spent a lot of time with his old police department buddies."

"He'll make out all right."

"I hope so. I just keep having nightmares about him building snowmen for company. But, at any rate, thanks for cheering me up. I . . . I'm glad we met."

"Me, too."

Christie unwillingly reached for the door handle.

"Christie?"

Her heart skipped a beat. She turned back and silently waited for David to continue, hoping she seemed more casual than she felt.

"I imagine you'll be spending the evening with your father and Kay?"

"No. I'd never crash anyone's wedding night. I'm seeing them in the morning—for breakfast. Their flight to Barbados doesn't leave until the afternoon. And neither does mine to New York. But all I'm doing after the reception is checking into my hotel."

David's smile swept her in a wave of warmth, making her feel the most incredibly strong . . .

No. Crazy. Can't fall in love on a look. It was merely his kindness that was making her—

"Would you like to have dinner with me then, Christie?"

She couldn't help smiling again. David Lawrence didn't fit her doctor stereotype at all. The gargantuan ego she'd expected him to have simply didn't exist. In fact, he was looking at her as if he were anticipating rejection.

"Yes. Dinner. Yes, I'd like that." In fact, she'd like it a whole lot. Until now she'd been thinking the McCloy's plans made sense. They were flying home to Denver tonight.

But, suddenly, Christie was very glad she'd decided to stay over.

CHAPTER TWO

"GOOD NIGHT, Mrs. Lambert. I hope everything was satisfactory."

"Everything was absolutely perfect. And thank you for staying so late."

Kay closed the front door behind the caterer. Mrs. Lambert. That was going to take getting used to. When Bill had died, she'd been certain her emotions had died with him.

But here she was, so crazy about Sid that she sometimes pinched herself to be certain he wasn't part of a dream. She was one of the lucky ones, finding twice what some people never found once.

She snapped the lock on, then turned back to the living room and smiled across at Sid. He looked tired, sitting there—or perhaps merely pensive.

He patted the couch. "Come and sit with me for a few minutes, Mrs. Lambert. It's been a long day."

"Long, as in tedious?" she teased.

"Tedious? Marrying you? Not a chance. Just long, as in I thought the guests would never leave."

Sid drew her down beside him once she'd crossed the room, then gently kissed her, sending tiny tingles racing through her. When the kiss ended, she snuggled against him, feeling loved and safe in the shelter of his arms. At her age she wouldn't have thought she'd still respond to a man this way. Sid made her feel like a teenager all over again.

"Happy, Kay?"

"Incredibly."

"That's good. Me, too. Even simply sitting here, holding you, makes me happy. Let's just relax and talk for awhile before we go upstairs."

Kay gazed at his face, wondering if he was feeling even a fraction as anxious as she was. Maybe so. It was difficult to tell with men—especially with Sid. He never looked the least bit nervous about anything.

But a wedding night was hardly a run-of-the-mill anything. And probably for a sixty-year-old man... well, sitting and talking a little was undoubtedly a good idea for both of them. With any luck, some of the butterflies inside her stomach would flutter off.

No wonder Holly called her Nervous Nellie. Right now she was nervous about going upstairs...about making love with Sid for the first time...about their future.

Maybe fifty-seven was too old to be starting a new life. Although she didn't feel old. Not in the least. In fact, she was often taken aback when she glanced into a mirror, surprised at being reminded that her ginger hair had faded to the color of pale sherry, that her face had developed tiny wrinkles.

But those things didn't matter. Sid loved her.

She looked up at him. "Do you think everyone enjoyed the wedding, dear?"

"They must have. The invitations said noon till six. Here it is past midnight and we're barely rid of the last of them."

"But what about Christie? She seemed awfully upset during the ceremony. She isn't unhappy that you and I...?"

"Naw. Nothing like that, Kay. Christie likes you. You know how women cry at weddings."

"But she left so early."

"She knew we wanted to be alone. If everyone else had been as sensitive to our feelings, we'd have been in bed hours ago." Sid gave Kay such an exaggerated leer that she laughed.

"You're trying to change the subject, dear. But are you sure Christie wasn't really upset? I'd hate to think she disapproved. Or maybe...do you suppose she made plans for the evening with David?"

"David?"

"Yes. I was hoping they'd like each other. And they seemed to. You noticed that they left together, didn't you? David was standing right beside her when you kissed her goodbye. He'd offered to drive her to the hotel. Do you think, maybe...?"

"Christie and David? No. Never. Working at the clinic, she meets a fair number of doctors—consultants mostly. But she never dates them. She's got a thing about them—about doctors and hospitals and the health care system in general."

"What do you mean, 'a thing'?"

"It...it's a long story."

Kay cuddled more closely to Sid. "That's all right. We need to take time to unwind. And you've got me curious."

"Well, it's just that Christie originally intended to be a nurse. She almost graduated, in fact. But she got turned off by the system—decided modern medicine sometimes does more harm than good. That's how she ended up studying naturopathy. She was looking for an alternative.''

''I see. I wondered how she'd gotten into the field. It's such an unusual...it's so...so...'' Kay paused, at a loss for words. She could hardly call Christie's profession *quackery*.

''Naturopathy's not as weird as people tend to believe,'' Sid offered, rescuing her from her discomfort. ''It's mainly that instead of focusing on symptoms, the way doctors do, naturopaths focus on the underlying roots of health problems—emotional, physical and environmental factors. And they use natural remedies instead of prescription drugs—or 'chemicals,' as Christie calls them.''

''And the remedies work? All those vitamins she has you taking actually do something? And all the herbs and powders she brought for you?''

Sid laughed. ''I'm honestly not sure. I used to be as skeptical as you just sounded. And I only started taking those things to make Christie happy—figured a few vitamins and plant leaves couldn't hurt me. I did start feeling healthier after a while, though. So who knows? And Christie swears by her approach. I suspect the only way you'd get her into a doctor's office would be to drag her.''

''That's ironic, isn't it? After her studying nursing, I mean. What made her drop out?''

''Kay...it had to do with her mother's death.... Look, honey, I don't want to get into this. And I'm sure it's not something you want to hear about on our wedding night. I shouldn't even have mentioned it.''

''It's all right, Sid. I asked the question. And we can't spend our life together trying to tiptoe around our pasts.''

"Tiptoeing? Me? That's pretty unlikely when I weigh more than two hundred pounds."

"Yes. I've been meaning to talk to you about that extra weight." She poked Sid playfully in his paunch.

He winced. She stopped breathing for a moment.

"Are you all right, dear?"

"Fine."

"You're sure?"

"Sure I'm sure. It's just indigestion."

Of course. Indigestion. Kay ordered her fears away, recognizing them for the exaggerated reaction they were.

When she'd belonged to her bereavement group, they'd talked about hundreds of problems that might arise in the future. And this was one of them. Because Bill had died of a heart attack, fearing Sid might do the same thing was to be expected—even though it might be irrational.

She glanced back at him. He didn't look well. She tried to convince herself that was simply her imagination but couldn't manage to do it.

"Sid?"

"Mmm?"

"This indigestion . . . do you get it often?"

"No. It's probably from drinking champagne when I'm used to beer."

"What does it feel like?"

"Kay, getting married didn't instantly transform you into a nag, did it?"

"Sorry, Sid. I'm just worried about you."

He smiled at her. "Sorry, myself. I should be glad you care. Guess I'm going to have to get used to it. But all I've got is a minor pain in my chest."

"In your chest?" The words came out a whisper. "Where? Exactly where?"

Sid tapped the left side of his chest. Kay's mouth went dry.

"Kay, it's not really a pain. Only a little pressure...a little tightness. Simply indigestion."

"Does it feel like someone's sitting on your chest?" she managed.

"I guess you could describe it like that. But not a very big someone."

"Sid...just in case this is serious...I think I should take you to the hospital."

"The hospital? Kay, I'll try to get used to you worrying about me, but let's not be absurd."

"But, Sid, I..."

Sid took both her hands in his. "Honey, I understand. I realize that after Bill...that your being overly concerned isn't surprising. But I'm not about to have a heart attack."

"Sid, in case—"

"Kay. If you think that when I've married a woman who insisted on waiting until her wedding night...if you think I'm going to spend that wedding night in an emergency room instead of in bed with my wife—"

"Sid, let's call David, then. You could describe your symptoms and—"

"Kay, honey, I don't have symptoms. I have indigestion. And I also have an overwhelming desire to make love to you. I love you, Kay. So come upstairs with me and stop worrying. The last thing in the world I intend to do, when I've barely found you, is die."

Kay tried unsuccessfully to smile. Sid's face seemed to be growing paler by the moment. And she wasn't

certain, but she suspected he was having a little difficulty breathing.

She'd feel a million times better if he'd listen to
her...if he'd at least let her phone David. But that
idea, she supposed, was an assault on Sid Lambert's
macho self-image.

She followed him up the stairs, thinking about how
stubborn he was, how bullheaded, how—

At the top stair, Sid suddenly sat down. His hand
went to his chest and an expression of pain crossed his
face. "Geez, Kay," he muttered, his voice hoarse.
"This is the worst case of indigestion I've ever had."

"So, the naturopathic college gave me credit for most
of the nursing courses I'd completed—ones like biology, psychology and anatomy. And that meant I only
had to take the more esoteric subjects."

"Such as?" David prompted. He could listen to
Christie's voice all night.

"Oh, such as acupuncture, massage and botanical
medicine."

"And after you graduated?"

"I've been at the Manhattan Health Styles Clinic
ever since. It gives me a nice variety, working with in-
dividual patients but also running programs on things
like family planning, stress management, general nutrition—practically everything and anything. But tell
me more about you, David. Except for what you've
said about your work, I've been doing all the talking.
Tell me about your family."

"Well, there are five of us. I'm the oldest and there
are two other boys and two girls. One of my sisters

lives in Vancouver now, and one of my brothers is in Toronto. The rest of us, and my mother, are still in Winnipeg."

"That's all I get? I don't even get names?"

"You wouldn't remember them."

She gave him a delicious-looking smile. "I might. And it hardly seems fair that all I get is a bare-bones family sketch after I told you the entire Christie Lambert life story."

"I wish I'd known it earlier—before I brought a vegetarian to a steak house for dinner."

"Well, I'm not a fanatic about what I don't eat, David. Mostly I just avoid red meat. Besides, the shrimps were wonderful...and the salad...and the company."

He continued to gaze at Christie for a moment after she stopped speaking, still scarcely able to believe she was real. She couldn't conceivably be as fantastic as she seemed—because she seemed to be the most incredible woman he'd ever met. She was gorgeous and funny and sexy...and flying back to New York tomorrow.

And that final fact, he firmly reminded himself, undoubtedly added greatly to her appeal.

He knew enough basic psychiatry to realize what was going on inside his head. Christie Lambert was an extremely attractive woman who'd walked into his life during one of his rare introspective moments. He'd been brooding about his inability to love and boom! There she'd been.

And the way he'd reacted, she might have been the legendary stranger across a crowded room—straight out of *South Pacific*'s "Some Enchanted Evening."

But what he'd felt the first moment he saw her, what he was still feeling, was merely the result of his subconscious trying to bolster his self-esteem, trying to reassure him that he was capable of falling for a woman as hard as any man had ever fallen.

Because his subconscious realized that Christie Lambert was perfectly safe to fall for. There was no possibility of a long-term relationship with her—a relationship that would end when he was finally forced to admit to himself that he didn't really love her, when he once again had to face the fact that he lacked the capacity to love.

She caught him watching her and smiled. "What are you thinking about, David?"

"Oh . . . just wondering if you'd be coming to visit your father very often."

What? Had he really been wondering that? Not consciously he hadn't been. She lived two thousand miles away. The prospect of seeing her again was awfully remote . . . but maybe he shouldn't be so darn certain what his subconscious was up to, after all.

"I'll be visiting Dad now and then, I guess."

He realized he was fidgeting with his empty wineglass and put it down. "You'll be coming back on your own?"

"I imagine so."

She offered nothing more.

Well, what did he expect? He should have come right out and asked what he wanted to know instead of starting a silly cat-and-mouse game.

"I . . . look, Christie, my real question is whether or not you're involved with anyone."

He held his breath. The odds against a woman like Christie not being involved were about a million to one—unless the entire male population of New York was crazy.

"No, David," she said quietly. "I'm not involved with anyone."

One in a million! He should rush out and buy a lottery ticket while he was on a roll.

She was smiling across the table at him. "You look surprised."

"That's because I am."

"Well, New York isn't the most ideal city in the world for meeting men—not men I want much to do with, at least. We're overloaded with aspiring Broadway stars and Wall Street wizards."

"And you're not into either the theater or money?" David teased.

Christie laughed. "You're being obtuse. I love the theater. But actors are generally either gay or in love with themselves or both. And the financial crowd works eighteen hours a day at making money and does drugs to keep going. I'll admit there's an occasional straight, relatively normal man but . . ."

The waiter materialized and slipped their bill onto the table.

Christie glanced at her watch. "Did you realize it's past midnight, David? We've been here for over four hours."

Four hours? How could four hours have seemed like four minutes?

"Your car won't have turned into a pumpkin, will it?"

"It never has before." Of course, he'd never had a *before* anything like this.

David paid the bill, collected Christie's coat from the checkroom and they started down the stairs.

Halfway down, he caught himself glancing back to be sure she hadn't lost a glass slipper.

His mind was going! If he didn't concentrate, he'd be asking the valet to get his pumpkin instead of his Mercedes.

The young man saw them coming, nodded to David, then dashed outside. A few minutes later he reappeared—the shoulders of his dark jacket lightly dusted in white.

Christie eyed him curiously. "It's not snowing out there, is it?"

"Sure is. Started a couple of hours ago."

She grinned at David. "And you were trying to convince me Winnipeg isn't part of the frozen tundra?"

"Just a freak spring storm, Christie. They happen here sometimes."

"In April? When the apple blossoms are already blooming in New York?"

"What color are they?"

"Some pink, some white."

"Well, then, there's no problem. Just pretend. White petals, white flakes. Use your imagination and you won't even notice it's dipped below freezing."

Christie paused in the doorway and began laughing. "David, I'm pushing my imagination to the limit, but my shoes still don't have any toes in them. And those cold white petals on the sidewalk are a good two inches deep."

David stepped past her. "Put your arms around my neck."

"What?"

"Come on. It's an old Eskimo trick."

"You don't look much like an old Eskimo to me, David."

"What do New Yorkers know about Eskimos? Just do as you're told."

Tentatively Christie obeyed.

Feeling like a reincarnation of Rhett Butler, David scooped her up in his arms and swept her outside. By the time he reached the car, she'd collapsed against his shoulder in a fit of giggles.

He struggled with the door handle, wondering what on earth had possessed him to risk a hernia, praying that he wouldn't drop her. Dumping her on her keister onto the snowy sidewalk would certainly be a wonderful climax to a romantic gesture. He managed to get the door open and maneuvered Christie inside. She was still giggling, her arms around his neck, her hair softly tickling his cheek.

"You're right, David," she admitted as he settled her in. "I don't know a thing about Eskimos. But I suspect I'd really like them."

David drew back a little—just far enough so that he could see her face. She smiled at him. In the glow of the car's light it seemed the most come-hither smile he'd ever seen. And her lips were irresistible.

He leaned forward again and kissed her. When she kissed him back, he knew it was the kiss he'd been waiting for all his life.

It was fireworks exploding and whistles blowing and sirens wailing. And Christie Lambert, warm and responsive against him, was the most delectable woman he'd ever held.

She tasted impossibly wonderful...and she felt, God, he couldn't think straight with her so close...so soft and desirable in his embrace.

He felt like...he felt like...there *was* no *like*. What he was feeling was like nothing he'd ever felt before...and he wanted the feeling never to end.

Vaguely he realized it would have to—that he couldn't spend the rest of his life standing in the street outside Hy's Steak Loft, half in and half out of his car.

Reluctantly he pulled away. Christie clung to him. Well...maybe he *could* give spending the rest of his life here a shot.

"David?" she whispered.

"Mmm?"

"David, do you know any more old Eskimo tricks?"

FROM THE DOORMAN and parking attendant to its marble foyer, David's building exuded elegance. A glass-paneled elevator whisked them up and opened onto a lushly carpeted hall. Its walls were sheathed in grass cloth and decorated with elegant prints.

Once inside his apartment, David closed the door behind them, banishing the hallway's muted light. Christie blinked, trying to adjust her vision to the darkness. The vestibule was pitch-black but, on the far side of the living room, moonlight was flooding through French doors.

David took her hand firmly in his and started across the shadowy room. "Come on. I want you to see the view from outside."

Beyond the shelter of his balcony, the odd snowflake was still drifting downward. Four stories beneath them the scene was a nighttime winter wonderland—a riverbank blanketed with pristine, shimmering snow, dropping off to a wide stretch of blackly flowing water. Moonbeams danced on the river's tiny ripples.

Christie stared down, intensely aware of David's hand holding hers. She hadn't wanted the evening to end, but she was far from certain that coming to his apartment had been a wise idea.

She was breaking all her rules tonight...well, no, she wasn't going to break *all* her rules, even though the thought of breaking them with David Lawrence was awfully tempting. His kiss had shaken her...or, rather, her reaction to it had shaken her. Even now, just standing beside him in the moonlight, her heart was racing.

"What do you think, Christie?"

What did she think? She thought he was the most exciting man she'd— No. He was referring to the view.

"It's beautiful, David. You were right. Looking out over this river is like being in the country."

"Did you think I was lying to you?" he teased. "Have I ever lied to you before?"

"A girl never knows." She gazed down at the river again. "From my apartment all I can see are bright city lights. And the noise of traffic never stops. Have you been to New York, David? We've spent so much time talking about me that I haven't even asked you that."

"I've been there a few times."

"Like it?"

"Well...well, it's a fascinating city."

"Yes. But do you like it?"

"The truth?"

"Of course. No point in starting to lie to me now," she added, smiling at him. Every time she looked at him she felt like smiling.

"Well, the truth is that it strikes me as *too* everything—too intense, too fast, too dangerous."

"It's not nearly as bad as its press, David."

"No. Probably not. But for a lot of people—me included—it's more than a little overwhelming. I suspect the saying about it being a nice place to visit but I wouldn't want to live there originally referred to New York." He shrugged apologetically for criticizing her city.

She should probably say something in its defense, but her brain seemed to have switched onto pause, mesmerized by the way David was gazing at her. If he kept watching her like that, she was going to melt. Even if it *was* below freezing out here.

She felt a surge of disappointment when he turned, without kissing her, and ushered her back inside. He flicked on a dim light. "Here, let me take your coat."

"I . . ."

David slipped the coat from her shoulders, then nodded toward the fireplace. "There's a fire set. Why don't you sit down while I light it . . . and open a bottle of wine?"

"Well . . ."

"Fine."

Fine. Right. Everything would be fine. They'd just sit on this chocolate leather couch, in this sunken conversation pit in front of the fire and drink a little wine and . . . and undoubtedly test her willpower as it had never been tested before.

David lit the fire, then disappeared. Christie glanced around. The living room was a clear statement of masculinity—wood, leather, a brown carpet so deep that she'd sunk to her ankles in it, and that gorgeous brick fireplace. Her entire Manhattan apartment would fit twice into this one room.

David could clearly afford the best—designer suits, a pricey apartment, his silver Mercedes. If it weren't for those trappings, she might forget that he was a doctor.

Not that it really mattered what he was. Being realistic, she knew she'd probably never see him again. By the next time she came to Winnipeg, he'd have forgotten about her.

That thought brought a strong twinge of regret. Strange how unkind fate could be. She so seldom met a man she really liked. Why did this one have to live so far away and in a godforsaken town where it snowed in April?

David returned with two glasses of white wine and handed her one. He sank onto the couch beside her, gazed at her for a long moment, then raised his glass.

Please don't spoil things, she said silently. *Please don't say anything corny or suggestive or—*

"To old Eskimos, Christie."

She laughed aloud. Since the moment he'd kissed her outside the restaurant, sexual tension had been practically crackling in the air between them. How had he come up with such a perfectly silly toast?

She touched her glass against his. "To old Eskimos, David. And to you. You've made my visit to Winnipeg far more memorable than it would have been without you."

He merely smiled…he had the most engaging smile she'd ever seen.

She forced her eyes away from his, sipped her wine and watched the fire, listening to it crackle. In the background David's stereo was whispering a love song.

"Christie?"

Her gaze returned to his face, half drawn by him speaking her name, half by the strong sexual pull between them—and she felt herself drowning in the deep blue of his eyes.

"Christie...I'd really like to see you again. The next time you're here. Well, actually, I'd far more than really like it. I'm not attracted to many women, but, with you...I...there's something I can't quite put my finger on but..."

"Pheromones."

"What?" He sat back.

She'd broken the romantic spell. She wasn't certain whether she'd wanted to or not, but it was probably just as well. Simply being alone with David was making her think and feel and want...well, the last thing she needed was the added magic of a spell.

"Pheromones, David. You likely only react to very select pheromones. That's my problem, too. I mean, I hope you don't think I go around kissing just any old Eskimo I meet. I kissed you because your pheromones were affecting me so strongly. But with most men...well, theirs don't do the slightest thing for me."

"Christie, what on earth are you talking about? Is this some naturopathic theory?"

"Not at all. You don't know about pheromones?"

"Never heard of them."

"What kind of doctor are you?" she teased. He looked so taken aback that she almost laughed. "Well, I'll admit they're not relevant to cardiology, David. More to sexology. But they're unique chemical substances that individuals produce—involuntarily, of course. They attract certain people of the opposite sex. But I'm not attracted to many. And, from what you said, you aren't, either.'' She shrugged, somewhat embarrassed. ''I guess we just happen to be attracted to each other's.''

Of course, there were a hundred additional things about David Lawrence that were attracting her, but she'd better stop talking while she was ahead ... or at least not too far behind.

He watched her skeptically until she felt obliged to break the silence. ''Really, David. 'Chemistry' between people actually *is* partly a chemical attraction. Pheromones are similar to the scents that animals emit.''

''Come on, Christie. You're making this up. Med school is top heavy in chemistry and biology courses and I didn't sleep through very many classes.''

''Well, scientists haven't known about pheromones for very long. Maybe they didn't make it into the textbooks you used. But, at any rate,'' she rushed on, feeling more foolish by the second, ''getting back to what I was saying about some people's reactions being very select ... well, I'm not sure what the right term is for *pheromone receptors* but, whatever they're called, some of them only react to one person in a million.''

''And why's that?'' David's grin said he still didn't believe a word she was saying.

She forced a smile, wishing she'd learn to keep quiet. Or at least not to raise offbeat topics. She should have stuck to something safe, like the weather.

This very moment they could be discussing an April snowfall instead of pheromones. And now she was out of facts about them and into conjecture. And David was probably on the verge of deciding she was an airhead.

She thought quickly, trying to come up with an intelligent-sounding explanation. "Well, David, the cause of response selectivity hasn't been established with certainty. But one possibility is that the sensitivity of people's receptors is somehow linked to their blood types. So, if you have a rare blood type, you might have rare pheromone receptors." She grinned at him, realizing she'd stumbled on an opportunity to change the subject. "You do know about blood types, don't you?"

"Of course I do. That's something," he added with exaggerated indignation, "far more relevant to cardiology than those damn pheromones I've never heard of before. And, as a matter of fact, I do have a rare blood type."

"Really? What? Me, too." Christie stared at him for a moment. She'd been half joking. The theory relating blood types and pheromones was simply a hypothesis she'd read about—nothing that had been scientifically proven.

David was eyeing her closely. "Back up a minute, Christie. When you started in on this, you said you kissed me because you were reacting to my pheromones—and that most men's don't do anything for you."

She shrugged, suddenly uncomfortable again. "It's all pretty theoretical, David."

He smiled slowly. "It's one of the most interesting theories I've ever heard. The first thing I'm going to do on Monday morning is hit the library and read up on this." He reached across the space between them and gently brushed her hair from the side of her neck.

The touch of his fingers against her skin set off a series of electric sparks within her. Whether it was pheromones or old-fashioned hormones or the magic of the moment, she was going to die right here and now if David didn't kiss her.

"Christie, between your personality and your sense of humor and your pheromones I've had an absolutely wonderful time tonight... the most wonderful time I can remember having." He leaned closer, and her heart began hammering. "Christie, I don't want you to leave Winnipeg without being certain you aren't walking out of my life. What are we going to do about seeing each other again?"

He'd murmured the words into her ear. She knew the murmur would echo the rest of the night. "David, I—"

Brrringg!

She jumped at the phone's ring.

"Damn it! Christie, I'm sorry, but I have to grab this. I'm not on call this weekend," he added, striding across the room, "so I won't have to go in. It's just that my chief of service is on vacation and I'm in charge of the unit. When there's an emergency, I get notified." He paused, his hand not quite on the phone, and smiled at her. "Don't move. I'll only be a minute."

Christie leaned back as he picked up the receiver. She had no intention of moving. She'd just sit and listen to David's voice. It was such a warm, deep voice.

"Dr. Lawrence here.... What? ... Well, try to re-lax.... It's probably not as bad as it seems."

Christie focused on David's face. It was reflecting the concern she could hear in his voice.

"Wait. Take a deep breath and hold it for a min-ute. We'll take care of things just fine. But I want you to calm down and tell me exactly what's been hap-pening." His frown deepened as he listened.

"How long ago did they start? ... And his breath-ing? ... Okay. Now listen. He's probably right. But just to be on the safe side, I want to see him. I'll go down to Mercy and meet you there.... No. That snow's made the driving bad, so I'm going to send an ambulance for you.... I don't care what he says. The streets are icy and you sound too upset to drive. I'll meet you there in fifteen minutes. Twenty tops. I'm going to phone for the ambulance as soon as we hang up. Then I'll leave and wait for you at the emergency entrance. He'll be all right.... You just try to stay calm. That's the best help you can be."

David cut off the connection, then pushed a mem-ory button. The sound of a number automatically dialing clicked across the room.

Christie rose, surprised that her impression of Da-vid had just gone up. She wouldn't have thought *up* was possible. "I'll catch a cab back to my hotel, Da-vid. I can ask your doorman to call one for me."

"Christie... wait just a minute."

She shrugged into her coat as David ordered an ambulance. He made a second call and spoke quietly into the phone—to someone at the hospital, she imagined—then he buzzed downstairs and asked for his car to be brought up from the garage.

Finally he crossed the room and took her hands in his. "Christie . . . this probably isn't nearly as serious as it may have sounded to you. But that was Kay who called me. Your father's having chest pains."

CHAPTER THREE

THE DOOR SWUNG OPEN, then closed again, and David stood inside the waiting room, his face revealing nothing. He was wearing a lab coat over his suit, transformed from friend to doctor.

Christie stared at him, not breathing, wanting—and not wanting—him to speak. Her mind flashed back an hour—pictured the ambulance screaming up to Mercy's Emergency entrance. Then that image faded into one of her father on a gurney.

She'd barely glimpsed him, had only seen that his face, half hidden by an oxygen mask, was pale and strained. Then he'd been raced to an elevator and up to the Coronary Care Unit, the CCU orderlies following David's instructions and bypassing Emergency.

Kay took Christie's hand, drawing her thoughts back to the present. The older woman was trembling. Or was Christie the one shaking? She wasn't certain. Shock. That was it; she was still in shock. Well, at least she was aware enough to diagnose her condition.

David cleared his throat, and Christie realized the door was still shuddering slightly. He'd only been standing there for a second, not the eternity it seemed. She closed her eyes, would have closed her ears if that were possible.

"Sid's resting comfortably. His risk appears minimal."

At David's words, she breathed again.

"We've done an electrocardiogram and run some blood tests, but it's difficult to make a diagnosis in the first few hours. You know how it is, Kay."

Christie glanced at Kay, reminded that her first husband had been a doctor—a cardiologist at this hospital, in fact. Over dinner David had talked about interning under Bill Russell. And he'd died of a heart attack. Right now Kay must be petrified. Christie squeezed the older woman's hand.

"What did the tests show?" Kay whispered.

"Not much so far. Sid's cholesterol's a little high, but that's not surprising in a man his age. As far as heart damage goes, well, he had too much to eat and drink tonight for us to begin testing just yet. We'll get going on that in the morning."

Kay nodded her understanding. "May I see him, David?"

"Yes. He's in a private room and I've asked the nursing supervisor to take you in. She'll be along any minute."

Christie glanced a question at David, not trusting her voice.

"Let Kay go in alone first. Your father hasn't been told you're here—and he's worried about how upset he's gotten Kay."

Christie nodded, reminding herself she was no longer first lady in her father's life.

"You need," David added gently, "to pull yourself together a little more before he sees you."

Pull herself together. Right. At the very least she had to be able to speak without fear of crying. She nodded at David again and he gave her a quick smile.

He clearly meant it to be reassuring, but it wasn't. She doubted anything could reassure her. She hated hospitals. People died in them.

David was speaking to Kay once more; Christie tried to concentrate on what he was saying.

"Sid's hooked up to monitoring equipment, so he looks like hell. But he's feeling a lot better and I think he's going to be fine. The equipment makes this look much worse than it actually is."

"Really, David?" The quaver in Kay's voice had diminished a little.

"Yes. Really. *If* he did suffer a heart attack, it was a minor one. And it may not have been that at all. He's right about the possibility of indigestion. I just don't want to take any chances."

"I appreciate that, David. So much. I didn't know what else to do but call you. He was being so stubborn and I was afraid—"

"It's all right, Kay. Don't worry. And try not to let him realize you're still anxious. Maybe you could mention that Christie's waiting out here to see him— tell him about the coincidence of her being at my apartment when you called, talk about anything that takes his mind off himself."

"I'll try." Kay took a deep breath. "I'll do just fine, David."

"Good."

The door opened again and a nurse appeared, a young woman with long brown hair. Her white uniform accentuated the darkness of her eyes. David nodded to her, then glanced back. "This is Jennifer Doyle, our night supervisor. She's been with Sid since the moment he arrived at the unit. Jenny, this is Mrs. Lambert . . . and Mr. Lambert's daughter, Christie."

The nurse flashed a friendly smile. "I remember meeting you before, Mrs. Lambert. I started on the CCU while your husband—I mean, while Dr. Russell—was our chief of service. But I told David I was sure you wouldn't remember me."

"Of course I do, dear. We met at a unit party and . . . and you'd just gotten a kitten, hadn't you?"

"That's right. And you told me the secret of keeping him from scratching my furniture."

"And did it work?"

"It sure did. Sammy's five now and I still have the same furniture. But you want to see your husband, not hear about my cat."

Jenny shot Christie a quick smile as Kay rose. Christie tried to return it. But the nurse was in her late twenties, at most. How could she be a supervisor? How could she be experienced enough?

The door swung shut behind the other women, and Christie turned back to David, still uncertain she could manage a coherent, intelligent question. He stepped forward and took her hands in his. She resisted the impulse to jerk them away, knowing he was trying to console her. But she didn't want consoling. She merely wanted the truth—the straight truth, not candy-coated with false assurances and wrapped up in David's bedside manner.

"I wasn't soft-pedaling with Kay, Christie," he said quietly. "I don't think this is serious. I honestly don't. But we'll just have to wait and see before we're sure."

"So you're doing nothing? Just waiting and seeing?" Oh, Lord! She hadn't meant to sound strident. And she knew there wasn't a lot that could be done. And David cared what happened to her father. She had to get hold of herself.

David took a deep breath, trying to think of the right words. He'd been forced to play this scene so many times before, with so many anxious people. And yet this was different.

The fear that patients' loved ones experienced always touched him. But not to this extent. He could feel Christie's emotional distress every bit as much as he could feel the physical trembling of her hands.

"We aren't doing 'nothing,'" he finally murmured. "Your father hasn't been alone for a second since he arrived and we're doing everything possible—using morphine in the IV drip to ease the pain and monitoring his vital signs. There's a TV screen in his room and another in the nursing station. The slightest irregularity will set off a warning bell. But I don't think anything's likely to happen, Christie. We aren't picking up any irregularities at all."

"So... so it looks as if this was a false alarm?"

Her voice told him how badly she wanted him to say yes.

"It... it's definitely looking that way."

She gazed at him as if she'd heard the unspoken "but" at the end of his statement. "You aren't sure, though, are you?" she finally pressed.

He glanced away from her for a moment, wanting to magically banish her fear. But he was a doctor, not a magician. "Christie, I can't be absolutely certain. It's possible he suffered some minor damage to his heart before he reached the hospital."

"How... David, how high is the possibility that's what happened?"

"His... well, the ECG reading showed an abnormality."

She drew her hands away from David's and wiped at her eyes.

"Christie," he offered, resting his hands on her shoulders, "it's the type of irregular heartbeat that might mean nothing—could be something he's had his entire life."

"Or," she murmured, "it could have resulted from a minor heart attack tonight."

"That . . . that may be what happened."

Tears began streaming down her face and he folded her into his arms. She pressed her face against his chest and sobbed quietly, making him feel helpless.

He hugged her more tightly and stroked her hair, wishing he could ease her pain. He'd spent the entire evening wanting to hold her. But not like this. In an ideal world he'd be holding her and kissing her. Not holding her and comforting her.

"Christie, with any luck at all, your father had nothing more serious tonight than indigestion. I'll get hold of an earlier ECG and compare them—see if what we picked up has been there all along. Does he have a family doctor in New York?"

She shook her head without looking up, swallowed audibly, then began speaking between sniffles, not making any move to draw away from the circle of his arms. "No. He's never been really sick. Never went to a family doctor. But being on the police force he had to have regular checkups. I'm not certain who did them—a doctor affiliated with the NYPD, I guess."

"And how long since he retired?"

"Only about a year."

"Then whatever medical files the police department keeps should still be available. Let's see, this is Saturday night. Sunday morning, really. I'll have someone get on the phone and track down his records first thing Monday. In the meantime we won't let a single thing go wrong.''

"David, I—'' Her voice dissolved into tears once more.

"Christie…Christie, your father's going to be fine. Even if the absolute worst was to happen now, even if he went into cardiac arrest, we'd know about it instantly—and be there to deal with it. He's hooked up to monitors and a nurse will be sitting by his side constantly. He's being watched over like a baby.''

Gradually her crying eased. Finally she shifted back a little and gazed up at him. Even with a tear-stained face, he thought fleetingly, she was gorgeous.

"Who's watching him, David? If anything does go wrong, who'd be there?''

"After you've seen him, Jennifer's going to be by his bedside—until eight o'clock when her shift ends.''

Christie gave him what almost looked like a smile. "The nursing supervisor? Should I take it that Daddy's getting extra special treatment?''

"Just a little. Jenny volunteered because she remembered liking Kay. And I jumped at the offer. Someone else can fill in at the nursing station and Jenny's so terrific with patients that your father will fall in love with her.''

"I'd like to stay with him, too, David.''

"You can see him, Christie, as soon as Kay comes out. But there's really not much point in sitting in a hospital lounge all night—''

"No, not a lounge, David. I want to stay in his room.''

David shook his head. "That's impossible. I've already bent some of the rules, but this one's not flexible."

"Nothing's impossible, David. I'll feel much better if—"

"No, Christie. Even after the night shift ends there'll be a nurse on constant until I'm certain he's not in the slightest danger. But you staying in the room during the night is out of the question."

"David, you don't understand! I...David he could die! My mother died in a hospital. And I wasn't there. I wasn't with her. David, it could happen again." She bit her lip and watched him—anguish written on her face.

He tucked a finger beneath her chin and tilted her face so that she was looking directly into his eyes. "Christie, listen to me carefully. Your father is not going to die. He's *not*. I promise. Just because I didn't know about pheromones doesn't mean I'm not a damn fine cardiologist, so believe me. Okay?"

He watched her attempt to smile. And when she couldn't quite manage it, he simply drew her closer once more and tried to hug away her fear.

CHRISTIE PAUSED outside the door of her father's room, telling herself she was overreacting. Rationally she knew she was. But emotionally...emotionally she was treading water that was so deep it terrified her.

This old hospital, with its antiseptic smells and its deathly colorless walls, was reviving too many painful memories—memories that threatened to drown her at any moment. And that moment might well come when she walked into her father's room.

She'd seen hundreds of intensive care patients. But the man lying in there, connected to machinery, was the person she loved most in the world.

"Come on," David murmured, resting his hand on the small of her back. "Just remember what I told Kay. He's feeling fine now. And this looks far worse than it is."

She ordered one foot in front of the other, barely aware of a nurse slipping out of the room and past them. Once inside, Christie froze, her attention riveted on her father. She eyed him closely, somewhat reassured that he didn't seem to be at death's door. Of course the room was dimly lit. And appearances could be deceiving. But his color was far better than it had been earlier. In fact, if it weren't for the ominous monitoring equipment, he'd appear more unhappy than unhealthy.

And *unhappy* was certainly understandable. Electrodes were fixed to his chest and wired to an oscilloscope. An IV drip was inserted into his right arm. Another tube ran from an artery in his left arm to a blood pressure monitor.

She realized how cautious David was being. Generally, in situations like this, blood pressure wouldn't be monitored constantly, just periodically with an ordinary family-doctor-type sphygmomanometer.

Her father smiled a forced-looking smile. "Hi, baby. They've got me trussed up pretty good, huh?"

David nudged her forward.

"I . . . I've seen worse." Thank heavens her voice sounded almost normal. Letting her father realize how upset she was wouldn't do him the least bit of good.

She crossed to the bed, kissed his cheek, then straightened up again, resisting the urge to throw her arms around his neck. If she did that, she'd undoubtedly be reduced to tears once more. "Actually, Daddy, it looks as if you're getting off pretty lightly—just hooked up to heart and blood pressure monitors and that skinny IV tube."

Her glance flickered to the oxygen and suction unit beside the bed. She quickly looked away, praying it wouldn't be needed, and forced herself to keep talking. "David was being kind. There are all sorts of gruesome things they could have stuck into you."

Sid snorted. "If David was being kind, he'd let me out of this wretched bed. I've spent the past three hours telling people that I simply have indigestion. And even it's practically subsided. But nobody's listening to me. From what they're saying, I won't be able to get out of here in time to have breakfast with you. I'm even liable to miss my own damn honeymoon flight!"

Christie checked her father's expression. He was a whiz at hiding his feelings, but surely he didn't actually think she'd fly home and leave him lying in a hospital.

"Well, maybe I'll stick around and have breakfast with you here. I might even stay in Winnipeg a little longer than I'd planned—say until your indigestion is entirely cleared up."

"Christie, I'll be fine. I *am* fine. Haven't they told you there's absolutely nothing showing up on these monitors? There's no point at all in you hanging around."

"Daddy, don't argue, okay? I'm not going anywhere until you're up and about."

"I'll be up and about in no time, baby. In fact," he added, glancing at David, "it would make sense for me to be discharged later today, wouldn't it? I'll be off this machinery in another hour or so, right? And, after that, there's no point in my taking up a bed—especially not when Kay and I are supposed to be heading for Barbados."

David grinned. "Barbados isn't going anywhere, Sid. And there'll be other flights. You're not getting off these monitors for about twenty-four hours. If nothing shows up by then, and assuming your heart scan and a few other tests we're going to run indicate there's been no damage, you can go home in a couple of days."

A couple of days? A fresh wave of concern swept Christie. Minor heart damage was sometimes difficult to detect. But, if her father'd actually *had* a heart attack, he'd be at high risk of having another over at least the next week.

She cleared her throat, not wanting to sound as anxious as she felt. "David? Realistically Dad has to resign himself to being in hospital for at least a week or so, doesn't he?"

David shrugged. "Let's wait and see."

She glanced at her father again, her anxiety increasing. As much as she distrusted hospitals, this was the best place for him at the moment. He should have complete bed rest unless the possibility he'd had an attack was entirely ruled out. And if he got out of here, he'd do precisely as he pleased. David had no idea how stubborn Sid Lambert was.

"David, I—"

"Christie, David's the doctor. Look, baby, would you mind letting me talk to him alone for a minute?"

"Ah...sure." Reluctantly she began edging toward the door.

"I'll come back to the waiting room," David offered. "I want to talk with both you and Kay again." The door closed behind Christie and David glanced expectantly at Sid. "What's up?"

"What's up is that I don't want you keeping me in here simply because Kay and Christie start nattering at you. I'm fine. Well, I am, aren't I?"

"Take it easy, Sid. You didn't feel so darn fine a few hours ago. So let's make absolutely certain there's nothing wrong before we start talking discharge."

David almost laughed at the glare Sid produced.

"All right," Sid finally growled. "So you do your tests and then I'm outta here. Right?"

"That's about it. I also want to get your medical records from New York—check that none of my test results show any recent changes."

"Wait for mail to come from New York? Damn it, David! This was my wedding night! But what with that indigestion and everyone staying so late and... and...David, Kay and I haven't...David, I've never made love to Kay! I just want to get out of this hospital bed and into a proper one. Do you really expect me to lie here for a month of Sundays, hoping some jokers in the post office do their jobs?"

"Fax, Sid."

"What?"

"I only need a few things. We won't have them mailed. We'll have copies faxed here the moment they're located."

"Oh...well...I guess maybe that's okay then. But you're going to have to be firm with Christie, David. I know Kay respects your judgment, but you heard the way Christie started in about keeping me here for at least a week.''

David grinned. "I'm sure I can cope with Christie's concerns.''

"Don't be too damn sure. She...well, nothing personal, but she doesn't figure most doctors are worth the price of their golf clubs. If she doesn't agree with what you're doing, she's liable to give you one hell of a hard time.''

"Everything's going to be fine, Sid. Christie already asked about staying in the room with you and I said no. End of discussion. She isn't going to give me any grief.''

Sid looked doubtful. "David, you might have thought it was the end of the discussion, but I wouldn't be certain. Maybe I should tell you about something—just so you'll understand if Christie becomes overbearing.''

"All right. Shoot.''

"When my first wife, Martha, died, Christie was taking nursing. And she got it into her head that Martha's death—well, that she shouldn't have died. That she got less than ideal care.''

"I see. And was there any basis for thinking that?''

"I honestly don't know. Martha'd had elective surgery and complications developed. Christie felt those complications only happened because the medical staff screwed up. She laid most of the blame on the doctor in charge. I have no idea whether she was right or wrong. At the time I was so broken up that I barely listened to her—figured her blaming someone was merely her way of trying to cope.''

David nodded. "Thanks for telling me about that, Sid.''

The door opened and Jenny poked her head in. "Ready for my company again, Mr. Lambert?"

Sid grinned. "Jennifer, if I was a year or two younger—or you were a year or two older—and if I wasn't a happy newlywed..."

"YOU GOING to sleep the day away? It's past nine."

David jerked awake and sat up, his mind scrambling to get its bearings.

The doctors' lounge. Of course. And Brent Wakefield standing at the end of the couch.

The CCU intern grinned. "What are you doing here? Aside from catching some beauty sleep."

"I did an emergency admission last night, then stuck around to check on him this morning."

"You did an admission? On a Saturday night? When you weren't on call? You're taking this acting chief business far too seriously."

"I knew the fellow." David pushed himself up from the couch, eyeing Brent curiously. "Speaking of not being on call, what are you doing here?"

"Came to pick up Jenny. We had plans for the day. At least I thought we did. But I haven't been able to find her, so either she forgot about me or she stood me up."

David resisted commenting, although Jenny doing either of those things was extremely unlikely. She practically drooled whenever she was within ten feet of Wakefield.

"Let's go and have a look at my admission," David suggested, grabbing his suit jacket and heading across to the door. "Jenny may still be with him."

"Yeah? She's sure a demon when it comes to work, isn't she?"

David merely nodded and started down the hall, Wakefield on his heels. Jenny was also a demon when it came to unit staff pulling their weight. But she seemed oblivious to the fact that Brent Wakefield was the laziest intern they'd had in years. She apparently couldn't see a millimeter beyond his dark good looks.

Their chief of service, Irv Rothman, had quietly nicknamed the guy "Dr. Dolittle." But David suspected that his own mild dislike of Wakefield stemmed more from the man's relationship with Jenny than from annoyance about his laziness.

Retroactive jealousy. That's what it was. Silly, when it had been at least five years since David and Jenny had dated. And, even then, there'd never been anything serious between them.

But he felt a residual affection for her—considered her as much a friend as a co-worker—and the idea of her and Dr. Dolittle being a hot and heavy item...well, Jenny deserved better.

David stopped in front of the door to Sid's room. He had it barely half open before Ruth Allison, a day shift nurse, greeted him by raising a finger to her lips. She glanced meaningfully at Sid, sleeping in the bed, and then at Christie, curled up in the armchair.

When David had left her, sometime after five in the morning, she'd been stiff-backed in the chair, clearly determined to remain her father's alert guardian. But now she was fast asleep, her blond hair mussed and falling across her face, looking as if she hadn't a care in the world.

"I think I see why you took a special interest in this patient," Brent whispered knowingly.

David ignored the remark and continued gazing at Christie. Asleep, she looked like an angel. But there had been nothing angelic about her a few hours ago. There had been no reasoning with her. Come hell or high water, she'd been determined to stay with Sid.

Her stubbornness had taken David somewhat aback. Now, seeing her so peaceful, he was glad he'd given in. And at least only Christie had insisted on spending the night in Sid's room. Kay, with her bad back, had realized that trying to sleep in a chair would have destroyed her.

Ruth quietly rose, crossed the room and joined the men in the hall. "Mr. Lambert seems fine, Dr. Lawrence. There've been no problems at all. Dr. LeBlanc's already been by on his morning rounds, but he merely checked the chart."

David nodded. He'd have to catch up with LeBlanc. The duty doctor would be wondering why David had taken charge of Sid's admission—and what sleeping beauty was doing in the patient's room.

"I'm going to my office for a few minutes, Ruth. Then I'll be back. But you took over from Jenny? At eight?"

"Yes."

"Any idea where she went?" Brent asked.

Ruth shook her head. "She just updated me on the patient's status. We didn't talk much. We didn't want to wake the patient . . . or his daughter."

David grinned at the critical edge to Ruth's tone. In her late forties she suffered from the delusion that she was everyone's mother. And she was perfectly aware David had broken hospital regulations.

Well, what the hell? Surely an acting chief of service was allowed to break the odd minor rule. But, for Ruth's peace of mind, it was just as well she didn't know Kay was still here, too—that she'd spent the night on David's office couch.

"Ruth, if Mr. Lambert's daughter wakes up before I get back, warn her off the cafeteria breakfast. Tell her that if she waits for me, I'll take her across to Benny's." He avoided the nurse's questioning glance by turning to Brent. "Sorry about the blind lead. I figured Jenny might still be here."

"C'est la vie." Brent gave an exaggerated shrug. "Guess I'm doomed to go home and catch up on my sleep—alone."

"You might consider hitting the library and catching up on your reading," David suggested, unable to resist the opening.

"That an order?"

"No. But it's a damn good idea. The next time Rothman starts discussing an article in *American Cardiologist*, it'd be nice to see a flicker of awareness cross your face."

"Okay, okay." Brent threw up his hands in mock surrender. "But, in my humble opinion, having hospital libraries open on Sundays should be illegal."

David manufactured a smile, then started toward the corridor of staff offices, certain that if Dr. Dolittle actually did hit the library, he'd spend the balance of the morning charming the librarian rather than reading.

LeBlanc's door was open, but he wasn't visible, so David continued along to his own office and knocked tentatively. "It's David, Kay."

"David?" Kay's voice was sleepy but anxious. "David, just a second. It's locked." A moment later the lock clicked and she opened the door, looking half asleep. "David, is Sid . . . ?"

"He's fine, Kay. I'm almost certain that was a false alarm last night."

Relief flooded her face. "Oh, David, I've been so worried. If you hadn't given me that sedative, I'm sure I wouldn't have slept a wink. Can I see Sid now?"

"He's still sleeping soundly. So is Christie. Probably the best thing you can do is grab a taxi, go home and freshen up. Doctor's orders," he added at her hesitant expression. "It'll make you feel better."

"Maybe it would. My clothes," she murmured, glancing down and smiling slightly, "look as if I've been sleeping in them."

David laughed. "I'm glad your sense of humor survived intact."

"Just barely. What about you, though, David? You're still wearing last night's suit. And looking at you in it is making me feel guilty."

"Don't. You know what a doctor's life is like, Kay. Last night was far from the first time I've been here overnight. In fact, it happens so often that I keep clothes here. And there's a shower in the doctors' lounge."

As he spoke, his gaze fastened on a sheet of paper that was lying on the floor. Computer paper—its edges still attached—with a few lines of print. Someone must have slipped it under his door. He picked it up and tossed it onto his desk, resisting the urge to read the message until Kay got organized and said goodbye.

"Well," she finally offered, "I guess if Sid's sleeping...if you're sure he's all right..."

"Pierre LeBlanc's on duty, Kay. He's a good man and he'll keep a close watch on Sid. I'll check in with you later," David promised, edging her to the door.

She paused in the doorway. "If Sid wakes up..."

"I'll tell him you're coming right back."

"Well..."

"I'll tell him I forced you to go home with threats of violence."

Kay smiled a half smile.

David waited while she assured him, at least fifteen times, that she'd be back at Mercy within an hour or two. Then, as she started down the hall, he closed the door and turned back to his desk to read the note:

Dear David,

   I won't be in for the next few nights. A personal crisis has come up that I simply can't delay dealing with. Sorry to leave you in the lurch, but it's imperative I get away for a bit.

   I'll be back as soon as possible and explain everything.

Apologies,
Jenny

David sat down and reread the words, trying to imagine what could be so serious—and have arisen so suddenly. If she'd known about it earlier this morning, surely she'd have said something.

He glanced at the message again. *The next few nights... get away for a bit.*

How many was a few? How long was a bit? Why hadn't she been more specific and told him how many shifts she'd likely miss? He continued staring at Jenny's note until his gaze lost focus, an uneasy feeling settling in the pit of his stomach.

Jennifer Doyle simply wasn't the type to leave anyone in the lurch. She might only be twenty-nine, but she was the most conscientious nursing supervisor he'd ever worked with. And she wasn't given to absences—spur-of-the-moment or any other kind.

Her dashing off, leaving only a vague explanation and a stood-up boyfriend, was completely out of character. Whatever her problem was, it must be awfully serious to make her...

Finally he checked for Jenny's home number, dialed it and listened to the endless ringing.

CHAPTER FOUR

As DAVID HAD FEARED, Jenny didn't answer her apartment phone. He hung up on the hollow ringing and glanced at his watch. Almost ten o'clock.

She lived barely fifteen minutes from the hospital. She could easily have gone home and already left again. Had she simply taken time enough to pack? To grab whatever she needed for her few nights away? Whatever she'd need while she was dealing with her problem?

Trying to shrug off his concern, he called Pierre LeBlanc's extension and talked with the duty doctor about Sid Lambert and a couple of the unit's other patients. But the conversation provided only a brief distraction. The moment David hung up, his thoughts wandered back to Jenny.

He gazed at the sheet of paper once more, his sense that something was very wrong growing stronger. Something was both very wrong and very urgent. Jenny had slipped the note under his door without even taking time to tear off the paper's perforated edges.

A personal crisis... can't delay. He hated to think of her being as upset as her message told him she was.

Her message? He stared at the print, searching his memory. Had she ever before left him a note with her name typed rather than scrawled across the page in her childish handwriting?

Come to think of it, had he ever gotten anything from her, aside from official reports, that wasn't handwritten? She rarely used the nursing station's computer—jokingly referred to herself as computer illiterate.

And that typed signature...

David tossed the page down, telling himself he'd read too much detective fiction. No one except Jenny had written the note. Under stress people often acted uncharacteristically.

He shook his head. It had been a long night. And, even on normal Sunday mornings, his brain tended to function at slow-verging-on-stop. Maybe, once he'd freshened up and had some coffee, he'd be able to make sense of this. Or, by that time, he might be able to reach Jenny.

Yes. He'd grab a shower, then take Christie across to Benny's for breakfast. With any luck Jenny would be home by the time they got back. And she'd explain what was going on. He pulled his jeans and a sweater from the office closet, then headed back to the doctors' lounge.

CHRISTIE GAZED through the window at the quiet streets below. It was amazing what the sun could do. It had banished every trace of last night's snowfall. And waking up to the bright glow that was merrily flooding the hospital room had done wonders for her state of mind.

Of course, it wasn't only the sunshine that was affecting her mood. She glanced across at her father, still unable to believe how well he seemed this morning.

This was definitely not, she reassured herself once more, going to be a replay of what had happened to her mother. This situation was completely different. And David was an entirely different type of man from the doctor who'd been in charge in New York.

David. Merely thinking of the hard time she'd given him last night made her feel guilty. She must have spent half an hour arguing with him about her staying in this room. In the process she'd probably convinced him that she was a complete shrew, when it was really just that last night...well, last night, she'd been fearing the absolute worst.

But this morning Sid Lambert was clearly back to his regular form. In fact, he'd been awake for less than half an hour and he already had Ruth Allison looking as if she'd like to throttle him. Christie had been fearful of leaving the two of them alone—even long enough for her dash into the bathroom—although she wasn't quite certain whom she was protecting from whom.

A quick tap drew her attention to the door. David opened it, strode in and smiled across at her, giving her a glimmer of hope that he hadn't decided she was a *complete* shrew after all. And then her father seized the moment.

"What the hell's a guy gotta do to get some food around here?" he bellowed.

"Daddy!" Christie tried to keep from smiling at his act. He certainly seemed to be feeling like his old self.

But his roar had sent Ruth leaping out of her chair. She stood, hands on ample hips, her dark eyes shooting daggers at the bed. Clearly the nurse didn't think much of Sid's old self. Or perhaps she simply liked her patients docile. Fat chance of that when it came to Daddy.

"So, Sid," David offered, "should I assume you're feeling better?"

"I'm feeling one hundred percent, except that I'm starving to death and except for these damn things stuck into my arms and except for these whatever-you-call-'ems taped to my chest. And getting the little suckers off is going to rip out half my chest hair, isn't it? And some vampire was just in here draining about twelve gallons of my blood!"

"Daddy, for goodness' sakes, take it easy."

David caught her gaze as she spoke. He had the most wonderfully blue eyes. And his smile was reminding her, in vividly delicious detail, of their time together last night. Until Kay's phone call they'd been having an incredible evening. And Christie had been feeling the most astonishing attraction...

Well, David's attractiveness certainly hadn't diminished overnight. Replace his suit with jeans and a navy blue sweater and all you did was replace sophisticated gorgeous with long, lean, casual gorgeous. There was no other word for him. Those broad shoulders hadn't just been padding in his suit jacket. And the way his jeans clung... he looked positively good enough to eat—obviously fresh from the shower with his blond hair dampened to dark bronze.

Self-consciously she tried to brush back her own hair. Her fingers caught in a tangle, making her realize how awful she must look. While she was in the bathroom, she should at least have taken time to check the mirror.

Her dress was beyond help, of course—the yellow silk incredibly wrinkled. But she could have combed her hair and washed her face. After her tears last night, any remnants of mascara were undoubtedly streaked halfway down her cheeks. She probably looked like a refugee from a horror flick.

Ruth cleared her throat loudly. David looked at the nurse, and Christie dived for her purse. She could practically feel that damn mascara on her skin.

"I thought I'd better wait for your okay, Dr. Lawrence, before I requested any breakfast for Mr. Lambert. And I did explain that he definitely couldn't eat before his blood samples were taken. In fact, I explained it *several* times."

David checked the progress chart on the bottom of Sid's bed, had a look at the monitors, then nodded to Ruth. "Breakfast will be fine now. And I think we've kept Mr. Lambert on constant for long enough."

What? Christie stopped rubbing at her face and clenched the Kleenex into a ball. David was taking Daddy off constant? She'd thought she'd almost entirely convinced herself that her father would be fine, but now she suddenly realized she still had a whole horde of worries.

The nurse was nodding, her short, bleached hair bouncing a bit with the motion, her expression saying she'd be only too happy to escape from Sid Lambert.

"Everything's looking good, Sid," David added, turning back toward the bed.

"David?" Christie murmured.

"Yes?" He looked over at her once more.

Now what did she say? She could hardly explain that her father was a consummate bluffer, that his hale-and-hearty act might be phony. At least she couldn't explain that while he was lying there listening.

"Ah...David, is it really safe to take Dad off constant yet? Don't you think...?"

Ruth cleared her throat again, so vigorously there was no doubt that she was demanding David's attention. "I'll order Mr. Lambert's breakfast when I get to the nursing station, Dr. Lawrence." She grabbed her sweater from the chair, then marched out with a frosty "Goodbye" to Sid and a withering glance at Christie. Ruth apparently didn't like interfering relatives any better than she liked feisty patients.

Sid grinned at her retreating back. "What game were you playing with me, David?" he muttered gruffly as the door closed.

"A hospital variation of Good Cop, Bad Cop? When I fell asleep, that sweetie pie, Jennifer, was hovering over me like Florence Nightingale. But when I woke up she'd been replaced by the dragon lady."

"Ruth's not that bad, Sid. She's just a little rule-oriented."

"Not that bad? She's got a glare that would shrivel half the NYPD at a single glance. The old bat's a definite man-hater. How long's she been divorced? Two years? Three?"

Christie smiled at the curious expression that appeared on David's face. Her father was up to his tricks.

"I guess three years would be about right," David admitted. "Why?"

"Just curious."

"I'm surprised she mentioned being divorced. It's a bit of a sore spot with her."

"She didn't mention it."

"Well, then..." David's expression was growing more puzzled by the moment.

"I was a detective for over twenty-five years."

David glanced a question at Christie.

"Ruth didn't say anything about being divorced that I heard."

"I think," David muttered, looking certain they were a couple of charlatans, "that you two are playing games."

"Her husband got involved with another woman, didn't he?" Sid pressed, clearly enjoying the conversation.

"Sid ... how the hell ... ?"

"Can't divulge trade secrets. But now that you've gotten rid of her, what about taking me off this damn machinery?"

"Daddy! Last night David said twenty-four hours. You're nowhere near that yet."

"Oh, come on, Christie. You can see for yourself that I'm perfectly fine."

"Let's not rush things, Sid," David murmured, stepping forward and putting a restraining hand on the IV tube. "All the indicators say you're okay. But I want you to stay on the monitors for a little longer. Just to be on the safe side."

David looked at Christie again, ignoring Sid's further protests. "Did Ruth pass on my offer to take you across the street for breakfast? Benny's isn't gourmet fare, but it beats out what your father's going to get."

Across the street? With Ruth gone? Did David really expect her to leave her father alone?

She forced a smile. "Thanks, but maybe another time. This morning I think I should stay and keep Daddy company."

"Christie, for God's sake go with David and get some fresh air. There's not a damn thing wrong with me. And you staring at me as if I'm about to breathe my last is making me antsy as hell.''

"I'm not staring at you as if you're about to breathe your last. I'm not staring at you at all. I'm just...well, I'm just going to stick around and keep you company until Kay wakes up.''

"She's already awake," David said. "But the last time I saw you two you were both asleep. So I sent her home for a couple of hours. Under protest," he added to Sid. "She was still pretty worried about you.''

"Between my wife and my daughter," Sid muttered, "I'm far more likely to be worried to death than to die of a heart attack.''

David glanced back at Christie. "You sure you don't want breakfast? I've got instant communication with the hospital." He patted a beeper attached to his belt.

The gesture drew Christie's attention back to the sexy way his jeans hugged his hips. She forced her eyes to his face, wishing she could take him up on his offer. But half the point of staying in Winnipeg was to ensure her father had a constant watchdog.

"Thanks, David. I'm not really much of a breakfast eater, though. But maybe after Kay gets back I could talk to you for a bit? Will you be in your office later?''

"Ah...sure. I'll be going back there as soon as I grab a coffee. Would you like me to pick up one for you?''

"Please.''

"What about me?" Sid demanded. "I'm the patient here. And that breakfast probably won't show up until lunchtime—if the dragon lady even remembers to order it.''

David shook his head. "Sorry. No coffee while you're on the monitors. Caffeine occasionally causes transient rhythm disturbances—they'd set off an alarm."

"It only causes them *occasionally*? Then I'll take my chances."

"Uh-uh. You'd regret it. One of the warning bells on that equipment goes off and you'll have Ruth back in here baby-sitting you again."

Sid was mumbling something about a conspiracy among sadists as David left. When he returned, delivering the coffee, he considered sitting in the room for a while. It seemed to be the only place he was going to get to spend any time with Christie.

Reluctantly he rejected the idea. He wanted to call Jenny again. And he'd see Christie later... in his office. Not that his office had been on his list of potential places to spend the day. He'd been hoping she'd be ready for a break from the hospital. But clearly she wasn't about to budge far from her father.

"See you after Kay arrives then, Christie?" he asked, handing her the coffee.

"Yes. See you then." She smiled one of her irresistible smiles at him.

He retreated down the hall, picturing that smile in his mind, deciding, as he dialed Jenny's number, that spending the day in his office might not be the worst thing in the world. But the image of Christie's smile gradually faded as he listened to the sound of Jenny's phone. After a dozen rings he hung up.

A personal crisis. The phrase kept repeating itself in his head, striking him as more malevolent-sounding with each repetition. Whatever her problem was, why hadn't she at least talked to him about being away?

He'd been in the hospital when she'd gone off duty. So why not at least a brief explanation? Had she told anyone what was wrong? Brent Wakefield perhaps?

No, David silently answered his own question. Brent had come to Mercy expecting to meet her. On the other hand, if anyone might have an idea about what was bothering her, it was probably Brent.

David shoved Jenny's note into his jacket pocket and headed down to Mercy's library, suspecting the odds that Wakefield had actually gone there were pretty low. Surprisingly enough, the intern was sitting at a study carrel, surrounded by cardiology journals. He grinned when he spotted David. "You here to check on my study habits?"

"No." David pulled Jenny's message from his pocket and handed it over.

Brent stared at it for a moment, then looked back up. "What's the story?"

"Haven't got a clue. That was slipped under my office door. I was hoping you'd know something."

Brent reread the note. "It doesn't sound like conscientious Jenny, does it?" He shoved back his chair and rose quickly. "Earlier, when I couldn't find her, I stuck my nose into my office. Thought maybe she'd left me a message. I didn't see one, but it's got to be worth a second look."

The two men rode up to the CCU in silence. A quick check of Brent's office told them Jenny had left nothing for him. "I'll try calling her," the intern offered.

"I already have. She wasn't home. But give it another shot. With any luck..."

Brent dialed, then stood leaning against the edge of his desk, the receiver to his ear. Finally he hung up and shook his head.

"You sure," David asked, "that you've got no idea what might be bothering her?"

"None. From her note it sounds as if something came up right out of the blue, doesn't it?"

David nodded, half convinced they should do something more, half suspecting they should mind their own business. Maybe Jenny wouldn't want them butting in. Maybe they shouldn't consider it. But the idea of her pulling a vanishing act was so completely out of character...

He eyed Brent closely, seeing his own concern reflected in Wakefield's expression. If he was even half as worried as he looked, they'd both feel better if they did something.

"I've got a key to Jenny's apartment," the intern volunteered, as if reading David's thoughts.

"Let's go," David muttered.

DAVID KNOCKED a second time on Jenny's door. There was still no response. They hadn't really expected one, of course. She hadn't answered her phone, so she probably wasn't inside. Unless...

David dismissed the thought. It was crazy. His imagination was running away on him. Wherever Jenny was, she was undoubtedly fine. He'd just be a whole lot happier if he knew precisely where she was. And if he was certain she could handle whatever crisis had arisen.

"Well?" Brent asked, his voice sounding anxious. "Time for our break-and-enter routine?"

"I don't think it counts as a break-in if you've got a key," David offered, stepping back from the door. Or did it? Something to ask Sid about.

David waited impatiently while Brent fiddled with the key.

The lock finally clicked open. How could that tiny noise sound ominous?

Brent shoved the door open, hesitated a moment, then preceded David in. Jenny's cat, Sammy, uncurled himself on the armchair and stretched, meowing a welcome. The two men glanced around the living room. Everything looked normal.

David exhaled slowly, suddenly aware he'd been holding his breath. Quickly they checked the rest of the apartment. No one. And nothing obviously out of order.

"Let's try the bedroom closet," David suggested. "See if any of her things are missing."

He stood in the doorway, anxiously watching Brent sort through Jenny's clothes. After a few moments Sammy appeared, loudly proclaiming his presence and wrapping himself, like a noisy gray fur piece, around David's ankles.

"Knock if off, Sammy," he muttered, absently picking up the cat. "We don't need you bringing new meaning to the word *caterwauling*."

For a moment Sammy continued to wail—apparently displeased about being captured. Then he busied himself sniffing David's sweater.

Brent shifted a few more hangers along the closet's rod, finally shrugging. "I can't tell whether anything's missing or not. If you asked me to identify a dress or something as Jenny's, I probably could. But this is backward. She might have taken things that I'm just not thinking of."

"Let's have another look around, then. See if anything strikes us as unusual." David turned from the bedroom and wandered to the kitchen.

When he reached it, Sammy began a fresh round of meowing and struggled to be set free. The moment David plopped the cat onto the floor, he stalked across the room, tail switching, and sat down in front of the fridge. Then he gazed back and let out a loud, pitiful mewl—obviously meant to convince David that no one had fed him for at least three years.

David glanced at the counter. Sammy's food and water bowls were sitting on it. Both empty. "Brent?"

Wakefield poked his head into the kitchen.

"Do you know what time Jenny feeds the cat?"

"In the morning. As soon as she gets home."

David gestured at the bowls. The two men stared at them for a moment.

"So much for her having come home to pack," David murmured. "I'll just feed Sammy before we leave."

"Maybe," Brent suggested quietly, "you'd better give him enough for a few days."

JENNY'S CAR wasn't in its space at her apartment building.

"Where do we go from here?" Brent asked as they headed back out to the street and got into David's Mercedes.

"I don't know. I guess we check Mercy's parking lot. But I don't know what we'll be proving—regardless of whether her car's still at the hospital or not. Maybe we should be thinking about calling the police."

Brent tapped an annoying tattoo against the dashboard, not replying until David had started the car and pulled away from the curb. "Do you think maybe we're overreacting, David? I mean, we're both worried about her, so we could be blowing this way out of proportion. She might have had a perfectly good reason for taking off. And it's not as if she simply disappeared into thin air. She did leave you that note."

"Yeah. But the whole thing bothers me—her not saying anything to either of us, the printed note, leaving Sammy the way she did. It's all so unlike her."

"You're right."

"So what are we going to do?" David glanced across the front seat, wondering how hard he should press about the police. For that matter, how hard should he press about anything?

When it came down to the bottom line, he was merely Jenny's boss—her temporary boss at that. Maybe he shouldn't be mixing into her personal life at all, let alone calling the shots. If anyone could figure out what was going on, it should be Wakefield. And yet, relying on Dr. Dolittle made David marginally uneasy.

"I think," Brent offered slowly, "that if Jenny's car is still at the hospital, then you're right. We should call the cops. I can't see her just walking out of Mercy and grabbing a bus to go wherever it is she's gone. If her car's still there, well..."

David nodded. There was no need to finish the thought. If her car was still at Mercy then, despite the note, vanishing might not have been her own idea. He was glad Wakefield had the brains to figure that out.

"On the other hand," Brent continued, "if she took off in her Mustang, she's probably all right. So, between that and the note and everything being okay at her apartment, I think if the car's gone we should maybe hold off for a little…not do anything more for a while. She might call the unit later to explain, or she might phone me. Hell, David, she could even have a change of heart and show up for work tonight."

David wheeled into the hospital parking lot, wondering how likely it was that they'd hear from Jenny today. The idea, he decided, was undoubtedly just Wakefield's wishful thinking.

"She usually parks to the right, David. As near as she can get to the north entrance."

He turned right and they drove slowly up and down the rows of parked cars near the hospital door, looking for Jenny's red Mustang. Then they widened their search until they'd covered the entire parking lot. The car wasn't in it. Finally David drove back toward the main building, pulled into his reserved space and cut the engine.

"Now what, Brent? Still think we should hold off for a while?"

"Well, I feel better, knowing her car's not here, but still… Look, maybe Jenny talked to someone before she left this morning. How about if I ask around the hospital a bit?"

"Good idea," David agreed as they got out of the car and started toward the entrance. "I have to go back up to the unit, so I'll see if anyone there knows anything. You try the other areas she might have hit. And someone in Security might recall her leaving. She sometimes chats with old Reg on her way out."

"Yeah. I'll catch him later. I'll go down to the cafeteria first. I looked for her there this morning, but I guess she could have grabbed a quick coffee and been gone before I checked.''

David nodded. ''We should get in touch later and compare notes.''

''Right. I'm going to go home after I've asked around—in case Jenny tries to reach me. So why don't you call me there?'' Brent paused, glancing at his watch, then opened the hospital's door. ''It's a little past noon. How about phoning me around three?''

''Good. Around three, then.''

David waited for the elevator, feeling better now that they had a plan of action. Surely one of them would come up with something. And, even if they didn't, surely Jenny would turn up soon—safe and sound.

Wakefield had probably been right. They were undoubtedly overreacting. There was no point in doing any serious worrying just yet.

The elevator arrived and David pushed the button for the CCU. He'd ask around the unit before he even checked back in with Sid and Christie. Then he'd be free...just in case Christie decided she wanted to spend a little time away from the hospital...just in case she wanted to spend a little time with him.

CHAPTER FIVE

"SOME HONEYMOON we're having, huh, Kay? We should be heading for Barbados this afternoon instead of being trapped in this damn room."

Kay patted Sid's hand. "I don't care, dear. Not in the slightest. I've been to Barbados. And all I care about at the moment is you being well."

"I'm perfectly fine," he assured her for the umpteenth time.

Christie reflected—also for the umpteenth time—that the truth of that statement still remained to be proven. It was difficult to correlate her image of a perfectly fine man with one who was lying flat on his back attached to a heart monitor and sporting an IV drip.

Kay leaned closer to Sid, murmuring something, and Christie resisted the urge to clear her throat. She doubted the lovebirds even remembered she was in the room. And if Kay got any closer to the bed, she'd be in it. But she so obviously adored Sid that Christie couldn't help smiling.

"Both David and that other fellow..." Sid paused, glancing at his daughter.

Well, at least one of them remembered she was here. "Dr. LeBlanc," she supplied.

"Right. Both David and LeBlanc are *certain* my ticker's okay. It was the champagne that did me in.

Damn bubbles gave me gas. That caused the entire problem.''

Kay looked at Christie with an expression that begged for confirmation.

'' 'Certain' is a bit of an exaggeration, Kay. But when LeBlanc came by he did say the indicators were pointing toward Dad being all right. He even took him off the blood pressure monitor.''

In fact, she'd gotten the distinct sense that, if not for David's orders, LeBlanc would have taken her father off all the monitors. But that suspicion wasn't something she intended to share with Sid. He'd read more into it than he should and then he'd be even more disgruntled about being here. Sid Lambert had never subscribed to the ''better safe than sorry'' school of thought.

''When will they be entirely sure it wasn't a heart attack, Christie?'' Kay pressed.

''Hopefully we'll have a pretty good indication by tomorrow. David said he'd see about getting a previous ECG reading from New York. If it's the same as the one they did last night—''

''Then I'll be getting out of this wretched place,'' Sid muttered.

''Not,'' Kay said sternly, ''until you give me your solemn promise that you'll never drink so much champagne again.''

''Kay, I don't even want to see another glass of the stuff for the rest of my life.''

Kay began to pat Sid's hand once more. Christie turned away, feeling like a third wheel, and gazed longingly out at the sunny spring day. Her father wasn't the only one who'd like to get out of this wretched place—at least for an hour or two.

He really did seem to be fine. Certainly he didn't need two baby-sitters. And she'd kill for a shower and fresh clothes. But she didn't want to leave until she'd spoken with David.

There was no guarantee he'd manage to get her father's medical records tomorrow. The NYPD was far from famous for its facility with paperwork. And until those records arrived . . . well, she wanted to be certain David understood how ornery and stubborn Sid Lambert could be. If he was handled the wrong way, he was liable to discharge himself—whether it was against medical advice or not.

She stood up, unable to sit for another minute. "I'm just going to phone the Sheraton and let them know I won't be checking out today—before they cart my things into the hall."

"You're welcome to stay with me," Kay said quickly. "I haven't been thinking straight since last night, or I'd have invited you before this. Why don't you check out of the hotel and take your things to the house?"

"Oh, no. Thanks, but you've got enough on your mind without the bother of a houseguest."

"You won't be any bother. And you don't count as a guest. You're family."

"Thanks, but—"

"Why not do that, baby?" Sid coaxed. "It would give you and Kay a chance to get to know each other better."

"I . . . well, that would be nice, Kay. If you're certain I won't be in the way."

"Of course not. It's a big house. And you can—"

David breezed into the room, his entrance cutting Kay off midsentence. He grinned at her sandwich, sitting on the bedside table. "Smuggling food in for my patient, Kay?"

"If I was doing any food smuggling, it wouldn't be that sandwich. You'll notice I only took one bite. The egg salad tastes as if it's two weeks old."

"Three."

"Pardon?"

"If you bought it from Mercy's cafeteria, it's more likely three weeks old. That's how we maintain a full patient load. If there are any empty beds, we alert the cafeteria staff and they give people food poisoning." He turned to Christie. "Sorry I was out of my office for so long. Were you looking for me?"

"I checked a couple of times," she lied. Actually, she'd wandered down the hall looking for him at least half a dozen times and had started wondering if he'd forgotten about her.

"Sorry," he repeated. "Something came up. Can I buy you lunch to make amends?"

"Buy me lunch? And give me food poisoning?"

"I thought," he told her, grinning an extremely engaging grin, "that we'd leave the hospital food to the newlyweds. I had a somewhat better lunch in mind."

"Well, tempting as that sounds, I'm afraid I'll have to pass. Once we've talked, I've got to head over and check out of my hotel."

"You've decided to go home today after all?"

The disappointed look that appeared on David's face sent a tiny ripple of pleasure through her. Crazy as it might be, she liked the idea that he didn't want her to be going home. She liked it a surprisingly large amount.

"No. I've decided to stay until Dad's out of the hospital. I'm moving into Kay's house for the duration."

David's grin reappeared. "What a coincidence. I just happen to have my moving van outside. We can talk on the way."

She gazed at David, knowing this was the place in the script where her line was a polite protest, where she was supposed to tell him she didn't want to disrupt his plans for the day, where she should tell him she could easily grab a taxi.

But he was so darn appealing that she didn't want to protest. She'd already turned him down for breakfast and lunch. What if she protested this time and he simply gave up on her? She'd be kicking herself all the way to Kay's.

She had to get there somehow. And David was still wearing his beeper. She'd be better off with him than on her own because, if anything happened while she was away from the hospital...

Sardonic laughter inside her head told her she was rationalizing like mad. She wanted to be with David because he just might be the most appealing man she'd ever met. It was as simple as that. But she was scrambling for other reasons because, deep down, she suspected her prolonging something that had no future didn't make much sense.

And she wasn't even certain what the *something* was that she was prolonging. In the blink of an eye last night David had gone from being her date to being her father's doctor. Where did that leave him—or, rather, the two of them—today?

She wasn't certain. But if fate, and David, were offering her a chance to spend more time with him...

"Well," she said, undoubtedly sounding about as casual as a grade-schooler who'd been offered a trip to Disneyland, "I'd hate to see your moving van go to waste."

Kay dug into her purse and produced a key. "I'll find you a spare key later, Christie. But take mine for now. And you know where things are, David—towels and everything. Christie can use Holly's old room."

Christie's glance shot to Kay. The woman was putting her in Holly's room? She wanted David to settle her into his ex-fiancé's old room?

She tried to decide whether she was being silly or if there was really something disconcerting about that idea. She peeked at David's face, but it told her nothing. He simply took the key from Kay and nodded.

Well...she probably *was* being silly. After all, it was just a room.

"And make yourself at home, Christie. There's a ton of food in the fridge. The caterer packed all the leftover hors d'oeuvres into it. If I'd been smart, I'd have brought my lunch from home instead of supporting Mercy's food-poisoning program."

Christie laughed, glad her father had married a woman with a sense of humor. "Thanks, Kay. And I'll be back soon with your key."

"Baby, don't make it too soon. You've already spent enough time here. I don't want you coming back for hours."

"But—"

"He's in the best of hands," David promised. "He won't get away with a thing."

"I don't have a prayer of getting away with anything," Sid muttered, giving Kay an affectionate smile. "I can see that this woman isn't going to take her eyes off me. And you need a good break, Christie. You look as if you haven't slept in a week."

"Thanks a heap!"

David grabbed her arm and propelled her toward the door. "I think," he whispered as they left the room, "you look great."

"In that case," Christie teased, "you need glasses."

"THIS IS THE PLACE," David said, opening a bedroom door and gesturing Christie in. "And the bathroom's at the far end of the hall."

"Great. I'm dying for a shower. I must look like a bag lady."

"I guess disagreeing with you is pointless when you've already told me I need glasses."

"Sorry," Christie offered, smiling. "Accepting compliments gracefully isn't one of my strong points."

David tossed her suitcase onto the bed. "You certainly travel light. That felt empty."

"It almost is. I didn't expect to be staying longer than overnight. If I hadn't been toting so many vitamins and things for Dad, I'd have made do with hand luggage."

She glanced at David's face as she spoke. When they'd talked about naturopathy last night, he hadn't offered his opinion on it. She hadn't yet determined if his attitude was the same as that of most doctors—whether or not he figured she bordered on Weirdsville.

"You mean all those vitamins and things that almost got you arrested?" he kidded, his expression telling her nothing except that the story of her airport experience had been the joke of the wedding. And she'd realized that practically the moment she'd arrived.

"Actually, the vitamins weren't a problem, David. It was a giant-size peanut butter jar full of white powder that almost landed me in jail. I swear I'm never going anywhere near Toronto again."

David shook his head, grinning. "You shouldn't vilify Toronto because of one customs officer. It's actually a great city. I've been to a few conferences there—and visited my brother a couple of times since he moved down."

"Well, *you* don't have to go through customs to get there. Now that I'm changing my flight home, anyway, I'm going to connect through Chicago. That man in Toronto got me so upset that I couldn't think straight. You know what I did?"

"No. What did you do?"

"While I was waiting for the next flight to Winnipeg, I took this good silk dress I'm still wearing—a dress that's probably ruined beyond hope by now—out of my suitcase. I felt so guilty about holding up the wedding that I figured I'd be clever and save time by changing just before we landed. But that man had me so rattled that I wasn't thinking about how small an airplane washroom is."

"You didn't really try to change in it, Christie? Not once you realized...?"

"Oh, yes, I did. And it practically turned into a Carol Burnett sketch. We hit turbulence just after I got into the washroom. The Return to Your Seat sign flashed on but, by that time, I already had my suit off. So, there I was in that tiny cubicle, balancing in high heels and struggling into this darn dress, certain I was going to rip it because the plane was bouncing up and down like crazy. And, the entire time, I was muttering away about how much I hated Toronto. I must have been muttering pretty loudly, too. When I finally came out, the people sitting nearby looked at me awfully strangely."

David gave in to his laughter. "You have to focus on the up side of experiences like that," he finally offered.

"Yeah? There's an up side to making an idiot of myself at thirty thousand feet?"

"Sure. At least you know that if you ever want to change professions you can become a contortionist."

"Some up side that is!" Christie snapped her suitcase open and peered in. "Getting back to the topic of this almost empty case, all I've got to change into is the suit I traveled in—up until those fateful minutes in the washroom—or the jeans and sweater that I threw in on spec."

"Go with the jeans," David suggested, looping one finger under the waistband of his Levi's. "We'll be a matched pair."

A matched pair. That was an interesting turn of phrase. Simply a figure of speech, of course, but an intriguing one.

Christie forced her gaze away from the sexy fit of David's jeans and feigned interest in the room. It looked like a teenager's. An old poster of John and Yoko decorated the wall above the bed and a pink, life-size plush dog stood guard beside the closet.

"Holly hasn't lived here for years," David explained. "Not since she went off to university. But I don't think Kay ever wanted to believe that her little girl had left home."

"She...Holly's living in Denver now. Right?" Christie eyed David closely, suspecting she was treading on dangerous ground but curious as hell about Holly. Or, more specifically, about Holly and David having been engaged until a few months ago. Or, even more specifically, about whether David was harboring a broken heart. Of course, that was none of her business. And she wasn't entirely certain why it seemed important for her to know. But there wasn't a whole lot she could do about her curiosity.

"Yes. Holly's living in Denver. She seems to be happy there."

Christie merely nodded. Curious or not, she couldn't think of anything else to ask about a woman she'd scarcely met.

"Holly and I were engaged, Christie."

She almost jumped at his statement. "Yes...yes, someone mentioned that to me...Dad...or Kay."

"I figured they would have. And I imagine, with Holly marrying Mac so quickly, people assume I was dumped. But the breakup was actually mutual—no major pain, no residual hard feelings."

She nodded again, wondering what she was supposed to say next. Good? That's nice? I'm glad? Those all struck her as pretty inane responses.

David shrugged. "Just thought I'd mention it— thought you might want to know that I'm not in the ranks of the walking wounded."

What? Could the man read her thoughts? She felt her face growing warm.

"If I'd met you first, Christie, it would have saved both Holly and me a lot of time."

Christie stared at him blankly. What was this gorgeous man saying to her? He couldn't be suggesting...not when they'd only met yesterday. There was most definitely a chemistry between them, but he must realize as well as she did that nothing long-term could ever—

"If I'd met you first," he repeated, smiling devilishly, "you'd have filled me in about pheromones and I'd have realized that Holly's and mine weren't doing a darn thing about attracting each other. Your explanation would have saved us a lot of time. We both sensed something was missing but weren't sure what."

Christie tried to smile, her face growing hotter by the second. Of course he hadn't been suggesting...he hadn't been suggesting anything at all. He'd merely been teasing her. She prayed he couldn't actually read thoughts and reminded herself that she wasn't the least bit certain how he was viewing their relationship at the moment. Maybe he'd just offered her a ride because he was kind or because of Kay or, well, whatever his reason, she'd better give him a chance to escape.

"Well, David," she managed, "I really am dying for a shower. So I guess...well, thanks for driving me here...and thanks for our talk about Dad...about the care he's getting. I know I worry too much sometimes. And I honestly didn't mean to imply that I don't think you know what you're doing."

"That's all right. I'm good at ignoring implications I don't like. For example, from what you just said, I could almost infer that you expect me to leave now. But since I'm so good at ignoring subtle hints, I'll just head down to the kitchen and dig out some of Kay's leftovers. You must be starving."

David turned on his heel and strode out of the room, leaving Christie with his image in her mind, the lingering echo of his voice in her ears and a smile on her face.

Maybe she should try a little ignoring of her own. Maybe she should try ignoring the fact that she'd be flying back to New York soon. Then again maybe she shouldn't do anything of the sort. When it came to David Lawrence, ignoring facts might be dangerous as hell.

"THIS TASTED even better than it did after the ceremony yesterday," Christie offered, polishing off the final chunks of lobster.

"That couldn't have anything to do with it being your first meal of the day, could it? When it's past two-thirty?"

"That doesn't mean it wasn't good." Christie brushed back her hair—still damp from the shower—and absently rubbed her stiff shoulder. Falling asleep in the hospital's chair hadn't been smart.

The next thing she knew, David was standing behind her, firmly kneading her neck. The gentle strength of his touch felt heavenly.

"Mmm...that's wonderful. Don't stop."

"Never?"

"Well...not until I beg you to." And that, she silently added, might be a long time off.

He began pushing with the heels of his hands...a rhythmic trapezius scooping...making her realize he'd been trained in massage.

"Where did you learn to do this, David?"

"Med school."

"Really?"

"Yes, really. Naturopaths aren't the only people who know something about massage therapy, Christie."

She could hear a teasing smile in his voice.

"Before I decided on cardiology, I flirted with the idea of specializing in rheumatology. Of course, if I'd ended up working with arthritic patients, I'd have made more use of massage. I'm pretty rusty now— don't get much practice."

"This sure doesn't feel rusty to me."

"Well, it is. There's not a lot of demand for massaging hearts. Stand up for a second, Christie. If we turn the chair around I can do a better job."

Better? What could be better than heavenly? Obediently she stood up, and David turned the chair's back against the table.

"Now straddle the seat and lean into me for support. Drop your neck forward."

She sat down again and...oh, Lord! She suddenly knew what was better than heavenly. The feel of his hips and lower chest against her back, the warm, hard maleness of his body pressing against hers was a quantum leap beyond heavenly.

Or was her body pressing against his? Whichever it was, the physical contact was making totally outrageous thoughts flash like neon signs in her mind— thoughts of David touching the rest of her, of his body being even closer to hers, of...

This shouldn't be happening! Any massage she'd ever had before, and those she'd given, had been strictly nonsexual. But not this one! How could David turn her on by merely kneading her shoulders when, normally, a whole body massage didn't do anything other than relax her?

She didn't know how. But David's touch was definitely sending erotic messages through her body. She was intensely aware that it was *his* hands on her, that it was David Lawrence who was standing so near that she could smell his faint, masculine scent, that it was *his* body supporting her back, *his* body heat that was making her so hot that her blood was beginning to sizzle.

Go with the flow... enjoy, a tiny voice whispered inside her head.

Right... enjoy. Christie let her body relax and simply savored the stirring warmth that was spreading all the way to her toes... even though it was probably indecent to enjoy anything so much.

David began to poke-and-press up the back of her neck, stretching the erector spinae muscle, working away at her last bit of tension. Vaguely she heard a three o'clock news break replacing the radio's music. But when the announcer began speaking, it could have been in a foreign language for all she knew. She was aware only of David touching her.

He began lightly caressing her neck... butterfly stroking... the final, relaxing ending to a massage. Ending?

She considered reminding him that he was supposed to keep this up until she begged him to stop, then thought better of the idea and remained silent.

"Take a deep breath," he murmured, brushing her neck with a slow stroke that was so light she barely felt it. "And relax. Why don't you rest your head on the table for a couple of minutes? I have to make a quick phone call."

Rest her head. Good suggestion. She was so relaxed that she'd probably keel over if she tried standing up. She put her head down, facing toward the phone, and watched David—liking what she saw.

He was standing by the counter, the phone in his hand, dialing. His legs were long and lean. But she imagined they were muscular because his chest certainly was. It looked every bit as broad and strong as it had felt when she'd been leaning against it.

And then there were his incredibly blue eyes . . . and the way his blond hair tended to angle sharply down across his forehead when he leaned forward. He struck her as positively irresistible. She could imagine becoming addicted to this man.

A sharp lecture from her common sense brought her back to earth. Becoming addicted to a man who lived two thousand miles away would be about as intelligent a move as becoming addicted to heroin.

The voice of common sense was right, of course. She just wished she didn't prefer the little voice that had told her to enjoy.

She ordered herself to stop listening to both imaginary voices before she began to think they were real. Instead, she concentrated on listening to David.

"Nothing at all?" he asked into the receiver. "No one? . . . No, I had no luck, either. Ruth Allison was the only day-shift person who talked to Jenny. And they just chatted about my patient. . . . Yeah. Yeah, I guess you're right."

David didn't sound the least bit as if he thought whoever was on the other end of the line was right.

"Yeah. She's probably fine. . . . Yeah, it's just a matter of waiting for her to get in touch. . . . Well, call me if you hear from her. I'll be going back to Mercy later. If there's anything new, I'll let you know." David hung up, his face a picture of worry.

"Problem?" Christie asked, now alert.

"Yeah. Problem."

"Jenny's the Jenny from last night?" she prompted.

"Right."

"She seemed nice. She was terrific with Dad."

David shrugged. "She's disappeared. She left me a cockamamy note saying she had a personal crisis and was taking off for a while. That was her boyfriend I just called. He's the intern on the CCU."

"And he doesn't know anything?"

"No. I talked to him this morning and we went over to Jenny's apartment. Everything seemed fine there, so after we got back to Mercy we each asked around a little—figured she might have said something to someone. I was hoping Brent had better luck than I did, but he came up empty, too."

"And you have no idea what her problem is? Or where she's gone?"

"No. And taking off . . . well, it's not like her. But I don't know what else I should do. Or even whether I should do anything else at all. What do you think, Christie?" He gave her a half smile. "Do detectives' daughters know how to deal with vanishing people mysteries?"

"I'm afraid this one doesn't, David. While I was growing up, there was so much police talk around the house that I perfected a method of blocking it out. Daddy's the one you should ask."

"Good idea. Why didn't I think of that?"

Christie's stomach knotted. "No, David. I was joking. Since Dad retired he's been like an old war horse put out to pasture. Tell him there's a missing person lurking about and he'll want to mount his own investigation. We'd have one hell of a time keeping him in that bed.''

"I was merely going to ask him a few questions." David's expression said he thought she was being unduly overcautious, but he didn't press the issue.

"Maybe you should call the police," she suggested, trying to make amends.

"Maybe I should. Brent and I talked about that, but he's in favor of waiting and seeing."

"And what are you in favor of?"

"I'm not really sure. No, that's a lie," he corrected himself, smiling fully this time. "What I'm in favor of is enjoying the rest of the afternoon with you. Standing here worrying about Jenny is stupid. Brent's right. She's undoubtedly fine. So what would you like to do?"

Christie gazed at David, suspecting the answer to his question was written all over her face. She'd like to do just about anything. As long as it was with him. But she couldn't push aside her nagging fear—couldn't quite believe her father was all right.

"David, don't take this the wrong way. I . . . I'd like to do something with you...I really would. But I think I should be getting back to the hospital soon."

He stepped across to where she was sitting and captured her hands in his. "Christie, tell me the truth. Was that simply a polite turndown, or would you really like to spend some time with me?"

"David, if I wasn't worried about Dad, I'd like nothing better."

"Nothing?"

"Nothing," she admitted with a grin, "that comes to mind, at least."

"Good. Then I'll call Mercy and get an update on our patient. They'll tell me he's doing great and that'll take care of your worries."

"But I—"

"Christie..."

David watched her face so intently that she felt herself beginning to dissolve under his gaze, melting at the way his eyes were saying things she wanted to hear.

"Christie, I'm not exactly sure what's going on between us. But when we met yesterday I felt ... well, I don't even know quite how to describe it. All I know is that I spent half my time last night worrying about never seeing you again, instead of simply enjoying our evening together."

"You did? Really?" Christie tried not to smile. She couldn't manage it.

"Yes, really. But my point is I wasted all that time worrying for nothing. Because here we are—together again the very next day. Of course, I wish to hell you'd stayed over in Winnipeg for an entirely different reason. But what I'm trying to say is that worrying's pointless. Your father and Jenny are both undoubtedly fine. And you and I are acting like a couple of worried idiots when we should be..."

Slowly he drew her up into the warm circle of his arms and traced the outline of her mouth with his finger, making her want him to kiss her. Instead, he began caressing the fullness of her lips with gentle, back-and-forth strokes that stirred a tiny throbbing deep within her. Then finally he began kissing her...kissing her as if he'd never stop...at least not until she begged him to.

She was suddenly sure that David was right. Everything was going to be fine. In fact, everything was going to be positively wonderful.

Her last fully rational thought was that David had come up with the most delightful way in the world for them to enjoy the afternoon together. After that, rationality began slipping away, banished by the certainty that she belonged in David's arms, by the realization she'd never before been kissed like this... never before responded to kisses in this way.

He was possessing her with his mouth. And she was reveling in the possession. He was kissing her deeply. And she wanted deeper. He tasted delicious; his tongue, playing sensual games with hers, was sending quivers of excitement racing through her.

She grew gradually aware of her entire body reacting to his. Of how aroused her nipples had become, demanding his touch, of how her arms, encircling his waist, were drawing him nearer as if they had a mind of their own...and that mind wanted the length of him against her.

And then he began possessing her with his body...with a slow, firm caress down the length of her back that drew her even more tightly to him, that crushed her breasts to his chest and settled his hard arousal firmly against her.

His closeness, his wanting her, her wanting him, was making her ache with desire.

Then David's kiss slipped to her throat and he discovered a sensitive area beneath her ear, setting off fresh shock waves of need.

"Oh, David," she murmured.

The longing in Christie's voice made David's erection grow impossibly harder—so that it strained against his zipper. He desperately wanted to make love to her. And her body was saying that was what she wanted, as well. Her shower-fresh scent was enveloping him in a mist of desire. The curves of her body begged to be touched, and her lips, soft and yielding beneath his, were heavenly. He'd never get enough of her sweet taste.

He cradled her behind, drawing her even closer, then slipped his hand beneath her sweater and up the silkiness of her back. She followed his lead, caressing his back so enticingly that he didn't know whether it was the touch of her hands or the way her lower body had begun moving against him that was more exciting. He unhooked her bra and cupped her breasts in his hands.

"Oh, David."

Her voice had become more of a sigh than a whisper.

He covered her lips with his own and gently stroked her nipples, loving the way their firmness assured him of her feelings. How could this gorgeous creature want him as much as he wanted her? It was so incredibly wonderful.

He tried to recall what she'd said last night but found thinking difficult. Something about the way his pheromones affected her. Something about most men's not doing the slightest thing for her.

He believed that—believed with absolute certainty that she wouldn't be here, doing what she was doing, with any other man she hadn't known for an awfully long time. And that belief made him even happier. But he had to let her know he understood...couldn't let her wonder whether he thought she would just... He forced his lips from hers.

"Christie . . . Christie I think something special has been happening between us. Something *very* special."

"Oh, David," she murmured, "I don't just think so. I'm certain of it. You're driving me absolutely crazy."

He kissed her a final, loving kiss, then nuzzled her neck. "Let's go upstairs," he whispered.

CHAPTER SIX

LET'S GO UPSTAIRS. Oh, Lord! David's suggestion brought rational thought racing back to Christie's mind at top speed. And just in time. She knew her body had been giving David the distinct message that she wanted to make love to him—and that was precisely what she did want. She'd probably never wanted anything more. But her desire was so strong that it frightened her. She had to think this through. First, though, she had to explain to David that... She tried to speak, but her voice wasn't working.

"Christie?" he whispered again.

"David...David, not now. I...I can't now."

His body tensed against hers. Then he stepped back a fraction of an inch and gazed down at her face. "Christie, I realize it's not very romantic to talk about how recently people have had blood tests, but if it's safe sex you're worried about, you don't have to be. Not with me. I'm not the type who fools around and takes chances."

She shook her head. "I never imagined you were. It's not that. I mean, I'm concerned, of course. And I'm careful...not that I've had very many occasions to be careful on but..."

Stop talking! she silently ordered herself, feeling her face flush. How could she possibly have let this get so embarrassing? She'd always been terribly uncomfortable in situations even remotely resembling this. But this was devastating.

"David, it's just too fast...too soon. My mother used to call me Cautious Christie. And the name fits. I...I hope you don't think..."

He cleared his throat, his body growing more rigid. "I guess I misread the signs," he muttered. "Sorry." His voice was strained; she wasn't certain whether he was hurt, embarrassed, angry or all three.

What was happening to her? How could she so desperately want to make love to a man when she didn't even know him well enough to read his emotions?

He dropped his arms stiffly to his sides and started to pull away.

"David..." She tightened her grip around his waist, not allowing him to escape, praying for the right words to say. Suddenly the most important thing in the world—in her world at least—was that David didn't walk out the door. And out of her life. Not before she'd had time to figure out precisely what was going on and what she intended to do about it.

She looked up at him, but he didn't meet her gaze. "David, you didn't misread the signs at all. I...I misled you. I didn't mean to, but I got more than a little carried away."

He glanced at her face, his expression telling her nothing.

"I think," she added, forcing a weak smile, "we just had an example of what happens when two people with extremely selective pheromone receptors are attracted to each other."

Why didn't he say something?

She pressed on, afraid he'd never speak to her again. "David, I need time to think. You and I are...well, this situation is so temporary. And everything was happening so fast...I felt incredibly aroused and...and, David, I really haven't had very many occasions to be careful on. And what I was feeling when you were holding me wasn't something I've experienced before...not so intensely and...well, it just frightened me that after so short a time..." She bit her lip. That seemed to be the only way she could stop herself from babbling.

David gazed down at her, and she felt his body relax slightly. "Is that the truth?" he asked.

"Have I ever lied to you before?" she managed. "It's not that I didn't want to...not that I didn't want *you*. I just need time."

David exhaled slowly, offering a silent prayer of thanks. She wanted him. She just needed time. He hadn't misread her feelings. He'd simply pushed too far too fast. And he was lucky she wasn't throwing him out instead of standing there with a pleading look that asked him to understand.

God! He deserved a swift kick in the butt. With Sid in the hospital, her emotions were undoubtedly already bouncing up and down like a yo-yo. She didn't need David Lawrence helping things along, coming on to her like a horny teenager. Of course she needed time. She wasn't the type of woman to...but what the hell did he say now?

Christie began to think David was going to stand gazing at her for eternity. And then he smiled. It was an extremely tentative smile, but it was enough to send her spirits soaring.

"What I was experiencing wasn't exactly commonplace, either, Christie. And I wouldn't generally suggest so soon...well, there haven't been all that many women I've ever cared to suggest to at all. I guess you weren't the only one who got more than a little carried away."

He leaned forward and kissed her lips. Gently...so exquisitely gently. When he finally stopped kissing her and shifted back a little, it was all she could manage to keep from drawing him nearer again.

"Look, Christie, I meant what I said about thinking something special has been happening between us."

"I know," she murmured. "I guess maybe it's so special that it's scaring me."

David smiled again. This time there was nothing tentative about it. "I'm not really a very scary man, Christie. And this something... well, I know it could lead to problems. With us living so far apart, I mean. And last night I kept telling myself there was no point in thinking about anything more than one enjoyable evening with you. One *incredibly* enjoyable evening. But I... well, I couldn't seem to make myself listen to that logic."

"I've been having the same problem, David."

He bent to give her nose a quick kiss. "I'll try to keep in mind your needing time, Christie."

She smiled, grateful for his understanding. But she didn't want to think about time. Time was something they didn't have a lot of.

David placed his hands on her arms and backed decisively out of her grasp. "Why don't I call Mercy and check on your father? And then let's get the hell out of here before... well, cool spring air's probably the next best remedy to a cold shower."

CHRISTIE GAZED across the front seat of the Mercedes at David's chiseled profile, then down at his hand resting gently on hers. Even that slight touch was making her incredibly aware of the residual darts of desire pricking at her. She still wasn't certain where she'd found the willpower to keep from making love to him.

The more he'd kissed her, the more she'd wanted him to kiss her. The closer he'd held her, the nearer she'd wanted to be held.

She'd never before felt such an incredible sexual longing. There was no doubt in her mind that making love to David would be absolutely, fantastically, wonderful. But it would also intensify her feelings for him. And they were already growing by leaps and bounds— without any added encouragement.

That was precisely why she had to figure out what she should do. The possibility of becoming addicted to a man crossed her mind again. No. Not *a* man. *This* man. Very, very specifically this man.

Because the sexual tug wasn't everything. *There's something special happening between us,* David had said. *Something very special.*

His words were still repeating themselves in her mind. She'd been feeling something happening since the moment they'd met. And so had David. Once she'd gone home, though, that something could be hazardous to her mental health.

Did she really want to become involved with someone she'd only be able to see a few times a year? Or maybe not even as often as that? David's job was hardly nine-to-five, Monday through Friday. It couldn't be easy for him to pick up and take off whenever he liked.

And she wouldn't be able to come to Winnipeg often. She didn't have an endless supply of vacation time, and the cost of living in the Big Apple didn't leave her with a whole lot of disposable income. She couldn't hop on a plane and spend a weekend here anytime the whim struck her.

Well, she could for a while—until American Express cut her off. But even if she ran her credit rating into the ground, where would it get her in the long run?

Nowhere, she answered herself realistically. Something special or not, the odds on a long run for her and David were extremely low. Long-distance romances must involve at least as much frustration as happiness. She couldn't imagine that many of them survived for any length of time.

So she should stop the *something* in its tracks before it grew too big to stop. Yes. She should walk away from the something special now and not allow this relationship to continue developing.

But how could she walk away from David when she could barely take her eyes off him?

She forced her gaze to the side window and tried to concentrate on the residential area they were driving through. The words *walk away* were floating before her.

She blinked them into oblivion and focused on the houses. She could hardly do anything about walking away right this instant. Not while David was in the midst of showing her around town. Aside from anything else, she'd be lost.

The old homes, sitting on huge lots along the curving drive, were virtual mansions. A quiet river flowed behind them. This had to be one of the nicest parts of town.

"Is this the same river your apartment overlooks, David?"

"Yes, the Assiniboine. We're west of my building now. This is Wellington Crescent we're on."

"It's lovely."

"Yeah. Winnipeg's a pretty city."

Christie merely nodded, glad she'd only called it a town in her thoughts. But that was what it was, at least in comparison to New York. There, everything was stacked sky-high and buzzing with activity—instead of sprawling, low and lazily, across a flat expanse of prairie.

"That's Assiniboine Park ahead," David offered, smiling at her.

Lord, she adored his smile.

"I thought we'd drive through it—figured you might be feeling lonely for Central Park."

"Now how did you know I was in need of a park fix?"

"Oh, I was just thinking about naturopathy... nature. And there's a tropical conservatory we could go into if you'd like. Unless birds flying around loose would bother you."

"Not at all. What made you think they might?"

He smiled again and she realized he was kidding her. "Did you see *The Birds*, Christie?"

"Yes. But it didn't leave me with ornithophobia."

"Is that actually the word for a fear of birds?" David's grin was skeptical.

"I wouldn't bet my life on it, but ornithology... ornithophobia. It makes perfect sense to me."

"Well, I don't know about your linguistics, but I thought that movie might have hit home—that you might have related to Tippi Hedren being attacked by the birds. You look a lot like her."

"I do?"

"Sure. When I first saw you, I thought of Candice Bergen, but I've decided you're more fragile-looking, like Tippi Hedren."

"I don't think I'm flattered, David. I mean, they're both beautiful women, but they're also both a lot older than me."

"Not in the films I catch on TV, Christie. I don't go to many movies, so if an actress hasn't made it onto *Midnight Cinema*, I generally don't even know her name."

"Don't you rent videos?"

"I used to. But I kept forgetting to return them on time, so I gave up on renting them—figured that if I didn't, the video police would batter down my door one day."

"Video police, huh? This must be a real law-and-order town."

David laughed.

She adored his laugh every bit as much as his smile. And there was nothing better than a man who appreciated her sense of humor. "Well," she offered, "I don't really think I fit the Tippi Hedren role. As I recall, she went through the entire movie dressed in designer clothes and a full-length mink coat. She didn't wear anything even a tenth as grotty as these jeans of mine."

"It wasn't your clothes that I was implying are beautiful, Christie."

"Oh...thank you." She snuggled into the glove-soft gray leather of the car seat, trying to look nonchalant, certain she wasn't succeeding. David thought she was beautiful!

THE CONSERVATORY PROVED to be a glass-and-concrete structure with long passageways that wound away from the main building like enormous, hollow glass snakes. And even at a distance brightly colored birds were visible inside, flying from tree to tree.

The entrance was a series of three doors—no doubt a system to prevent the birds from escaping. Walking through the third doorway was like walking into paradise. The air was hot and humid, almost muggy, reminiscent of Manhattan in July and August, but without any trace of the staleness that hung over city streets. The smell was pure tropics—the sweet, heavy scent of lush vegetation and flowering shrubs.

Christie smiled up at David. "It would be easy to forget the coolness outside, wouldn't it?"

"Very easy," he agreed, taking her hand.

She silently revised her thought. Never mind just the coolness. With David holding her hand, it would be easy to forget almost anything.

They walked along the narrow pathways, serenaded by birds. Sunlight streamed down through the glass roof and danced like tiny diamonds across the surfaces of fish ponds. Polite signs reminded visitors that metal coins poisoned fish. But one of the ponds was designated as a wishing pool.

David dug two quarters from his pocket and handed one to Christie. Wordlessly they tossed them into the water. Whatever his wish was, the expression on his face told her it had to do with them. She squeezed his hand affectionately as they wandered on.

"I know it's early," he said when they neared the exit, "but would you like to have dinner before we go back to the hospital?"

The hospital. She'd almost forgotten why she was still in Winnipeg.

"I...I would, but maybe we shouldn't, David. I should check in soon and see how Dad is. Kay would probably like a break."

"Your father really doesn't need someone with him every second, Christie."

"I know." At least that was what David kept telling her. She just wished she could be certain she should believe him. "I'm afraid I feel guilty, David. Here I am thoroughly enjoying the afternoon while Dad's lying in a hospital. I can't help thinking I should be with him."

"You can't spend every minute there, Christie. Your father doesn't expect you to."

"I guess you're right, but—"

"Tell you what. Why don't we look in on them and then, if they don't mind, go out again. I...I'd really like to take you to dinner."

"Even though I look like a ragamuffin?" she teased, brushing her free hand across her jeans.

"Well, neither of us is dressed for a jazzy restaurant. But there's a pizza place near Mercy that makes a mean vegetarian pizza—right down to great pineapple chunks."

"Ugh! Your taste in pizza leaves a lot to be desired."

David shrugged. "So we'll skip the great pineapple chunks. We'll still have the great company."

Right. And *great* was an understatement when it referred to David's company.

He paused, leaned closer to brush her cheek with a kiss, then wrapped his arm securely around her shoulders as they began walking toward the door.

The lingering, tingling warmth on her cheek told her that *great* was likely an understatement when it came to *anything* relating to David.

"So? What do you think about dinner?"

"Well...let's see how Daddy is. I guess if he's okay...and if they don't mind..." Agreeing made her feel guilty once more, but she couldn't resist. And if the pizza place was near the hospital, they wouldn't be gone for long.

David kissed her cheek again, and her heart began to pound. In the deepest recesses of her mind, she heard a little voice murmuring something about walking away. But that was silly. She couldn't walk away from David when his arm was securely around her shoulders.

Besides, the little voice was speaking so quietly that she wasn't really certain what it was saying. It was barely audible, in fact. And the thumping of her heart was beginning to drown it out entirely.

THEY CHATTED about silly nothings during the drive back to Mercy. It was just as well David had been content with nothings, Christie mused as he pulled the Mercedes to a halt in the parking lot, because she couldn't focus her full attention on anything but him.

He switched off the ignition and turned to her, lightly resting his hand on her shoulder. "I'm just going to stick my head into your father's room for a minute, then I want to see if there are any messages for me—from either Jenny or Brent.''

''And if there aren't? What are you going to do then?''

''I haven't really been thinking about that. I've been too busy thinking about you.''

Christie smiled. She seemed to have been smiling since the moment they'd left Kay's house.

''I guess,'' he went on, ''it would make sense to have a look at last night's nursing notes—see if there's any clue in them.''

She couldn't imagine any clue David might hope to find in the nursing notes. But he'd begun caressing the side of her neck and it was difficult to think. She needed all of her concentration to keep from leaning across the space between them and kissing him.

She wasn't about to give in to that temptation, though...at least not without a lot of thought. Because the way she'd felt when he'd kissed her earlier...well, if she decided not to walk away, there wouldn't be much more stopping at kissing.

David was speaking again and she forced herself to listen.

''Then, maybe, if we haven't heard from Jenny by later tonight, I'll come back before the night shift staff goes on duty and see if any of them know anything.''

''You'd come back at midnight?''

''That's when they go on duty.''

''Do you ever sleep?'' she teased.

David didn't smile. Absently she wondered if it was merely her imagination or whether David was overly concerned about Jennifer Doyle...and whether his concern for her was merely because she was part of his staff.

Jenny was a pretty woman. And she *had* seemed to be, in Sid Lambert's vernacular, a sweetie pie. And even though this Brent Wakefield was supposedly her boyfriend...

Christie suddenly realized where her musings were leading and pulled them up short. Surely the green-eyed monster wasn't rearing its ugly head. Surely Christie Lambert wasn't suffering an attack of completely unfounded jealousy. That wouldn't be the least bit logical.

But, of course, this entire *"something"* with David wasn't the least bit logical. When she was with him, logic practically fell over itself, beating a hasty retreat.

"Christie, the thing is that even though Jenny left a note I've got this funny feeling..."

"Yes?"

"It's probably crazy. But I keep thinking that maybe she didn't write the note. She simply isn't the type to disappear like this—note or not."

Christie nodded, trying to ignore her ridiculous pangs of jealousy. Not only did they not make any sense, they were terribly petty. As she and David headed into the hospital, and while they waited for the elevator, she gave herself a stern lecture about jealousy being one of the seven deadly sins. Actually, she wasn't entirely certain it was. But, if it wasn't, it should be.

By the time the elevator door opened at the CCU, Christie was hoping that David's funny feeling really was crazy... hoping that nothing had actually happened to the nurse who'd been so kind last night. David ushered her along the corridor to her father's room and opened the door.

"Hi, baby. Have a nice afternoon?"

She breathed a tiny sigh of relief. Silly. She'd known he'd be fine.

David shot her an "I told you so" grin.

She ignored it and said hello to Kay before answering her father. "We had a great afternoon, thanks, Daddy. I figured I'd better come back and let Kay get some dinner, though."

"That was thoughtful," Kay said. "And what about you?"

"I...well, I..."

"I've invited Christie out for a pizza," David said casually. He was standing at the bottom of the bed, reading Sid's progress chart.

"That's a good idea, baby. You can't live on those damn vegetables all the time. You should eat more food that'll put a little weight on you."

"I—"

"Good," David said, cutting her off. "Then it's settled. We'll go out after Kay gets back.

"Oh, by the way, Kay..."

"Yes?"

David tapped his finger against the chart, determined to look and sound as nonchalant as possible. "Sid will probably still be in this room when you get back. But don't panic if it's empty. I'm going to talk to the duty doctor about taking him off the monitors. He'll be moved then."

"Well, it's about time I got off these damn things! But what's this about another room? If I'm well enough for you to unhook me, why aren't I well enough to go home?"

David pretended not to notice that both Christie and Kay were staring at him anxiously. "You actually might be well enough to go home, Sid. But I can't take any chances. If you did have a minor heart attack, you need medical care and bed rest for the next little while."

"But, David, I—"

"Sid, I know you feel fine now, but I've got to be certain that what happened to you last night wasn't serious. And to be certain I need the ECG reading we talked about getting from New York. We have to check that there hasn't been any recent change in your heart's activity. And we also have to do a series of cardiac enzyme tests. We did the first one this morning, but the process involves taking fresh blood samples for the next couple of mornings and repeating the analysis."

"You mean that vampire will be back?"

"'Fraid so."

"Exactly what do the tests show, David?" Kay asked.

"We check certain values in the blood to see if their level's constant each day. If it is, everything's fine. But if the level decreases over the next few days, that indicates tissue repair is taking place in the heart—because there's been some damage."

"It would mean that Sid did have a heart attack," Kay murmured.

David nodded. "But a very minor one, Kay. He couldn't have bounced back from anything major the way he has. And, from what I've seen, I really don't think the chances of it having been even a minor heart attack are very great. It's still a possibility, though," he added, turning back to Sid. "And that's why you're confined to bed until we can give you a clean bill of health. I don't want you exerting yourself. Just in case."

He glanced at his watch. "I've got a few things to do in my office. Will you come by once Kay's had her dinner, Christie?" He gazed across at her, wishing she didn't look as if she'd begun worrying all over again.

"David...I think with Dad coming off the monitors and being moved and all...well, I think maybe I'll just stay and get something to eat here."

"Don't be ridiculous, baby. You know how awful hospital food is. And you've got to stop worrying about me. David just finished saying he doubts there's a thing wrong. Keeping me in here's just a formality."

"But—"

"You sit here with me while Kay's having dinner— tell me what you did this afternoon. But then I want you outta here. Go for pizza with David."

"I'll bring you back here after dinner," David offered. "Your father will be settled into his new room by then."

"Good idea. That way," Sid added with a grin, "she can see I'm still breathing."

"Daddy! That's not funny!"

"Baby, take it down a thousand, okay? I'm just fine. And you're going to give David the idea you don't trust his judgment."

"That's right," David agreed. "I'm getting the distinct feeling that you doubt I'm even a doctor. There's a medical degree hanging on my office wall, you know. And a specialist certificate to boot."

The corners of Christie's mouth twitched; he imagined the movement was meant to be a smile. "Sorry, David," she murmured.

"He'll still be on close, Christie."

"On what?" Sid demanded.

"Close. It's standard procedure when you're first off the monitors. A nurse will be looking in on you every fifteen minutes."

"Hmmph! Still no damn privacy! Well at least, after midnight, it'll be that sweetie pie Jenny doing the looking."

"Ah...no, it won't be Sid. That's not really her job and...and she may not even be in tonight."

"No? I'll be disappointed if she isn't. Before I fell asleep last night she told me she'd be dying to see me again by tonight."

"Are you trying to make me jealous, dear?"

David stared at Sid, barely hearing Kay's words. "Exactly what did she say?"

"What?"

"Jenny. Before you fell asleep. Exactly what did she say about seeing you tonight?"

"Just what I said. She was implying she'd fallen for me, that she couldn't wait to see me again. She was joking," Sid added slowly, looking at David as if he was a particularly dense child.

"Yes. Yes, of course." He glanced at Christie and saw his thoughts reflected on her face. "Walk me into the hall?"

She followed him out.

"What do you think?" he asked as the door closed behind them.

"I don't know, David. It might have meant nothing—could simply have been a throwaway line. Or..."

"Or in the wee small hours of this morning Jenny had every intention of being at work tonight."

"What time did you find her note?"

"Around nine-thirty, I think. Maybe a little later. But Wakefield had been looking for her before that. He'd come down to Mercy to meet her after her shift ended. Of course, he's invariably late getting places, but still..." David shook his head, wishing he knew what was going on in Jenny's life. When he got back to his office, he'd call Brent again. Maybe Dr. Dolittle had heard from her. "So," he said, shoving his hands into his pockets, "I'll see you when Kay gets back from having dinner?"

"Well...I guess. Although I didn't like the way my father was practically shoving me out the door."

"I liked it just fine. It's nice to have an ally."

Christie made a face at him, but he merely laughed, hoping, but not convinced, that he'd seen the last of her anxiety. He reached across and brushed back a silky strand of her hair. "Your father's all right, Christie. If all my patients looked even half as healthy as he does, I'd be worried about my job security. So you'll come and collect me once Kay's back?"

"Right. Unless Mercy's cafeteria manages to poison her. I don't know that she should be giving them another chance at her."

"Don't worry. I'll bet they won't get her tonight, either."

Christie turned to the door, then glanced back at David. "You *will* be in your office when I come looking this time," she teased quietly, "won't you?"

"Definitely. I wouldn't want you running away with some other guy." And that was putting it mildly, he thought, starting down the hallway. If some other guy tried to run away with Christie, that other guy would run the risk of being dead. Briefly David wondered how many potential other guys lived in Manhattan, then forced the thought away and paused at the nursing station to check for messages.

There were half a dozen, and when he saw one from Wakefield his hopes soared, then plummeted as he read the two words: "Haven't heard."

The time on the slip was 6:30, barely five minutes ago. He'd just missed the call. Not that it mattered when there was no news.

He scanned the other messages again, wondering why he was bothering. Was he expecting one of them to magically turn into something from Jenny? Thinking that maybe he'd find a message reading: "Ha, ha, April Fool." Not likely. They were too far into the month for that.

A quick review of the nursing notes did nothing to ease his concern. Jenny had made her standard, brief entries. He could undoubtedly read them upside down or sideways and still not see any clue. Some detective he'd make.

He continued along the corridor, pausing only to speak to the duty doctor about Sid. Then, once inside his own office, he began skimming through a file of consultation requests, telling himself it was simply the room's stuffiness that was affecting his concentration.

He reopened his door and shoved the window up a couple of inches, creating a breeze that wafted across to the hall...a breeze that caught up several papers from his desk and deposited them on the floor.

Apparently the fates didn't want him to work. He sat down again to wait for Christie, thinking of what Sid had said. Jenny had told him she'd see him tonight. But if she'd intended to be here...or had

Christie's thought been right? Had that merely been a throwaway line?

David pulled Jenny's note from his drawer and re-read it. Then he gave in and tried her apartment's number. As he'd expected, it was an exercise in futility. So what should he do next?

What he'd like to do was ask Sid's advice. But if he did that, Christie would have a fit. She was clearly still frightened that the slightest thing might cause Sid to drop dead—right here in the unit.

Not much of a vote of confidence. Of course, with her mother having died in a hospital . . . well, he probably shouldn't take her apprehension personally.

He gazed at his phone, deciding he'd played Brent's wait-and-see game long enough. It was time to find out what the police had to say.

CHAPTER SEVEN

TEN MINUTES LATER, David was staring unhappily at the page of doodles he'd made while talking with the constable. Here and there, amid the meaningless scrawls, he'd written words and phrases as the man had spoken them: "Overreacting. Intelligent woman. Happens all the time. Left a note. No need for concern."

Well, maybe he *was* worrying for nothing. The police had to know what they were talking about. If ninety-nine percent of people who disappeared reappeared shortly, then why was he trying to play Philip Marlowe?

He picked up the receiver again, called Wakefield and told him about Jenny's remark to Sid. "So," he continued, "I decided to phone the police."

There was a long pause at the other end of the line. "Do you mean you've already called them?" Wakefield finally asked.

"Yes. I just hung up." David underlined "No need for concern" on his page of doodles, waiting for Brent to ask about the conversation.

"I . . . I thought we'd agreed to hold off on that, David."

"I did hold off. I held off until ten minutes ago."

"Yeah . . . well, I guess I had a little longer in mind. I wish you'd talked to me first."

"Why? I got your message—knew you hadn't heard anything."

The pause was even longer this time.

"Brent, what's up? Has Jenny phoned you?"

"No. But what did the cops say?"

"Basically that it's senseless to worry about an intelligent woman who left a note, that we should take it at face value and expect her back in a few days."

"Yeah. Yeah, that's probably true, David. She'll turn up. I . . . I'm certain she will. Everything's fine."

David felt his annoyance level rising. He was getting the distinct impression that Dr. Dolittle was holding something back. "What's made you suddenly certain, Wakefield?"

"I'm not really *certain*. I shouldn't have said that."

"Well, you sound as if you know something."

"No. I don't *know* anything. I just have an idea."

"What idea?" Silence. "What idea?" David repeated more sharply. He felt himself moving beyond annoyance, heading quickly into anger, and he wanted to control that feeling. Both Brent's and his concerns about Jenny were more personal than work-related. So he didn't want to seem as if he was pulling rank. But what kind of game was Wakefield playing?

"David . . . it's barely even an idea. It's really nothing."

"If it was nothing, it wouldn't have made you decide that everything's fine." Good. He'd managed to sound reasonably calm and logical.

"Well, it's nothing I can talk about. It . . . it's actually none of your business."

David tapped his pencil on his pad so hard that the point broke—and with it his temper. "None of my business? It sure as hell is my business!" Well, there went reasonably calm and logical. But at least he hadn't sounded quite like a raging maniac.

He took a deep breath and began speaking more slowly. "Brent, aside from anything else, I'm in charge of the unit at the moment. And that makes one of our nursing supervisors taking off very much my business."

"Look, there's no point in getting agitated, David. I've got things figured out. Trust me."

"No. You trust me. Tell me what's going on."

"I can't. That's one thing I *am* certain of."

"Look, Wakefield, the last I heard we were working together. What do you expect me to do now? Sit here for the rest of the night, wondering what you know that I don't?"

"David, Jenny made me promise not to talk about this. That's why I didn't say anything this morning."

"What? You knew what had happened this morning? And you put on that know-nothing act? Went through the charade of going to her apartment with me?"

"No. You've got it all wrong. I mean, I realized what problem her note was referring to. But her leaving so suddenly took me as much by surprise as it did you. Like I told you, I expected her to be waiting for me. And going to her apartment was no charade. The note got me worried. I thought she might have . . . I wanted to be certain she hadn't done anything crazy. But she hasn't."

"What makes you so damn sure of that? This afternoon you said you hadn't turned up anything, that nobody you talked to had seen her after her shift ended."

"Nobody had. But I've been mulling this over all day and...and, well, I've decided that she's just gone off someplace to think."

"Think about what, damn it!"

"David, she wouldn't want me to tell you."

"Look, Wakefield, I'm not going to keep putzing around this with you. You can tell me now, or you can tell me when I come pounding on your door. What the hell's going on?"

The silence lasted so long that David began to think Wakefield had hung up.

"If I tell you, you'll keep it to yourself?"

"Of course I'll keep it to myself."

"All right, then . . . Jenny's pregnant."

"What?"

"She's pregnant. As in, with child. My child."

"Pregnant? Jenny? You're not serious!"

"Jeez, David! Do you think I'd joke about this? You're a doctor. You know how it happens. And it happened."

"Son of a bitch! You're a doctor, too, Wakefield. You're supposed to know better."

A motion caught David's eye and he glanced up. Christie was standing outside his office, her expression saying she'd heard at least the last part of the conversation. She mouthed a "Sorry" and he waved her in.

"Yeah . . . well, anyway," Wakefield was mumbling, "she's pregnant. And when she told me about it she hadn't decided what she should do."

"What *she* should do? What the hell? It's your baby, too. Or don't you care about that? Or about her?"

"Hey, she didn't want my help, David. In fact, I wondered why she'd even bothered telling me when she didn't want to listen to what I had to say about it. I . . . damn it, I said we should talk about getting married. What more was I supposed to do?"

"Son of a bitch," David muttered again. Jenny shouldn't have to be off all alone trying to deal with this. Surely Wakefield could have done *something* more than he had.

David consciously relaxed his grip on the receiver, realizing he wished it was Dr. Dolittle's neck he was gripping. But there was nothing to be gained by ranting and raving at the guy. "When did she tell you, Brent?"

"A couple of days ago. It didn't occur to me she'd take off, though."

"No. It wouldn't have occurred to me, either. That's not Jenny's style."

"I've decided she just wants time alone to think things through, David. When she's done thinking, she'll be back. And she'll probably be ready to discuss it then. I . . . I really don't think she'd do anything drastic without at least talking it over with me."

"Yeah. Time alone to think. Let's hope that's all it is. I'll see you in the morning."

As he hung up, Christie glanced at him apologetically. "Sorry, David, I couldn't help overhearing."

"I know."

"At . . . at least you got your explanation."

"Great explanation, eh? You'd think a doctor and a nurse would be more careful."

"I guess . . . well, trite as it sounds, accidents do happen."

"Yeah. I guess."

They sat in silence while David tried to assimilate the news. He was probably being absurd, but something...

"Christie, it's been a couple of days since Jenny told Wakefield she was pregnant. It's not as if she only found out this morning. She's had time to think, time to plan. And she's conscientious as hell. So why didn't she tell me she wanted a few days off?"

"Not saying anything doesn't strike me as odd, David. Not in this circumstance. I can understand a pregnant, unmarried woman wanting to get away by herself—without having to explain to anyone why she was going. And maybe... well, maybe she decided on an abortion. Maybe that's what this is all about. And, if it is, do you really think she'd have wanted to come to you and say, 'David I need a few days off to have an abortion'?"

"No. No, I guess not. But she could have given me a cover story. And what about the cat?"

"What about the cat?"

"Oh. I guess I didn't mention Sammy. When Wakefield and I went to Jenny's apartment, her cat hadn't been fed."

Christie gazed at David as if he'd taken leave of his senses.

"According to Wakefield," he elaborated, feeling more like an idiot with each word, "she normally feeds Sammy in the morning. But he was wailing for me to feed him while we were there."

"Weren't you the man," Christie asked with a trace of a smile, "who was lecturing me, only this afternoon, about worrying for nothing? And now you're worrying about a cat? A cat that got fed a little later than usual?"

"No, you don't understand. What I mean is that Jenny would never—"

"David, she probably asked a neighbor to feed Sammy while she was away. And you simply beat the neighbor to it."

Of course. That was a logical possibility. Why hadn't he thought of it? And what kind of a clue was a hungry cat, anyway?

He forced a grin, certain he must look the epitome of sheepishness. "I guess it's a good thing I went into medicine rather than police work, eh?"

"I don't think there's any guessing about it, David. Any self-respecting police academy would have turfed you after week one."

CHRISTIE ABSENTLY POKED her spoon at the marshmallows floating in her mug. Hot chocolate had been her mother's way of wrapping up a long day. Strange coincidence that it was Kay's, as well.

Sitting here at the kitchen table was almost like... She glanced across it. Kay was staring at the phone. "Kay?"

The older woman started, then smiled. "Pretty foolish, aren't I?"

"Well, that makes two of us, because I've been watching the phone, too."

"I don't know why we are. I certainly don't want it to ring. If it did, I'd jump out of my skin—even though Sid seemed perfectly fine when we left Mercy. I'm just having a lot of trouble believing he really is, Christie. And I keep thinking that I'd never be able to cope if he... I just couldn't stand losing someone I love. Not again. I guess that sounds awfully selfish."

Christie reached over and patted Kay's hand. "No. It just sounds normal."

"David seems to think your father's all right, though."

"He seems certain. So I guess both of us should stop this silly worrying."

"You're right. I'm glad you decided not to go back to New York yet, dear. It's reassuring to have someone around to tell me when I'm being silly. While Holly was still living in Winnipeg that was her job."

"You must miss her."

Kay nodded. "I phoned Denver while you and David were out for dinner, and she offered to fly back and stay with me. But I told her I'd be fine, that you'd be here." They sat quietly for a few moments. Then Kay hesitantly cleared her throat. "Christie...you seemed so upset at the wedding. I hope that...well, I...I do love your father. Very much."

"I know you do, Kay. I've never doubted that. I could see it written all over your face when you visited him in New York. And as far as those darn tears go...well, I'm really sorry about them. I didn't mean to do anything to spoil the ceremony. Bad enough that I delayed it."

"Nobody seemed to mind the wait."

"Well, anyway, I wasn't upset because Dad was marrying you, Kay. It was...oh, several things. I'll miss him. I guess I feel like you must have felt when Holly left Winnipeg. Dad's always been nearby if I've needed him. And New York's always been his home."

"I think he'll like living here, Christie. And if it turns out that he doesn't, then we can always go someplace else. Maybe check out condos in Florida or Hawaii or who knows where."

"Footloose and fancy-free, huh? There are definite advantages to being retired, aren't there?"

"Mmm," Kay murmured, smiling. "Four months ago I'd never have considered moving away from Winnipeg. And Sid says he'd never even thought about leaving the Bronx. But he could see that New York terrified me and...well, I guess falling in love can turn people's lives upside down."

Christie nodded, intensely aware of David's image in her mind's eye. Unexpected as it might be, fast and foolish as it was, she was falling in love with David Lawrence.

Perhaps the potential for falling in love in the blink of an eye was something she'd inherited. It had happened to her father twice—first with her mother and then with Kay.

But whether or not a genetic predisposition was to blame, it was definitely happening to her. Sometime over their pizza tonight she'd admitted to herself that the "something special" they seemed to have was definitely the initial stages of love.

Despite being worried about her father, she felt so incredibly euphoric when she was with David that it couldn't possibly be anything else. And when he'd kissed her good-night before taking her back up to the unit... well, that had been euphoria *plus*.

She hadn't intended to find herself in David's arms tonight. She still hadn't thought this situation through—hadn't decided whether letting nature take its course would be totally insane. But, when David had begun kissing her, all she'd been able to think about was how wonderful it would be to spend forever kissing him back.

If only...

She pushed the wish into a dusty corner of her mind. Wishing couldn't make the impossible possible.

"I'd better get to bed, Kay. I want to call the clinic first thing at nine. With New York being an hour ahead, I'll have to be up before eight."

"How long are you going to tell them you'll be away?"

"I guess I'll have to say I'm not sure, that I'll be home as soon as Dad's out of the hospital. Hopefully that'll mean being back at work before the week's out."

"You're welcome to stay here a little longer if you'd like, Christie. I was thinking you might want to stay through next weekend."

"Oh, no. Thanks, but I know you'll take good care of Dad. And you two are newlyweds. I'd simply be in the way once he's home."

"Well, I wasn't thinking of you being in the way very much, dear. I was thinking you might want to see a little more of the city... spend more time with David."

Christie glanced at Kay, wondering if she could be clairvoyant. No. More likely, what was happening between herself and David was just incredibly obvious. "Dad didn't warn me you were a matchmaker, Kay."

"I'm not normally. But I have to plead guilty in this instance. I suggested David not bring a date to the wedding. When you said you'd be coming here on your own, I thought maybe...

Well, I did make a good match, didn't I, Christie? You and David did hit it off."

Christie couldn't help laughing. *Hit it off* seemed an awfully pale phrase to describe what had happened.

"Yes, you made a good match, Kay. You could definitely say David and I hit it off. I should take you home with me and put you to work finding me a man in Manhattan."

"Oh, I'd never manage it a second time. Good men are awfully hard to find."

"I've noticed. I'm twenty-seven years old and, believe me, I've noticed."

"Well, as I said, dear, if you'd like to stay longer, you're welcome."

She was awfully tempted to take Kay up on the offer. Instead, she shook her head. "Thanks. But it's probably not a good idea. A few more days would only...well, regardless of whether we hit it off or not, there's no real future for David and me. Besides, we barely know each other. It's crazy to even think about..." Christie's words drifted into silence. The discussion was pointless.

Kay sipped her hot chocolate, looking pensive, as if she wasn't certain she should pursue the topic. "Christie," she finally offered, "perhaps I'm being silly again, but I can see that you and David... Oh, dear, I don't know quite how to put this because it's undoubtedly none of my business. In fact, I can practically hear Holly saying so. But I want to tell you about Holly and David—to explain why I suggested you stay."

Christie inched back her chair a fraction, uncertain she really wanted to hear about Holly and David. But she had no choice. Kay was beginning to tell her.

"They'd known each other for years, Christie— from the time David interned under her father. And they gradually drifted into their engagement. But there was something missing between them. I call it tingles, although Holly says that's an old-fashioned term. She calls it fireworks. Whatever you want to call it, though, it wasn't there. And Mac coming along made Holly realize that.''

So, it was precisely as David had told her, Christie reflected. There had been no pheromones at work between him and Holly.

"But it wasn't only that David wasn't the right man for Holly," Kay went on. "She wasn't the right woman for him, either. Christie, I know it's sometimes difficult to be sure what a man is really thinking or feeling. And what I'm trying to tell you is that the way David's been looking at you . . . well, I never saw him looking at my daughter that way. And that's why I thought you might like a little extra time here."

David had never looked at Holly McCloy the way he looked at her. Christie suddenly felt as if tiny bubbles were invading her veins—as if champagne were replacing her blood.

At the wedding, she'd noticed the loving way her father had been watching Kay. Were there special looks that went with tingles?

And the way David looked at her . . . well, she certainly adored the way David looked at her. When he gazed at her with those incredibly blue eyes of his, she felt as if she was the most desirable woman on earth. And she was sure she'd never looked at another man the way she looked at David.

But even if their looks rated twenties on a ten-point scale, the fundamental problem wasn't going to go away. She and David weren't going to have much opportunity for looking at each other.

What was the saying about east being east and west being west and never the twain meeting? Well, *never* might be an exaggeration in their case. But any future meetings they had wouldn't happen very darn often.

"I guess falling in love with your father has turned me into an old romantic," Kay mused. "But those tingles seem to be so rare that I thought I should . . . well, now that I've gotten into the match-making game, I feel I have a vested interest in you and David. I hope you don't mind, dear."

"No. No, I don't mind. But don't be disappointed when . . . well, don't forget David and I normally have two thousand miles between us. I can't imagine tingles are able to transmit anywhere near that far."

"Two thousand miles," Kay murmured. "One of you in New York and the other in Winnipeg. Precisely the way your father and I were."

Christie shook her head. "Your situation was completely different, Kay. Getting together wouldn't be as easy for David and me. In fact, I can't see that it would be possible—not on any permanent basis. I . . . Kay, I'm not even sure why we're talking about this. Just admitting that the thought has crossed my mind makes me feel ridiculous. I only met David yesterday."

"I don't think tingles have any respect for the concept of time, Christie. In fact, zapping people who barely know each other may be their specialty. Nothing's impossible."

"Well, I think any shared future for David and me is about as close to impossible as you could get. He has his practice here. And I'm only licensed to work in New York. And he's already told me he doesn't like New York and I don't—"

She caught herself and stopped. She couldn't even imagine living in a small city. That option was out of the question. But telling Kay that Winnipeg seemed like a dreadfully ho-hum little town would hardly be tactful.

"New Yorkers are a strange breed, Kay. When you grow up there it's difficult to think about living anyplace else. And, anyway, I've got to be logical about this. The likelihood of my seeing David again after this week isn't very great. By the next time I visit, he'll probably have forgotten about me."

"You know, Christie, I think that people sometimes try too hard to be logical. And I think that sometimes they're too frightened to take chances when it comes to emotions, that they pass things by because they're afraid to risk being hurt and that sometimes they miss out on very important things in life because they're too cautious."

Cautious. Cautious Christie. Her mother's pet name for her. Fleetingly she wondered if her father had mentioned that to Kay—wondered if she'd been speaking in generalities about people being afraid of risk or if—

"Christie, I know I shouldn't be going on like this. It's just that I'm fond of both you and David and I'd hate to see two people who just might…well, as I said dear, nothing's impossible. Sometimes circumstances just make things difficult."

Christie managed a smile. Kay was being silly again. All kinds of things were impossible.

Kay glanced at her watch. "I guess eight o'clock's going to come awfully soon for you. You can't have gotten much sleep in that chair last night."

"Right. I really should get to bed. I'll try not to make any noise in the morning."

"Oh, I'm always up before eight. I can wake you about a quarter to if you'd like. The alarm in Holly's room is awfully jarring. And what do you prefer first thing? Coffee?''

"You're spoiling me rotten, Kay. But I love it. And, yes, coffee would be great."

"Well, good night then, dear. I'm just going to sit here for a few more minutes. I'll see you in the morning."

CHRISTIE PUT HER MUG into the dishwasher, wished Kay good-night, then headed upstairs, expecting to fall asleep in seconds. Instead, she tossed and turned with Kay's words echoing in her mind: *Too cautious... miss out... the way David's been looking at you...*

Was Kay right about people trying too hard to be logical? But, even if that was what was happening here, could there be even a pinch of logic in becoming involved in a long-distance love affair?

Christie punched the pillow, wondering what she should do. She'd told David she needed time. And he hadn't pressed her tonight. He'd kissed the daylights out of her and left her longing for more, but he hadn't pressed.

Yet she was absolutely certain where any future kissing would lead. She wouldn't be able to resist the inevitable. Because simply looking at David turned her on. And his every touch left her craving the next.

But where they went from here was obviously up to her. And the luxury of time was one thing she didn't have. She had to make a decision—quickly.

She could back off and go home without letting things progress any farther. But if she did that, David would undoubtedly fall in love with someone else. Or she could reach out and take...

Take what? The chance of her life? She didn't want to love and lose. She didn't want a brief affair, followed by a not-so-brief broken heart. She wanted to love and be loved.

But if she became more involved with David, the odds on getting hurt—somewhere down the line—would be awfully high. Probably at least two thousand to one. Those damn two thousand miles between New York and Winnipeg. Those damn two thousand miles that tingles couldn't possibly transmit over.

She didn't know what to do. All she knew was that she'd never felt anything even remotely close to what she was feeling for David.

If she walked away from that feeling, if she refused to chance being hurt, she just might miss out on something wonderful. And simply imagining how wonderful the something could be made her wish that she was back in David's arms again.

She finally fell asleep... only to dream about how absolutely incredible David Lawrence was... and how she didn't want to walk away... didn't want it even a little bit... and that, in this instance, there were only two possible directions she could walk. And standing still wasn't a viable option.

CHAPTER EIGHT

"GOOD MORNING."

David glanced up from his desk and gazed at Christie. "Good morning, yourself."

It was impossible to look at her without smiling. She was wearing a slim white dress—plain except for a small lace collar. Yet both the dress and the woman wearing it looked as if they belonged in a fashion magazine.

The fabric fit smoothly across her hips. And the top buttons were undone, opening the neckline to a most interesting level. Christie might be thin, but her figure struck him as perfect.

And she was absolutely beautiful. Framed by his office doorway, with her pale hair hanging loosely on her shoulders, she could be a life-size portrait of an angel. But portraits were stiff and lifeless while Christie Lambert was warm and soft and felt like heaven in his arms. Watching her, all he could think about was the way she'd kissed him yesterday...and how desperately he wanted to kiss her again.

"I'm not disturbing you, am I, David?"

Not disturbing him? She had to be joking. She must realize that the mere sight of her disturbed the hell out of him.

"Of course not," he managed. "You look . . . you look terrific. That almost-empty suitcase of yours must be magic."

She smiled one of her sensational smiles, then struck an exaggerated model's pose. "This is the latest style from the fashion capital of western Canada. At least that's what the salesclerk told me. Kay raced me in and out of a store on our way over here."

"But only after she'd called to check on Sid."

"Of course. How did you know that, though?"

"I've been boning up on the art of detecting. You hurt my feelings yesterday, telling me that no self-respecting police academy would have me."

"Well...I simply meant that you didn't have much detective potential. I suppose you might possibly make it with those video police you mentioned. I wasn't thinking about them."

"Very funny. Have you been in to see your father yet?"

"Yup. But Kay sent me off to get an update on his condition. That's the only reason I'd come by and bother you when you're working."

David tried to decide whether she was kidding. He couldn't tell from her expression, but he certainly hoped she was. He'd be happy to have her coming by and bothering him twenty-four hours a day. A more enjoyable way to be bothered probably didn't exist.

"An update," he offered. "Okay, then. Sid's still doing great. We ran another cardiac enzyme test this morning, but I haven't seen the results yet. And, as far as that ECG reading goes, I spoke to someone in New York who's promised to track one down. We should have it . . . well, the fellow wasn't prepared to guarantee when."

"You'll have it whenever he manages to cut through the bureaucratic red tape. Right?"

"I suspect that's about it. Which brings you as up-to-date as I am. And that's the only reason you came by to see me, eh?"

"Well . . . no. Actually, there was another reason."

"Oh?"

"Yes. I had to come down here because Ruth Allison was at the nursing station. I thought she might bite my head off if I asked her about Dad."

This time Christie's smile assured David that she was teasing.

"I see. So you're only here because you were afraid of what Ruth might do to you."

"Right. I'm terrified of dragon ladies."

"But you're not afraid of what I might do to you?"

"Of course I am. I learned yesterday how dangerous you can be. You'll notice I didn't close the door."

"I was just thinking about that very thing. Anyone ever tell you you're a spoilsport, Christie?"

She reached back and shoved the door shut. "Better?"

"Depends on what happens next."

"Did you have anything in mind?"

Be cool, he told himself. But apparently he wasn't listening to himself, because he set a new personal best for rising and getting from behind his desk.

Christie's expression was saying precisely what he wanted to hear. And if she kissed him now the way she'd kissed him yesterday, he'd be floating on air for hours.

She took a step nearer—drew so close that he could smell her intoxicating perfume, so near that he could see the sparkle in her blue eyes, so near that she was setting off a four-alarm alert in his pheromone receptors.

Before he could move, she reached up, encircled his neck and kissed him into an eight-alarm alert. He hugged her closely, certain he wouldn't be floating on air for merely hours. He'd be floating for the rest of April.

Her body was soft and yielding against his. Her tongue gently teased his lips, then began probing more intimately, arousing him so intensely that it was all he could do to remember she wanted time. Because the only thing he wanted, the only thing in the world he wanted, was her. A more enjoyable way to be bothered *definitely* didn't exist.

"I...David I think," she finally murmured, breaking their kiss, "that the something that's happening between us has been working overtime."

He swallowed hard, hoping he wasn't reading something into her remark that she didn't mean. "Do you figure there's such a thing as double overtime, Christie?"

"I wouldn't be at all surprised. I've never before met a man who I simply couldn't seem to keep my hands off."

David drew her closer again, wishing they were in his apartment instead of his office. She couldn't seem to keep her hands off him! If she couldn't keep her hands off him and he couldn't keep his hands off her...God! How much more time would she need? Holding her this way was driving him mad.

He slid his hands down her back and pulled her against himself. She pressed her body even closer, sending an incredible rush of desire through him. Then she slipped her hands down and rested them on his thighs, leaving no doubt about her message. No doubt in *his* mind at least. But he'd misread her before. He wasn't going to make that mistake twice. When she'd had enough time, she'd have to tell him—with words rather than with this sexy body language that was practically making him drool. He could feel his heart hammering and tentatively began caressing her hips.

"I . . . I spent the entire night thinking about you, David," she whispered.

His heart stopped hammering and began racing a mile a minute. How could he have specialized in cardiology without ever learning about all the unbelievable things hearts were capable of? Since he'd met Christie he'd discovered that his could do all kinds of things he'd never believed possible. He doubted his voice was going to work, but it did. "I'm glad, Christie. Because I spent the entire night thinking about you."

"I . . . David, maybe there's such a thing as triple overtime because . . . oh, saying this makes me feel like a wanton woman, but I want to spend as much time as I can with you. I could keep on kissing you all day and . . . and . . ." She stopped speaking and rested her cheek against his chest.

He could scarcely believe it. He'd been so afraid that once she'd had a chance to think she'd decide to hightail it back to New York and he'd never see her again. But that wasn't going to happen. Here she was—snuggled warmly in his arms, the fresh scent of her hair and her perfume driving him crazy.

And impossible as it seemed, she must be feeling about him the way he was feeling about her. She'd said she could keep on kissing him all day. And her body was making even more intimate suggestions. And this time she'd thought things through, had spent the entire night thinking about him.

"You're not a wanton woman, Christie," he whispered. "There's nothing wanton about...about special somethings."

He'd managed to catch himself. He'd almost said there was nothing wanton about falling in love. That had to be what was happening, because nothing like this insanity had ever struck him before.

But it was too soon to tell her he loved her. What was going on between them had developed so fast that it seemed unreal. And he didn't want Christie to think he was saying something he didn't mean, didn't want her to think he was...

But, given the way she was looking at him, she didn't think he was anything other than terrific. How fantastically fantastic that was!

He kissed her once more, then forced himself to stop. His office wasn't very private, but if she said the word, he knew they'd be making love on his couch.

"I'll rearrange my schedule, Christie, so I can take a few hours off today."

"Mmm. That sounds wonderful."

He kissed her a final, loving, lingering time, certain a few hours with her would pass like a few seconds. If he could, he'd make those few hours a few days, or weeks, or months or...

His arm still around her waist, he leaned across his desk and began checking his appointment book, deciding what was absolutely essential and what could wait. Christie snaked her fingers up under the back of his jacket and his number of absolute essentials decreased substantially. She was only going to be in Winnipeg for a few more days. And come hell or high water he was going to spend every possible second of those days with her.

He'd only booked a couple of consultations for the week. And he'd taken several on-calls for Pierre LeBlanc recently, so he wouldn't feel guilty about asking him to handle most of the unit's routine administration.

Just as he finished skimming through his entries for the next few days, the telephone rang. He felt Christie tense and glanced at her.

She shrugged. "The last time your telephone interrupted us it was..."

"It won't be this time. Your father's right down the hall. If anything was wrong, someone would come knocking on my door." He nuzzled her neck, wanting her to relax again, then snuggled her against his hip and picked up the receiver. "Dr. Lawrence."

"I'm calling about Jennifer Doyle," a voice rasped.

The tension he'd been feeling in Christie's body seemed to be seeping into his own. "What about her?"

"I figured you'd be the one to tell what's happened to her."

SECONDS AFTER he answered the phone Christie felt David's body stiffen. She shifted away from him and watched him listen, watched his face gradually pale to the color of ash.

"All right," he finally said, his voice sounding strained. "I'll be here at four."

As he hung up, she thought his hand was trembling slightly. "What?" she demanded anxiously. "What's wrong?"

"It's...it's bizarre."

"David, what's bizarre?"

He ran his fingers through his hair. "Jenny. Jenny's been kidnapped."

"What?"

"Kidnapped. And whoever that was says he wants twenty-five thousand dollars to set her free."

Christie's mind began buzzing but she couldn't seem to put the right words together to form questions. "Exactly what did he say?" she finally managed.

"Just that. He wants twenty-five thousand dollars and I'm supposed to act as intermediary, convince the hospital to come up with the money. He's going to phone me back at four. He said if I don't have the money then, or if we call the cops, he's going to kill her."

"Kill her?" Christie wasn't certain she'd actually spoken aloud. Her voice had become a mere whisper.

David's nod told her that she'd indeed repeated his words. He picked up the receiver again, looking ill. "I have to talk to the hospital's administrator. We've got to decide whether or not to contact the police. We have to decide where we go from here."

"But this just doesn't make sense, David." Simultaneously the realization popped into her head and the words popped out of her mouth. Her voice had returned to near-normal.

He paused, the receiver in his hand, gazing blankly at her.

"Jenny's note, David. People who are being kidnapped don't leave notes saying they'll be back in a few days."

"Well, the kidnapper must have left the note, then."

"That's doesn't make sense, either. Why would a kidnapper write a note saying what that one did? Why wouldn't it have said she'd been kidnapped and he wanted a ransom?''

"I...I don't know. Damn it, Christie, I haven't got the foggiest idea what makes sense here.''

David began dialing and Christie concentrated on sorting through the bits and pieces he'd told her about Jenny's disappearance. He'd found the note slipped under his office door. Then he'd talked with Brent Wakefield and the two of them had gone to Jenny's apartment. Then they'd checked for her car in the parking lot and asked around the hospital about her.

That was it: *they'd asked around the hospital about her!*

David slammed the receiver down, jolting Christie's attention back to him. "Daley's not in the hospital right now. His secretary's going to try to track him down for me, but she didn't sound very hopeful. Damn! We've only got until four to decide what we're going to do. That's less than six hours from now.''

"David, something just struck me. How many people did you and Brent talk to yesterday?''

"What?''

"You told me you'd asked around about Jenny. So how many people knew you were looking for her, knew that she'd disappeared?''

"I don't know. I spoke with each of the unit staff who'd come on at eight. And Brent said he was going to check with the cafeteria and security people—and anyone else he thought might have seen her. But what does that have to do with—''

Christie could almost see the light bulb click on above David's head.

"A hoax, Christie? You think that might have been a crank call?''

"I think it's possible. Manhattan can't have cornered the entire market on weirdos."

"A weirdo. If the guy was just a weirdo, then Jenny's all right ... at least as all right as we decided she was last night. Lord, I hope that's the case."

"With luck it is, David. I can't see how her being pregnant and leaving that note could suddenly have become a kidnapping. But anyone who works at Mercy might know she's disappeared. They wouldn't know she'd left a note, though. So maybe somebody simply figured the hospital would be willing to cough up twenty-five grand."

David began to pace his office, muttering something about a slimy weasel.

Christie followed him with her eyes for a few moments before speaking again. "I don't imagine the voice sounded the least bit familiar, did it?"

"No. It was disguised—a raspy whisper. Could have been anyone. I just wish we knew if there was really something to worry about, knew whether that guy was on the level or simply a crank. If he's for real, Christie.... Oh, damn! I don't even want to think about him being for real. What if he's actually got Jenny? Should I contact the police? But if I do phone them, how seriously do you suppose they'll take that creep's call? I mean, you realized his story might not be kosher. They will, too. What the hell am I supposed to do?"

"I don't know what to tell you, David. I wish I'd paid more attention to some of Dad's detective tales."

"Your father. Of course. I'm not thinking straight. He's the obvious person to ask for advice."

"Pardon?"

"Your father. He's our best bet for making some sense out of this. Look, I'm going to talk to him before I do anything else. So, if you wouldn't mind getting Kay out of the room, hustling her off for coffee or something..."

Christie eyed David in disbelief. He was serious. He intended to lay a story about a disappearance and an extortion call on her father. Just what Sid Lambert needed to get his adrenaline pumping and his heart racing a mile a minute!

She took a deep breath before objecting, ordering herself to calm down. "David...I realize how worried you are, but hold on a minute. Getting Dad involved isn't a good idea. Why don't you simply go ahead and phone the police?"

"Because I'm suddenly involved in something I don't know a damn thing about, that's why! And that jerk might really have Jenny. And what do I know about kidnappings or threats or what might happen if I call the cops rather than come up with the money? I simply don't know what I should do, Christie. And I've got a retired detective down the hall who will."

"David, you've got a retired detective down the hall who's flat on his back! And I specifically recall you telling him that he shouldn't excite himself."

"Exert. I didn't say excite. I said he shouldn't exert himself."

"Exert! Excite! Don't give me a semantics lesson when he shouldn't do either!"

"Oh, for God's sake, Christie! Stop overreacting!"

"Stop yelling at me!"

"I'm not yelling at you. I'm merely trying to tell you that he won't be either exerting or exciting himself. I'm simply going to tell him the basic facts and ask him what to do. There's no reason in the world not to."

"There certainly is!" Oh, damn! Her last shred of control had just vanished. But David was an idiot if he thought that hearing about what had happened wouldn't get her father going. Of course, David was a doctor. And doctors always thought they knew everything.

"Christie, you realize you're being absurd, don't you?"

"I'm not being absurd!"

"You are! The medical facts thus far say there's absolutely nothing wrong with your father. You saw that the monitors didn't pick up a thing. And I know you've been sneaking peeks at his progress chart. You probably even had a look this morning before you came to talk to me."

Christie felt her face growing warm. David's guess was bang on, but her annoyance that he was right merely heightened her anger. "Damn it, David! All the medical facts aren't in yet. You haven't got that ECG reading from New York. And you haven't looked at the latest blood enzyme results. And you aren't entirely sure Dad didn't have a heart attack."

"If he did, it was an extremely minor one. And my talking with him isn't going to do the slightest harm."

"In my opinion you can't be certain what might harm him."

"Well, heaven forbid we should allow my medical knowledge to interfere with your opinion, Christie."

"Don't be sarcastic!"

"Don't tell me how to be! And I'm also getting more than a little tired of you having absolutely no faith in me when I tell you your father's going to be fine."

"Well I'm getting more than a little tired of you playing God!"

David opened his mouth, then closed it again and cleared his throat. "Christie...let's cool off here. I...I'm sorry I raised my voice. But Jenny's a friend. I'm terribly worried about her. And I feel frustrated as hell. I can't even figure out whether there's something seriously wrong. If there is, though, I want to do whatever I can to help her. But, hell, Christie, I don't know what I should be doing. For all I know we should just quietly pay the ransom instead of calling the police. I don't know anything about this sort of situation. I can't assess the risks. But your father can."

David paused and gestured across his office. "Look. There they are, just like I told you. My medical diploma and specialist certificate. Christie, I'm certainly not about to endanger your father's health. If anything, the way I feel about you is making me overly cautious."

Christie stood looking at David, her stomach churning crazily. What on earth were they doing fighting? David was a competent specialist. She had to trust his judgment. And she could see his point about Jenny. If the woman was in serious trouble, then of course they had to do what they could. But still...

"David, I...I'm sorry, too. And I'm sure you know what you're doing as far as Dad's concerned. It's just that he's so..."

David reached across and took her hand. "It's okay, Christie. I understand. I didn't mean to upset you. I know you've been having a hard time with him being in here. And I shouldn't have called you absurd when you were merely being concerned. End of argument? Still friends?"

She forced a smile, feeling like a fool—a fool who'd just thrown a childish tantrum. She likely *had* been absurd. But that didn't mean she didn't want to see for herself that her father wasn't getting excited or exerted or excessive or any other damn *ex*.

"Just one more minor detail, David. I want to sit in on your conversation with Dad. I'll feel a whole lot better if I'm there than if you shuffle me off to have coffee with Kay."

"Christie, I . . . I didn't mean to give the impression I wanted to shuffle you off. I was only thinking that it probably wouldn't be appropriate to talk about this in front of Kay. And I can hardly ask her to leave her husband's room while you stay."

"Does it really matter if she's there, David?"

"You know, I can't even answer that," he admitted with a slight grin. "See how little I know about criminal matters? No wonder I want to talk to your father."

Christie managed to return David's grin. "Guess I've been right about your lack of detective potential then, huh? So you'd better keep close track of those diplomas of yours."

"I'll let that unkind remark pass. Come on," he added, wrapping his arms firmly about her. "Let me give you one big, reassuring hug. Then we'll go see the expert."

THE OTHER THREE SAT in silence while Sid read Jenny's note for what must have been the tenth time. Despite Christie's fears, and much to her relief, he'd remained perfectly calm while David recounted the story's details. She had to admit she'd been wrong, that her father could obviously handle this.

In fact, sitting there propped up in bed, he looked as if he was ready to get up and handle anything that came his way. But Kay clearly wasn't the least impressed by this little meeting. She kept shooting David black looks that said she thought he should never have involved her husband.

Sid finally handed the note back to David. "There's no doubt that you should phone the police. It's the only sensible way to proceed."

"But what do you think about my caller, Sid? Was he legit? Does he really have Jenny?"

"I'd say he doesn't. I'd say he's simply a joker who figures he might be able to make some fast bucks."

Christie looked at David. The same relief she felt was flooding his face.

"Christie was perfectly right, David. A kidnapping and that note simply don't add up. Even so, the police will probably want to put a recorder on your phone. Whether your caller actually knows anything about Jenny or not, they'll want to get their hands on him. Attempted extortion isn't a joke. But he'll more than likely get cold feet between now and four o'clock. Odds are you won't hear from him again."

"So," Christie murmured, "if you don't think the kidnapper's for real, then we shouldn't worry? You figure Jenny's probably all right?" She waited for her father to say yes, then felt a fresh flutter of concern when he didn't.

"Well, the note does fit in with the boyfriend's conclusion that Jenny's gone off to think. It's just her leaving so suddenly.... No, it's not *just* that. It's several things. You've got good Sherlock Holmes instincts, David."

Christie almost groaned at the "so there" glance David gave her and decided she'd better cut the cracks about his lack of detective potential.

"You've pinpointed some interesting inconsistencies," her father went on. "You're right that Jenny suddenly rushing off doesn't make sense when she's known about the pregnancy for a while. And she mustn't have planned ahead about leaving. Otherwise why arrange to meet Wakefield? That makes me think something unexpected happened toward the end of her shift. Or just after she went off duty."

"Such as?" Christie prompted.

"I don't know, baby. But the same things that bothered David bother me. Why would Jenny write a note on a computer when she doesn't normally use one? Anything out of the ordinary like that is suspicious. And it makes me wonder if... well, I do think it's possible she's run into trouble of some kind... not necessarily related to her being pregnant. There are so many little things that don't make sense. For one thing, David's right about those edges being left on the paper. They probably indicate that someone was in an awful hurry. But that someone wasn't necessarily Jenny. Because typing her name rather than signing it is definitely something to wonder about, too. And the cat not being fed—noticing that was good work, David."

"I could hardly have missed it," David said. "People must have been able to hear Sammy complaining a block away. But Christie thought Jenny might have asked a neighbor to look in on the cat."

"That's certainly something to check."

"Sid," Kay murmured uneasily, "what do you mean, 'check'? You can't get involved in this. I don't even like your talking about it. David said you're not supposed to get the least bit excited."

Christie glared at David. She'd kill him if he started lecturing Kay about the difference between excitement and exertion.

"I won't let Sid get excited, Kay."

Ah. Fine. Glares were effective with the good doctor.

"But . . . but shouldn't David be phoning the police now, Sid? Instead of talking to you, I mean."

Christie patted Kay's hand. She'd obviously like nothing better than to see David end this session and leave—whether it was to phone the police or to do anything else imaginable.

"Of course he'll call the police, dear," Sid said. "In a minute."

"And what are they likely to do?" David asked.

"Well, at the moment I'd be surprised if they did much more than take a report and record your calls. They'll likely proceed on the assumption that this guy who claims to be a kidnapper is a phony and that Jenny will turn up on her own. Basically they'll probably just wait and see. I don't expect the loose ends you've picked up on are going to be enough to alarm them."

"So that's what we should all do? I phone the police and then we wait and see?"

"I . . . yes. For the moment at least, David. We can't do anything that might hamper a police investigation. On the other hand . . . if there's no investigation to hamper . . ." Sid paused, looking thoughtful. "David, is it really so out of character for Jenny to just take off?"

"Completely. That was what initially got me worried."

"Well, first things first. You go call the police and let's see where that gets us."

CHAPTER NINE

IT WAS ALMOST an hour before David returned to Sid's room.

"You get an A for predictions, Sid," he offered, slumping into a chair. "Basically the police are going to play wait and see."

"They aren't going to do anything?" Christie asked.

"Well, your father was right about them wanting to put a recording device on my phone. They're sending someone over to do that. 'Just in case,' the fellow said. But he didn't figure the ransom call was for real any more than you did, Sid. And taping my calls is all they're prepared to do at the moment."

"Sid?" Kay murmured, her voice anxious, "I didn't think you were being serious about them not doing anything. A young woman's disappeared."

"She left a note, Kay. And wanting time away to think because she's pregnant sounds like a perfectly acceptable reason for taking off. You can't expect them to worry about her."

"But you and David seemed to think she might not actually have written that note."

"Well, she probably did. And, anyway, there's an enormous difference between being a little suspicious and having hard evidence."

"They said they'd become concerned if Jenny's gone for a substantial length of time," David muttered. "However the hell long that is."

"Her note said a few nights," Sid offered. "A substantial length of time is going to be longer than that."

David shook his head. "You know, all those little loose ends we talked about didn't seem the slightest bit significant to the police. But they're still worrying the hell out of me."

"Well, rather than sitting around and worrying, I've got a few ideas about what would make sense to do—"

"Sid!" Kay exclaimed. "You'll do absolutely nothing! This has gone far enough."

Sid gazed at her with a henpecked expression. "After that sweetie pie took such good care of me the other night? What if she's in serious trouble? I owe her."

"Don't worry, Kay," David said, shooting her a reassuring glance. "I'm beginning to think that Sid's home free. His test results are looking good. I had a glance at them while I was gone and his enzyme levels are holding steady. So he's probably fine. I'm not going to let him move from that bed, though—not until I get those records from New York. But," he added, turning back to Sid, "if you think there's something I can do...I was planning on freeing up some time today, anyway." David looked at Christie as he finished speaking, his expression asking her to understand.

She forced a smile. Of course she understood. It was hardly David's fault he'd been dragged into a mess that they couldn't figure out. And there was no question about doing whatever their own personal detective advised. Not after he'd said he thought Jenny might have run into trouble. If only there was a fairy godmother lurking about who could wave a magic wand and make Jenny materialize before them.

"Well, the first thing *you* should do, David," Sid said, glancing at Kay as he emphasized the *you*, "is try to establish whether Jenny's actually okay. You should call her friends and see if she mentioned anything about being away for a few days. She might even be staying with someone you phone."

Christie gazed at David for a minute longer, at the man she wanted to spend every free moment he had with. He apparently wasn't going to have many of them for the next little while.

"And does Jenny have relatives in the city?" Sid asked.

"Her parents live in Saskatchewan," David said. "But I think there's an aunt here."

"She's worth contacting, too. And maybe even the parents if you can do it without alarming them. Then, if that turns up nothing—"

"If there's something else for David to do," Christie interrupted, "I can do the phoning."

David rewarded her with a grateful smile that made her wish even harder for a fairy godmother.

"I can say I'm a friend of Jenny's from out of town, that I'm trying to locate her."

"Good. That would be better than David calling—wouldn't get anyone worried."

"And if I don't have any luck on the phone, I could go banging on her neighbor's doors with the same story—see if anyone knew she was going away. I might even turn up someone she asked to cat-sit Sammy."

"Good idea. I'll make a detective out of you yet, Christie. We can get a list of people to call from the boyfriend. I'm going to want to talk to him, anyway."

"Sid!" Kay interjected.

"I said talk, Kay. I'm merely going to talk. Have you seen me getting excited?"

"Well . . . no."

"Fine, then. And I won't move a muscle. You can sit right there and keep on watching me."

"I don't want to, Sid. I don't want to hear any more than I've already heard. The idea of a possible kidnapping—or *anything* happening to Jenny—and the police not being concerned and you . . . well, listening to you playing detective is just upsetting me."

"Kay, I'm not playing. I've been a detective practically my whole life. And I'm simply—"

"No," she said firmly. "I married a retired detective, not an active chief investigator. And the idea of you directing an investigation from a bed in a cardiac care unit is . . . well, you shouldn't be involved in this."

"But David just said I was fine."

"David did *not* just say you were fine. He said that your test results were looking good. And that you were probably fine. Probably isn't good enough, Sid."

Christie eyed Kay guiltily, wanting to say something that would make her feel less upset but unable to think of anything. Now that Sid Lambert had his teeth into Jenny's disappearance, he'd be as tenacious as a bulldog about sticking with it. They all might as well accept that. Not that she didn't think Kay was right. A patient on the CCU directing amateurs on how to search for a missing person *was* more than a little ludicrous.

On the other hand, her father wasn't getting excited, and if David really thought . . . and there was Jenny to think about and . . . and it was too late to say anything reassuring anyway because her father was speaking again.

"Kay, honey, I'm not involved. I'm just giving David and Christie a few pointers."

Kay shook her head. "The thought that something might have happened to Jenny makes me feel awful. But it's only a *possibility* that something's happened, isn't it?"

"Well . . . yes."

"Yes. And you're a hospital patient, barely off monitoring equipment. And I think you're being stubborn and unreasonable by pursuing this."

Kay paused, glancing at David as if she was about to give him a piece of her mind, as well. Instead, she turned back to Sid once more. "I didn't realize exactly how bullheaded you were, Sid Lambert. But me sitting here being upset about what you're doing isn't helping either of us. I'm going to go home for a couple of hours and have lunch. I couldn't face Mercy's cafeteria food again, anyway. And maybe, by the time I get back, you'll have finished with your foolishness."

"Kay, I—"

"Here, Christie," Kay said, cutting Sid off and digging in her purse. "I turned up a spare house key for you so that you can come and go as you like. And it's just as well I did. I won't be surprised if Sid has you sleuthing until the wee hours of the morning."

Christie leaned forward to take the key and whispered that she'd make sure her father didn't get carried away.

Kay gave her a weak smile and stood up. "I'll be back in a while, Sid. You be good."

"I *am* being good, Kay. And neither David nor Christie are going to let me be bad."

David rose hastily and walked Kay to the door, murmuring reassuring-sounding phrases to her.

"Damn," Sid muttered quietly. "I didn't mean to get her so wound up."

"She'll be okay, Dad. She's just worried about you. And she's still pretty stressed out."

"I guess she didn't quite realize what she was getting into by marrying me, huh, baby? Guess that's one of the dangers that goes with whirlwind romances."

"Yes...I guess there could be a lot of dangers that go with whirlwind romances," Christie murmured, watching David.

"I do want to talk to this Wakefield," Sid said once David had closed the door behind Kay. "What's he like?"

"He's...he's all right. Kind of a nonchalant type to be a doctor, but not a bad guy."

"Well, don't say anything to him about the ransom call. He's likely to get upset when he learns about it and I want to hear his story before that happens."

"All right. He's in the unit. I'll get him. Come with me, Christie? I want to talk to you for a minute. Then we can collect Wakefield."

Outside her father's room several people were standing in the corridor. David motioned toward his office and headed down the hallway. Christie silently trailed after him.

He closed the office door behind them and wrapped his arms about her, drawing her into the warmth of his embrace. "I didn't really want to talk at all," he whispered. "I simply wanted to hold you."

Christie pressed her cheek against his chest, inhaling his enticing, male scent, feeling the faint thudding of his heart. She simply wanted to hold him, too. If only there was no need to move from the secure shelter of David's arms, she'd be happy.

"I wish to hell things hadn't gotten so crazy, Christie. Because there's nothing in the world I'd rather do than be alone with you."

"Me, too," she whispered, but she'd begun doubting they'd ever be alone together again.

"Anyway, thanks for understanding. And thanks for offering to help. With both of us working on this, we'll check things out twice as fast. We'll still have time for us."

Would they? In no time at all her father would be discharged from the hospital, and she'd be back in New York, and David would still be in Winnipeg. Even the couple of days she'd thought she'd have with David were quickly slipping away. Maybe fate was trying to run out their time clock.

David tucked one finger under her chin and drew her gaze upward. "There'll be time for us," he promised, as if he'd been reading her thoughts.

"I . . . I'm not so sure, David. When we met, when we hit it off so well, I wondered if some mysterious power hadn't brought us together. Now I'm wondering if some mysterious power isn't throwing obstacles in our course."

"I don't believe in mysterious powers, Christie. I believe in special somethings."

He bent and kissed the top of her head, then cuddled her closely against him, making her wish she didn't believe in mysterious powers, either, making her wish she couldn't hear that imaginary time clock ticking away.

"I GUESS IT'S POSSIBLE Jenny's run into trouble," Brent agreed, echoing Sid's words. "But I don't really think so. David and I talked about that but...well, the more I consider it the more unlikely it seems. I'm sure she'll be back in a day or two."

Brent's voice, Christie thought, sounded decidedly strained.

"You're probably right, Brent," her father offered. "Just in case, though, I'd like you to tell me what happened yesterday—right from the time you were supposed to meet her."

Brent glanced a question at David.

"Go ahead. We're probably the only CCU in the country with an in-house detective."

"Ah...all right. Well, Jenny wasn't waiting for me at the nursing station—"

"Wasn't waiting?" Sid interrupted. "You were late, then?"

"Yes. A little. We were planning on having breakfast out. And we'd decided to use Jenny's car, so I took a bus over. But they don't run very frequently on Sundays and I didn't get here till quarter after eight— maybe even half past. At any rate, I couldn't find Jenny on the unit, and she hadn't slid a note under my office door the way she sometimes does, so—"

"She leaves you notes fairly often?"

Christie felt a surge of pity for Brent. She hadn't heard her father in such a fine detective mode since she'd lived at home and had come in from a date several hours past curfew.

"Well...sometimes she leaves a note. I wouldn't say fairly often. But Jenny goes off duty at eight and, unless I'm on night duty, I don't usually come in till nine. Shift work sometimes makes connecting difficult."

"And are these notes typed or handwritten?"

"I...they're usually handwritten, I guess."

"Usually or always?"

Brent cleared his throat and grinned an unhappy-looking grin. "Why do I feel as if I'm being interrogated?"

"Sorry, Brent. Try not to take any notice of my interrupting. It's just years of habit. The fastest way to get the information you want is to ask questions. Questions like: are Jenny's notes usually or always handwritten?"

"Well, in the past it was always. But recently I'd say they're fifty-fifty. She's been trying to conquer her fear of computers."

Sid's glance flickered to David for an instant. "And when she types a note, does she write her signature or type it?"

"I...I'm not sure. It's been a while since she's left me one."

"All right. And then? After you couldn't find Jenny on the unit and there was no note?"

"Then I checked the cafeteria for her. And when she wasn't there..."

Instead of concentrating on what Brent was telling her father—basically a rerun of things David had already told her—Christie focused on the intern's body language. He was leaning forward in the bedside chair, his hands on his knees, visibly upset. But she was pretty sure he'd been worrying before David had hauled him in here. Since he'd realized that Jenny had disappeared, Brent probably hadn't stopped being concerned for a minute.

His clothes were her clue. The white dress shirt beneath his lab coat was crisp. And his tie was carefully knotted. But his casual wool pants should have been on their way to the cleaners. They'd lost most of their crease and were terminally wrinkled—as if he'd tossed them onto the floor last night, then grabbed them without thinking this morning. She doubted wrinkled pants were his norm. He struck her as the type of man who was particular about his appearance.

He was thirty—maybe a bit older. Definitely older than the average intern. And that, Christie suspected, was because he'd spent more time with the ladies than he had with his medical books. She'd bet he'd never lacked an active social life.

Not only had he turned on the charm the moment David had introduced them, but Brent Wakefield was Mr. Tall-Dark-and-Handsome personified.

As far as she was concerned, his attractiveness paled beside David's chiseled profile. But he had the sort of brooding good looks that made a lot of women drool—deep brown eyes, curling hair the color of tar, a cleft in his chin and a tan that was positively indecent for April.

Either tanning parlors were still the rage in Winnipeg or he'd been south recently. Of course, when Sid Lambert finally got around to telling Brent about the ransom call, he was undoubtedly going to lose three shades of that tan.

She glanced at her father, wondering how much he was picking up from this session that she and David weren't, then returned her attention to Brent and began listening intently. He'd finished talking about the trip to Jenny's apartment, had outlined his theory that she'd disappeared "to think things over" and had started in on facts that Christie hadn't heard before. He was telling her father precisely who he'd talked to yesterday afternoon, who had known he was trying to locate Jenny.

"So I asked the women on duty in the cafeteria if Jenny had stopped by for coffee in the morning. I'd gotten to thinking that maybe she'd been and gone by the time I'd checked it earlier. But they didn't recall seeing her."

"And after the cafeteria?" Sid asked. "Where did you go next?"

"I just wandered around the hospital for a bit—asked a few people if they'd seen her. But none of them had."

"Did you tell them she seemed to have disappeared?"

"I guess I did . . . more or less. I said she hadn't met me when she was supposed to and that I hadn't been able to track her down."

"And then," Sid prompted, "after you finished wandering around?"

"Well, then I went to talk to the security guard at the north entrance—Reg something-or-other."

"Crosnoch," David supplied. "Reg Crosnoch. He's an old guy. He's been at Mercy for years."

"Jenny parks her car near that entrance," Brent explained, "and she sometimes chats with Reg on her way out. But he didn't see her yesterday morning."

"And yet her car was gone from the parking lot," Sid mused. "So she obviously left the building."

"Well, it turns out Reg was away from the entrance for a while. The security people had a brief meeting that started at quarter to eight."

"And ended?" Sid demanded.

"I...I didn't think to ask that. At any rate, their boss had come in..." Brent paused for a moment and a peculiar expression crossed his face.

Christie couldn't read it. She glanced at her father, but if he'd found it interesting, he wasn't giving the fact away.

"Mercy's security is contracted to an outside firm," Brent went on. "And Reg said that the company's owner had come in to talk to his staff. Early Sunday mornings are usually quiet, so they apparently schedule the occasional meeting then—catch the tail end of one shift and the start of the next." The intern paused once more and cleared his throat. His glance flickered meaningfully to David, then quickly away once more.

"What?" David demanded.

"Nothing."

"Wakefield, for God's sake don't start in with your *nothings* again! What's up?"

Brent slowly shrugged. "I just thought of something. Well...actually, I first thought of it when I was talking with Reg yesterday. But it's probably crazy."

"Let Sid decide that, okay?"

"I...look, David, I don't like this. I mean, I know everyone's worried about Jenny and that you're all trying to help. But...well, I don't mean to take your concern lightly, Sid, but I'm not entirely convinced that Jenny either needs or wants any help. I keep coming back to this all having to do with her being pregnant, keep thinking that she'll show up soon. And when she does she's going to be spitting mad if she finds out we've been sorting through her dirty laundry."

"What dirty laundry?" David pressed immediately.

Brent stared at his shoes for a long moment. When he spoke again, his voice was so quiet that Christie leaned forward to hear his words. "Dirty laundry like Austin Allison."

The others waited for Brent to say something more. He didn't.

"Austin Allison," David finally said, "who was in Mercy yesterday morning around eight. I think you'd better elaborate on what you're getting at."

"David, like I told you, it probably means nothing—just a crazy thought."

"It's time," Sid said in what Christie recognized as his most official, no-nonsense tone, "to fill the chief investigator in on who Austin Allison is and what he's got to do with Jenny's dirty laundry."

Brent gazed at the floor once more.

David watched him with obvious annoyance for a moment, then looked at Sid. "Austin Allison is the owner of the company that has Mercy's security contract. They've had it for longer than I've been here, for at least fifteen years, in fact. I know that because Austin is also Ruth Allison's ex-husband. She introduced me to him while they were still married."

"Ruth Allison," Christie murmured. "The nurse who took over watching Daddy on the morning shift? The one Daddy called the dragon lady?"

David nodded. "But I don't catch the connection between Ruth's ex-husband and dirty laundry. Wakefield, you're going to have to tell us about that."

Brent glanced up once more, looking extremely uncomfortable.

"Well?" Sid demanded.

"Well, I only know what Jenny told me. And that was just the bare-bone facts."

"Go on," Sid ordered.

"Well, we got into the wine pretty heavily one night and started reminiscing about past loves...precisely the kind of thing you should never do with a current one...and, well..."

Sid began tapping the top sheet with his fingers, clearly irritated by Brent's hesitant manner.

Christie resisted the impulse to tell her father to remain calm. Instead, she reminded herself that David wouldn't let him get too excited and consciously sat back in her chair.

Brent leaned toward the bed, his hands on his knees once more. "A few years ago—about four, I guess—Jenny had an affair with Austin Allison."

The room fell still. Christie looked at her father's face. He hadn't done very well at concealing his interest in Brent's revelation.

"Four years ago," David finally said. "You don't mean that Jenny had this affair while Austin was still married to Ruth, do you?"

Brent nodded.

"Wakefield, are you sure about that? It doesn't sound like Jenny."

"No. No, it wasn't what you probably think, David. I mean, she didn't realize he was married. Not right away."

"She didn't recognize his name?" Sid asked. "Austin Allison isn't exactly John Smith."

"Well, yeah. I mean, she did know that Ruth's husband was called Austin. But she'd never met him. And what she didn't know was that Austin had a nickname. Ruth always referred to him as Austin. At any rate, he was introduced to Jenny as Bud Allison and he told her he was divorced. I don't know what other lies he told her, but she apparently had no reason to connect him with Ruth. Not at first. Not until after they'd started—"

"Lord," David muttered. "Austin's practically old enough to be Jenny's father."

"Well, I don't know what the attraction was. She didn't go into details, just referred to the affair as a stupid mistake. Anyway, eventually she and Bud ran into someone who called him Austin and the game was up. Jenny broke off with him. But by then Ruth had discovered that old Bud had been running around and she filed for divorce."

"But Jenny and Ruth work together," Christie protested. This entire story seemed to be getting more convoluted by the moment. "I realize they're on different shifts," she added. "But still...how could they even work in the same unit after all that?"

"Well," Brent explained, "Ruth found out about the affair but she didn't know who Austin's girlfriend was. At least he had the decency not to tell, or Ruth would likely have dragged Jenny into the divorce proceedings. Anyway, for a long time Jenny was uncomfortable whenever she saw Ruth. But she likes the CCU and didn't want to leave. And, of course, by then Austin was past history to both women. It was just when Reg told me that Austin had been here...well, I thought that possibly he'd seen Jenny...that maybe he had something to do with ... But, like I keep saying, it was just a crazy thought.''

"I wonder,'' Sid muttered. "Anything else, Brent? Anything happen after you spoke to the security guard?''

"No. That's about all I can tell you. Once I'd talked to Reg I went home, hoping Jenny would call me.''

"Well,'' Sid said, expanding the word into three syllables as he glanced from Christie, to Brent, then finally at David. "I guess it's time to fill Brent in about your phone call.''

"Phone call?'' Brent's gaze turned to David, but Sid's remained on Brent. Christie focused on him, as well. David cleared his throat. "Look, Wakefield, take it easy, because Sid and I don't think this is as serious as it's going to sound to you. But earlier this morning I had a call from a guy who said he'd kidnapped Jenny.''

Brent's face didn't lose the three shades of tan that Christie had expected it would. It lost five.

"What?'' the intern choked out, staring hard at David.

"He said he had Jenny and wanted twenty-five grand from the hospital. But we don't believe she's actually been kidnapped. We don't believe the guy was for real.''

"But that's...this is insane! Why didn't you tell me about it right away?''

"I asked him not to,'' Sid explained. "I wanted you to tell me calmly about what you did yesterday and I assumed the news would upset you.''

"Upset me? That's putting it mildly! Oh, jeez! What are we going to do?''

"We've already done it," Sid offered. "At least we've done what we're officially required to do. David called the police."

"I . . . I . . . oh, jeez. What are they going to do?"

"Not much," David replied. "Look, Brent, neither Sid nor the police believe Jenny's been kidnapped. They doubt the guy will even call back. Someone's coming in to put a recording device on my phone, just in case, but the police are convinced that Jenny will turn up on her own."

"But this call, David. How do you know whether the guy's for real or not? What if the police are wrong? Maybe Jenny . . . how did they explain the call?"

"They figured it the same way Sid did, that some jerk was hoping the hospital would pay twenty-five grand for nothing."

"I . . . I see. And you really don't think this guy has Jenny, Sid?"

"No."

"How can you be sure?"

"Nothing adds up to a kidnapping. Especially not the fact that Jenny left a note. Whoever called David couldn't have known about that. Otherwise he wouldn't have tried the bluff."

"Right," Brent mumbled, looking marginally reassured. "Tell me what the guy said, David."

Christie continued to watch Brent as David repeated the extortionist's words. When he reached the part about the threats, Brent almost jumped out of his chair.

"Said he'd kill her? Oh, jeez! No offense, Sid, but this is Jenny we're talking about. What if you and the police have this figured wrong? What if that guy left the note himself? Maybe he just wanted a little lead time to decide what to do. Maybe we should have come up with the money instead of calling the cops. Maybe..."

The intern was clearly panicking; Christie caught her father's eye and silently urged him to reassure Brent.

"Wakefield, I spent over twenty-five years as a detective. And I'd bet my bottom dollar that caller didn't kidnap Jenny."

Brent stared at Sid, clearly trying to put facts together in his mind. "If that's really what you think," he finally said, "then why is everyone in this room so worried? If the police are certain Jenny's going to turn up on her own, why are the four of us sitting here trying to reconstruct every detail of what happened yesterday?"

"Because," Sid answered quietly, "even though I don't believe the fellow who called David was legit, I do believe there's a chance—maybe just a slim chance but a chance nonetheless—that something unexpected happened in Jenny's life yesterday morning...and that she might be in trouble because of it."

Brent swallowed audibly.

"If she is, though," Sid continued, "I'm sure David's caller has nothing to do with it. Although...well, it is possible he saw something or heard something we don't know about. Maybe he even knows what actually happened. That could have been what got him thinking an extortion call might bring results."

Christie stared at her father, wondering how long ago he'd thought of that possibility. If the caller knew something...and if they could figure out who he was...

"Dad, what sort of person would make a phone call like that? He'd have to be a psychopath."

"You live in New York, baby. You know that psychopaths are a dime a dozen."

"But this is Winnipeg."

Sid smiled a little. "Well, maybe in Winnipeg psychopaths are a dollar a dozen. But I'm sure they aren't an endangered species in any city."

"So there's no guarantee the guy was even someone that Brent or I spoke to," David murmured. "Maybe he simply overheard Jenny talking to someone."

"But he has to be someone on Mercy's staff," Brent said. "Doesn't he? I mean, he phoned you rather than Rothman—knew that he's away and you're acting chief. An outsider wouldn't know that."

"Good thought," Sid offered. "David, is there a way of checking whether that call came to you direct or was rerouted from the chief of service's office?"

"I imagine Rothman's secretary would remember talking to the guy if he called there first. The voice was so unusual she'd have wondered about it."

"Good. I want you to ask her about that."

"But the voice, David," Brent said, his words tumbling out. "If it was someone on staff, an unusual voice, then maybe there was something familiar about it that just didn't click with you at the time. What if we run through the names of everyone that either of us spoke to yesterday? Maybe that would trigger recognition."

"I guess that's worth a shot. But I doubt it'll work. The voice was unusual because whoever called was whispering. And he was obviously disguising his voice.

"His or her," Sid corrected.

CHAPTER TEN

"WHAT?"

Christie, David and Brent uttered the word simultaneously, then sat staring at Sid.

"I said your raspy-voiced caller wasn't necessarily a man, David. There's a rule in police work: never assume."

David shook his head. "It was definitely a male voice. It didn't even occur to me that it wasn't."

"Remember Deep Throat?" Sid asked. "Helped blow Watergate wide open? That hoarse whisper sounded like a man's. But a lot of people in Washington believed they knew Deep Throat's identity—and that she was a woman. Which brings me to another question, David. Christie and I didn't wake up until about ten o'clock yesterday morning. And Ruth Allison was sitting in my room then. But she could have left it sometime between eight and ten, couldn't she?"

"No. You were on constant, Sid. A nurse could be dismissed for leaving a patient alone who's on constant."

"But it would have been possible, wouldn't it?"

"Sid, it's just not—"

"And if she'd gone out, would anyone necessarily have seen her? Or would anyone have looked in and noticed she wasn't there?"

"Well...no. I doubt anyone would have looked in. And maybe no one would have seen her if she'd left. But what are you getting at?"

"Maybe nothing, David. Just a thought. Thinking aloud helps solve cases. And so does tossing around possibilities. For example, Jenny was assuming that Ruth never found out who Austin's girlfriend was. But that brings us back to 'never assume.'"

Christie eyed her father uncertainly. "Daddy, are you suggesting that Ruth sneaked out of your room and had some sort of major confrontation with Jenny? Major enough to send her running?"

"I was simply throwing out a thought, baby. And let's follow it along for a moment. Suppose that, at some point, Ruth did learn Jenny was Austin's girlfriend. Now, from what I saw of Ruth, I'd say she's a very bitter woman. She simply exudes anger. And women like her always want to blame someone else when things go wrong in their lives. So, I'd bet she lays the blame for her marriage breaking up directly on Austin's girlfriend. And if she found out that was Jenny—"

"But Jenny wasn't to blame at all," Brent protested. "I told you. She dumped Austin the minute she learned he was married."

"That's not the point. The point is how Ruth would view things. And then there's Allison himself to consider," Sid continued. "He might have seen Jenny after her shift yesterday. Maybe he arranged his early staff meeting with that in mind. Could be he asked her to meet him."

"Daddy, if that's true, why wouldn't Jenny have told Brent she'd be late meeting him? Or left him a note?"

Sid shrugged. "Well, maybe nothing was pre-planned at all. Maybe Jenny simply ran into Austin while she was waiting for Brent. Or Austin could have had a spur-of-the-moment notion that he'd like to see her. Who knows? He might still be carrying a torch for her."

Brent cleared his throat. "I guess there's something else I should have mentioned earlier, Sid. A couple of years ago, after his divorce was final, Austin came crawling back to Jenny, wanting to marry her. She wasn't having any of it, but he *is* still carrying a torch, still phones Jenny the odd time. I've been at her place when he's called."

"How often is the odd time?"

"I don't really know. She never mentions him call-ing. But I can't imagine the only time it happens is when I'm there."

"I see," Sid said.

Christie glanced at David, wondering what he was making of this, wondering whether she was the only one who didn't have the slightest sense of what her father was actually seeing. She hadn't the foggiest idea which, if any, of those darn thoughts he was tossing around might be on target.

"I can't believe," Brent offered hesitantly, "that Jenny would have gone off anywhere with Austin."

No, Christie thought. She couldn't believe it, either. Not when Jenny knew Mr. Tall-Dark-and-Handsome was coming to meet her. At least, she wouldn't have gone off with Austin voluntarily... and that was an extremely unsettling thought.

"Perhaps neither of the Allisons had the slightest thing to do with Jenny vanishing," Sid said. "But maybe one of them did."

"If you really think that's possible, then shouldn't we talk to them?" Brent suggested.

David shook his head. "There's no point in talking to Ruth again. I spoke to her after we got back from Jenny's apartment, and she basically repeated the same things she'd told you and me earlier—that all she and Jenny talked about yesterday morning was Sid's condition. And she says she didn't see Jenny again after the shift change."

"But what if she's lying," Brent pressed. "What if Sid's thought was right and Ruth actually *did* have some sort of run-in with Jenny? We should ask Ruth—"

"Wakefield," David interrupted, giving Brent a dim look. "Don't get carried away. What would you ask her? Whether or not she knew Jenny had an affair with her husband? That would be a terrific question to ask if she *didn't* know, wouldn't it?"

"Well . . . well Allison, then. One of us should talk to him. Not me, I guess. I don't imagine he'd want to talk to Jenny's boyfriend. But—"

"No," Sid objected sharply. "We've got to keep in mind that there's a chance something has actually happened to Jenny. If it has, the police are going to end up investigating. And if that happens, and they figure I had a hand in jeopardizing a potential investigation, they'd have me barred from retired detectives' heaven.

"So I don't want any of you talking to either of the Allisons about this. In fact, I don't want any of you talking to a damn soul about it without clearing things with me first. I probably shouldn't have been thinking out loud in the first place. Must be getting senile," he added in a mutter.

"Well, if we can't talk to people, what can we do?" Brent demanded.

"For starters, David can check with the chief of service's secretary—see if our raspy-voiced caller tried that office first. If not, we can be pretty certain he's on the hospital staff."

"*He*, Daddy?" Christie interrupted. "What happened to 'never assume'?"

"I'll admit a man is by far the most likely guess, baby. And if he *is* on staff here, it'd be worth trying to figure out who he is and whether he might actually know something."

"How would we do that?" David asked.

Sid merely shook his head. "First things first. Brent, you can make a list of everyone you think Jenny might possibly be staying with or might have confided in. Christie's going to call them."

"Why don't I do that, Sid? I guess I probably should have done it already."

"No. Just as well you didn't. People would wonder why Jenny's boyfriend is having trouble locating her. If Christie phones, it won't get anyone worried. And with any luck, she'll at least talk to someone who knew Jenny was intending to go off for a few days. Then we probably have nothing to worry about and can stop there."

"And if nobody Christie talks to knows anything?" David asked.

"We'll deal with that situation if we come to it. But step one is checking with Jenny's friends. There's no point in doing anything more until Christie's talked to all of them. In the meantime I want both you and Brent to make up a list of the people you asked about seeing Jenny—while yesterday's still fresh in your memories. Even if we don't use the names...well, it's still a good idea...just in case the police might want them later."

Christie glanced from her father to the others, wishing detective Sid Lambert would stop implying there might be a future police investigation. The idea of this situation coming to that must be making Brent feel ill. She was trying to think of something comforting to say to him when a teasing male voice drifted into the room from the hall.

"Toot, toot, mama. Gotta keep alert when Walt's doing the driving or you'll get nailed."

The door was shoved open and Christie caught a momentary glimpse of Ruth Allison backing away from the doorway. An instant later, an orderly sauntered in, pushing a food cart before him. He kicked the door closed again with his heel.

Christie glanced quickly at the others. Their attention was focused on the orderly. Was she the only one who'd been sitting at the right angle to see Ruth? And what had the nurse heard while she'd been out there? Anything? Nothing? Everything?

"Hey, Doc," the orderly offered, grinning at David. "Hey, Wakefield," he added, nodding.

"Have you got a Mercy special for my patient, Walt?" David asked.

"Right on." Walt swung out the metal table attached to the bed and set a tray on it.

"Hey, man," he said cheerfully to Sid, "you're looking one whole lot better."

"See," Sid said pointedly as the orderly sauntered back out. "I'm looking one whole lot better. I should have been discharged by now."

"This is our cue to adjourn," David said. "I've heard that line before."

Sid was eyeing the food suspiciously. "What is this?"

"That," David answered, grinning slightly, "is what we fondly refer to as a Mercy special—a low-sodium, low-cholesterol, low-fat special."

"Well, you can add low appeal to your description," Sid muttered. "And, no doubt, low taste, as well. I should have asked Kay to bring me something from the house."

"Uh-uh," David said firmly. "You're on a special diet until we've finished checking you out."

"Special? This stuff looks like something you'd feed a dog."

"Well, despite what it looks like, eat it. Then get a little sleep if you can before Kay comes back."

"Be sure to check in with me between now and four, David. I've got a few ideas about what you should say if that guy does phone back."

Christie leaned across and kissed her father's cheek. If David wanted him to get some sleep, this was no time to fill his head with thoughts of what Ruth might have been up to in the hall.

"We'll be by again before four, Daddy. But you heard what David said about sleeping, so don't spend every minute plotting what he should say to Raspy Voice."

"Well?" Christie demanded, once they'd walked a few steps away from her father's room.

"Well, what?" David asked.

Brent's face wore the same blank expression as David's.

"You didn't see her?"

"See who?" the men asked in unison.

"Ruth. Ruth Allison. When Walt opened Dad's door, she was standing right by it. She must have been listening to us. And if she was there long enough, she heard every single thing we said about her and Austin and Jenny."

"Lord!" Brent exclaimed. "If she didn't know about Jenny and Austin before this, she sure does now. And she heard those suspicions Sid was tossing around about her being out of his room while he was on constant."

"Hold on," David said quietly. "First of all, are you certain it was Ruth that you saw, Christie?"

She nodded.

"You got a good look?"

"Yes. I mean, just for a second. But I'm sure it was her."

"Well . . . she may have simply been passing by."

"I don't think so, David. Remember hearing Walt say, 'toot, toot'? Don't you think that would have been because someone was standing in his way—not merely passing by?"

"I . . . I don't know what to think," David admitted. "But I do know that Sid specifically told us not to talk to either of the Allisons about things. And, hell, I wouldn't know what to say, anyway. If I asked Ruth what she'd been doing in the hall, she'd probably just remind me that she works on the unit. We'll talk to your father about this later, Christie, and see what he suggests. In the meantime I think we'd better just let him rest and follow his last instructions. I'll go and have a chat with Rothman's secretary and you two go and make up that list of Jenny's friends."

Christie trailed down the corridor after Brent and sat in his office while he copied names and numbers from his address book. The image of Ruth's face seemed to be etched in her mind's eye. The nurse had looked startled, as if the moment she'd seen Christie staring at her she'd felt guilty about being caught doing something she shouldn't have been. Or was that startled expression merely a figment of Christie's imagination?

Brent completed the list and looked across his desk, tapping the paper against the old wooden surface. "I feel awkward about not doing this phoning around myself, Christie."

"I don't mind helping out. You and David have work to do."

"Well, I really appreciate it when you barely met Jenny."

"That's all right. She . . . she seemed awfully nice."

Brent merely nodded. "You'll let me know what you hear? Right away?"

"Of course. If one of these people knows anything, I'll zip right back here and tell you the moment I hang up."

"Well, I won't hold my breath waiting. All of Jenny's friends work, so her aunt's probably the only one you'll get hold of before dinnertime."

"It's worth trying now, though, Brent. If Jenny's staying with someone, she might answer their phone. But why don't you give me your home number? If I don't learn anything this afternoon, I'll call you there once I've talked to everyone."

The intern was scribbling down an additional number when David walked into the office.

"Well?" Brent asked anxiously.

"Well, I finally got hold of Daley and told him what's been going on."

"And he said?"

"He said he figured I'd done the right thing by calling the police. And that Mercy's administration will cooperate with whatever they think we should do."

"Which at the moment," Brent muttered, "is nothing. But what about the caller? Did the guy try Rothman's office first?"

David shook his head. "No. She must be someone who knew I'm acting chief. The only other possibility that occurred to me is... Lord, I hate to even think about this, but if the police are wrong, if Sid's wrong... if the guy does have Jenny, then she might have told him to call me."

Brent swallowed hard. "I hadn't thought of that."

Christie gazed from one man to the other, feeling slightly nauseated. She hadn't thought of that, either.

"Oh, damn, that just can't be it," Brent snapped. "Sid must be right. That guy has to be some weirdo who doesn't have Jenny at all, who's simply hoping for the money."

"Well, I'm going to start trying these numbers," Christie said, taking the list and joining David by the door. "Is there a phone I can use, David?"

"Sure. There's a vacant office just along the hall. Do you want to get some lunch first, though?"

"I'm not really hungry. I don't normally eat breakfast, but this morning Kay insisted I have some. I'd rather just start calling. At least we'll be doing something."

"David?" Brent said hesitantly. "Would you mind if I wander down to your office a little before four?

I ... well, I'd like to be there in case that guy does phone back. Maybe I could listen in on a bit of what he says. His voice might sound familiar to me."

"Sure. Good idea."

David took Christie's arm, then paused, glancing at Brent. "Try not to look so worried, Wakefield. Odds are that Jenny's safe and sound. And if you do your rounds looking the way you are now, we're going to have our patients thinking they're about to die."

"Yeah. Yeah, right. I'll manage smiles for them. It's just that I didn't get any sleep last night. I was worrying about what Jenny might be up to. I wasn't really thinking she could be in trouble, but after talking to Sid ... the way things stand now ...

"Oh, hell, David! I was so sure this all had to do with Jenny being pregnant. Now I just don't know what to make of it. But whatever Sid figures we should do...well, I want to help any way I can, so don't leave me out of anything. I just wish ... oh, damn." Brent dug a Kleenex from his pocket and wiped at his eyes, clearly embarrassed.

Christie felt badly just watching him. She wished men didn't view crying as a sign of weakness. Brent was clearly worried sick. And thinking that he should be hiding his emotions could only be adding to his distress.

She looked down, pretending she hadn't noticed his tears. A small gold object was lying at his feet; she bent and picked it up—an earring in the shape of a sea gull.

"Sorry," Brent mumbled, shoving the Kleenex back into his pocket. "You're right, David. I've got to pull myself together and ..."

He noticed the earring on Christie's outstretched palm and stared at it as if he was trying to figure out where it had come from.

"It was lying on the carpet," she explained.

"Oh. Oh, yeah. I must have pulled it out of my pocket with that Kleenex."

"You aren't toying with the idea of wearing an earring, are you?" David joked, clearly trying to lighten the other man's mood. "Rothman doesn't approve of that sort of thing."

Brent shook his head. "No. No, I can live without a pierced ear. I picked that up in the hall a few days ago, then completely forgot about it. But I think it might be Ruth's. When I found it, I recalled her wearing ones that looked like that. I meant to check with her. You know, though," he added thoughtfully, "maybe forgetting I had this was a lucky stroke. Taking it down to Ruth would give me a perfect excuse for chatting with her. Maybe," he added, reaching for the earring, "I could casually ask her about being in the hall and—"

David quickly grabbed the tiny gold bird from Christie and stuck it into his own pocket. "Forget it, Brent. Unless Sid says we should talk to Ruth, then we don't talk to her—not casually or any other way. I told you. I'll ask him if her being out there changes things. But, in the meantime, let *me* see if this is hers. If it's not, I'll turn it into the nursing station. It has to belong to either a nurse or a visitor."

David walked Christie along the hallway to the vacant office, closed its door behind them and shot her a rueful smile. "I'm starting to feel like an extremely frustrated teenager, Christie. All I want to do is be alone with you—and not just for a few minutes now and then in one of Mercy's grungy offices. How can spending time alone together be so difficult for two adults to manage?''

Christie shook her head. ''The theory about a mysterious power throwing obstacles in our course was the best I could come up with.''

David took her hands in his. ''I told you. I don't believe in mysterious powers. And whatever's going on here can't last forever. I only wish I didn't have the feeling that Wakefield wants to stick to us like glue until this is sorted out.''

''He's just worried, David.''

''I know. But that doesn't mean I want to play Siamese twins with him. Look, Christie, why don't you make those calls and I'll finish getting my schedule reorganized? Then, if you have no luck, we can drive over to Jenny's apartment and talk to her neighbors. We could easily make it there and back before four o'clock.''

''I think we might as well plan on doing that, David. Brent only had home phone numbers and he figured all of Jenny's friends would be at work. I'm liable to be making calls into the night.''

''If that's the case,'' David murmured, drawing her closer, ''I just happen to have a phone in my apartment that you could use.''

''Oh? Well . . . I guess I could do that all right. But only,'' she teased, ''because your apartment's a tiny bit nicer than Mercy's grungy offices. Working into the night won't seem half as bad if I'm at your place.''

David's smile almost melted her on the spot. And it made her think they just might beat that mysterious power's obstacles yet.

"I wouldn't want you working too far into the night, Christie. Isn't there a saying about the evils of all work and no play?"

She opened her mouth to reply but didn't get the chance. Instead, she got a kiss that sent her pulse racing and made her long for the afternoon to be over and the night to arrive.

IT WAS PAST FOUR and David's phone hadn't rung once during the twenty minutes they'd been in his office. David glanced at Christie, sitting to one side of his desk, then across to where Brent was slumped in a chair by the wall. Christie's expression was worried, but there was no contest as to which of them seemed more anxious.

Brent was looking more upset by the moment— probably hadn't expected the waiting to be so nerve-racking. It was just as well they hadn't filled him in on Sid's instructions. If they had, he'd be climbing the walls by now.

This entire situation seemed to be an unnerving wait-and-see game. First it had been wait and see because Jenny would probably turn up on her own. Then Sid had told them not to ask Ruth what she was doing in the hall. "Wait and see whether she does anything else suspicious," he'd said. "If she does, let me know."

And now they were waiting to see whether the phone would ring.

David wasn't even sure that he wanted it to, wasn't certain he could carry off Sid's plan. What if he blew it? What if the caller got angry...got angry and actually did have Jenny?

He didn't, David silently reassured himself. Neither Sid nor the police thought there was a chance of that. But Sid did believe the guy could have heard or seen something that might explain Jenny's disappearance. At least, if he called again, they might find out something useful.

"Keep him talking," Sid had advised. "If he does know anything, the more he says, the more likely you'll learn something."

And that would certainly be more than they'd managed to do thus far. Of everyone Christie had called, only one of Jenny's friends had answered her phone—another nurse who worked the night shift. And she'd known nothing.

Neither had the aunt. And when Christie had finally phoned Jenny's parents in Saskatchewan and given her mother the "friend from out of town" story, Mrs. Doyle had suggested that Jenny was probably just out for the day and told Christie to keep trying the apartment.

Instead, they'd gone over and talked to Jenny's neighbors.

But they hadn't known anything, either. Of course, not all of them had been home. Sammy's regular cat-sitter had been, though, and the fact that she hadn't known Jenny was away wasn't good. The only good thing had been the way the woman had immediately hustled a disgruntled Sammy into her own apartment and—

David started as the phone rang, then stared down at the silently turning tape in the recording device. It had activated instantly.

Brent leaped to his feet, crossed to the desk in two long strides and leaned across it. "Let me listen in as soon as there's a chance, David."

He nodded, took a final glance at the notes he'd made of Sid's instructions, then picked up the receiver. "Dr. Lawrence speaking."

"You got the money?" a voice whispered hoarsely.

David moved the phone an inch or two away from his ear the moment he heard the raspy voice. Brent leaned nearer so that his ear was almost as close to the receiver as David's.

"I...I've almost got it. We just ran into a minor hitch—need a little more time."

There was a pause—so lengthy that David could feel the receiver growing slick in his hand.

"Almost got it ain't good enough, Doc," the voice finally said. "What's the hitch?"

"We couldn't get hold of the chairman of the hospital board. He's in Toronto for a meeting and we haven't been able to reach him yet. And Daley's adamant that we can't release the funds without an okay."

David held his breath, waiting to see if Sid's trick would work. If their caller didn't ask who Daley was, then he undoubtedly recognized the hospital administrator's name. And that would leave virtually no doubt about him being someone on Mercy's staff.

"Can't reach the chairman, eh? Don't know if I believe that. You've had all day."

"He's due back tonight. Give me till the morning. We'll be able to contact him tonight for sure. If you call back in the morning—after the banks have opened—I'm sure I'll have the money for you."

The caller snorted. "Yeah. After the banks have opened. Guess I don't want no check. And I don't want no big bills, either."

"Right. No big bills. But listen. Daley wants me to talk to Jenny so we know she's all right. Put her on."

There was another long pause.

"No can do, Doc. I'm calling from a pay phone and she ain't here."

The caller's voice had just changed entirely. It was still a raspy whisper, but its tone had slipped from arrogance to uncertainty.

"I'll wait here," David offered. "You can call me back. I have to speak to her . . . or there's no deal."

He swallowed hard, praying that Sid knew what he was talking about. Those final words had almost choked him on their way out.

"What . . . who the hell are you to tell me there's no deal?"

"All I'm telling you is what Daley says. I talk to Jenny or there's no money."

The man uttered a string of obscenities, then began muttering so rapidly that David had trouble catching all the words. "You don't get to make the rules, buster. And you don't get to talk to her at all. The deal is you give me the money and I give you Jenny. You can talk to her all you want to after that."

"I can't make that deal. Daley's absolutely firm. I have to hear from Jenny, have to be certain she's okay, before you get the money."

"Well, keep your damn money then! Who needs it? And you won't ever be talking to Jenny again! You just signed her death certificate."

The phone clicked as the line went dead. David closed his eyes, praying he'd done the right thing.

"Well?" Christie asked anxiously.

He shook his head. "I hope to hell your father was right. If he was, then that guy doesn't have Jenny. But if Sid was wrong... No, he couldn't have been. What would have been the big deal about talking to Jenny if she'd been available to talk to?"

"Daddy's always right, David. I don't think he's been wrong about anything in the past twenty years. It's one of his more infuriating qualities. But not in this case. And you did just great."

"Thanks. I didn't learn anything useful, though. I was hoping he'd drop a clue about who he was."

"Maybe he said enough to give the police some leads, David. I mean, even though Dad figures you have Sherlock Holmes instincts, the police do have more experience with this sort of thing."

"They're welcome to it. I'm not cut out for subterfuge, Christie. I was so busy trying to remember my lines that I barely heard what the creep was saying. And I feel as if I've been through a wringer. What do you think?" he asked, turning to Brent. "The guy reacted the way Sid predicted he would. Does that make you feel better?"

"I...I think so. He sure sounded taken aback when you wanted to talk to Jenny. And he'd have put her on if he actually had her, wouldn't he? When he heard he wasn't going to get his money otherwise? He'd have had to, wouldn't he?"

David nodded. "That's what Sid said."

And, according to Christie, Sid was always right. David exhaled slowly, consciously relaxing, feeling somewhat relieved. Whatever was actually going on couldn't possibly be as bad as the worst scenario he'd been imagining.

"If only you'd recognized the voice," Christie murmured. "The police could pick him up and we'd be certain he doesn't even know anything about what Jenny's up to."

"It still didn't sound the least bit familiar to me. Strike any chords with you, Brent?"

"No. You were right. Even if he's someone we talk to every day, we'd never have recognized his voice from that whisper."

"Well," Christie said, "the important thing is that we're certain Jenny hasn't been kidnapped."

"I'd better call the police." David reached for the phone once more. "They said they'd send someone right over to listen to the tape. If they can figure out who he is, they're going to lay some sort of charges."

"They'll probably want to talk to you while they're here, David. And Dad will be itching to know what's happening."

David glanced at Christie and smiled, glad that she wasn't as anxious as she had been about Sid's involvement in this. Seeing her upset made him feel so damn protective that—

"You'll let me know?" Brent asked. "Both what the police have to say and what Sid thinks we should do next?"

"I'll let you know right away."

Brent glanced at his watch, then started for the door. "I'll be here for a while yet. But if I've left by the time the police get here, you can get me at home. I'll be going straight there. I still keep hoping that Jenny will call."

"Maybe she will," Christie said. "I'm certain she'll be back soon. Woman's intuition," she added, giving Brent a reassuring smile.

"I sure as hell hope you're right, Christie."

"Tell me," David said as Brent closed the door behind himself, "is your woman's intuition really saying that Jenny's safe? Or was that line simply for Brent's benefit."

"I . . . I'm afraid I'm actually pretty weak in the intuition department, David. Sorry," she added, rising. "I guess I'll head along to Dad's room and give you some privacy while you phone."

David reached across and took her hand, drawing her back down into the chair. "I don't want privacy. What I want is you to stay right here beside me."

Christie smiled, unable to imagine any place she'd rather be. She watched David as he spoke to the police, intensely aware how perfect her hand felt in his, thinking how much had happened since she'd left New York Saturday morning.

She might as well be living through a story from *The Twilight Zone*. She'd arrived in a strange town and become involved in a mystery and involved with a man she scarcely knew. Scarcely knew, yet felt she knew so intimately.

It seemed as if a year had been packed into the past few days, as if she'd entered some kind of impossible time warp that caused events to rush along at breakneck speed and sent emotions on a never-ending roller coaster ride.

Maybe that explained why she'd fallen so hard and fast for David.

He hung up the receiver and squeezed her hand. "Someone will be here within half an hour. And you were right. He'll want to talk to me briefly. So why don't we go and fill your father in now? Then I'll talk to the police. And then let's get the hell out of here.

And I don't even want to share you with any restaurant staff tonight, Christie. On the way to my place we can pick up something to cook."

She managed a smile, wishing her nervousness would disappear. Feeling nervous was silly when she was so crazily, deliriously in love with David. But the prospect of being alone with him, in his apartment, was incredibly exciting and scary as hell at the same time.

Maybe she'd been too hasty in thinking this situation through. But every time she looked at David she wanted him so desperately that not having him seemed impossible.

She'd made the right decision. Her heart was reassuring her that this was one time she should let caution fly out the window. So she was darn well going to shove her worries aside. There would be time enough to worry about the future when it became the present. And surely there wouldn't be any more surprising obstacles ... unless ...

"David, you don't think Dad's going to want us to play detective tonight, do you? I mean he never did take that extortion call seriously, but there are still all those little loose ends ... and now Ruth ..."

"No. We'll be off the hook tonight. Don't you remember? He said he doesn't want us doing anything more until you've gotten hold of Jenny's friends."

Christie shook her head. "He said so many things my brain went on pause somewhere along the way."

"Well, I remember. So I'd say that after a few phone calls we're going to have the entire night to ourselves."

"Not the *entire* night," she teased quietly. "I can't have Kay thinking her newly acquired stepdaughter is a loose woman."

"I stand corrected then," David murmured. "We're going to have the entire evening. And I can hardly wait," he added, leaning forward and brushing Christie's lips with a gentle kiss, banishing her nervousness and making her certain she could hardly wait, either.

CHAPTER ELEVEN

DAVID OPENED his apartment door and ushered Christie inside. She gave him an uneasy little smile that cranked his own uneasiness level up another notch.

When they'd left Mercy, he'd been feeling great about the prospect of spending the evening alone with her. He'd even felt somewhat better about the situation with Jenny. Marchman, the detective who'd arrived, had been hopeful about identifying Raspy Voice. "There can't be many people on the hospital staff with speech patterns like these," he'd said after listening to the tape.

So the police would likely be able to question the guy and learn if he knew anything. And Marchman had sounded as if he might even follow up on some of those worrisome loose threads—assuming none of Jenny's friends knew where she was. David and Christie had left him talking to Sid about the disappearance—to Sid's obvious delight.

Yes, when they'd left Mercy, David had been feeling damn good. But that feeling had gradually slipped away during the trip home; he'd begun sensing mixed messages from Christie again.

Earlier he'd been positive she was every bit as crazy about him as he was about her—had felt certain that she wanted to make love to him. Now he wasn't sure whether she was merely nervous about the prospect or if she'd had second thoughts.

He prayed it wasn't the latter. Because simply looking at her was making him want her. But his looking at her only seemed to be increasing her anxiety.

Cautious Christie. She'd said the nickname fit. Well, there was nothing wrong with being cautious. It could be a commendable trait, in fact. At the moment, though, it had the potential for driving him insane.

More than anything he'd ever wanted in his life, he longed to take her into his arms and tell her he loved her. Maybe it was too soon for that, though. Maybe she'd think...how could he know what she'd think? She might believe he was sincere or she might decide he'd simply been on the make all along.

He so desperately wanted to hold her that he was convinced her pheromones must have gone into overproduction. But she looked so damn uncertain.

Earlier today...well, this wasn't earlier today. This was right now. And right now her expression wasn't even saying, "Kiss me," let alone, "I want to make love to you."

And damn it all, anyway! He needed far more than her expression to give him messages. After he'd made a complete jackass of himself at Kay's, he wasn't about to try sweeping Christie off her feet unless he was darn sure she wanted to be swept.

He had to keep in mind that they really hadn't known each other for very long. And that kind of issue was more important to women than to men. And, as far as this particular woman went, it was apparently making her as ambivalent as hell.

If only he wasn't so absolutely insane about her. But he was. And that made looking and not touching downright painful.

Well, he could hardly sweep her off her feet and into the bedroom while he was holding a bag of groceries, anyway. "I'll just put these things away, Christie."

"Right. And I guess I should try phoning Jenny's friends again."

David glanced at his watch, thinking that if he had to sit through a torturous half hour, watching Christie on the phone, he might explode. Whatever she was thinking and feeling, he had to know.

"It's not quite six, Christie. Maybe we should wait for a bit—give everyone a chance to get home. Marchman said there was no point in your getting back to him until the morning, anyway."

She merely nodded, then silently wandered into the living room.

When David returned from the kitchen, she was standing in front of the balcony's French doors, gazing at the river below. He paused, taking off his suit jacket and tie while he waited for her to say something. When she didn't, he crossed the room and stood beside her, looking out without seeing, resisting the urge to put his arm around her.

"What are you thinking about?" he finally asked.

"You," she said, turning to face him.

"Me? Should . . . should I be flattered?"

"Yes."

His heart began pumping harder. But he wanted far more than a little flattery. He wanted to know precisely what was going on inside her head. "Is that all I get? A one-word compliment? Couldn't you elaborate a little?"

"All right. I . . . I think you're an exceptional man, David . . . a very special man. I've never met anyone like you."

"I, well, thank you. I've never met anyone like you, either." But where the hell was she leading with—?

"I only wish . . ."

"Yes?" he pressed.

She bit her lip, as if unsure how to say what she wanted to.

Whatever it was, it was something awful. He just knew it was. She wished they had more time, probably. Yes. That was going to be it. If Cautious Christie had more time to get to know him, then maybe there'd be a chance for them. But the way things stood—

"David . . . David, here I go sounding like a wanton woman again, but my problem is that I don't want an affair with you. Not a meaningless affair."

Damn it all to hell! He'd known that was what she was going to say. That was the decision she'd reached with all her dratted thinking things over. She'd decided that all he wanted was an affair. And she wasn't buying. Well, she had him figured all wrong. And what did she expect him to do now? Shake her hand and tell her to have a nice life? Let her walk out of his world when she was the only woman he'd ever truly loved?

"Christie . . ." He paused, forcing his arms to remain at his sides instead of reaching for her. "Christie, there could never be anything meaningless between us. Never."

"Well . . . maybe meaningless is the wrong word. But what I'm trying to say is that I want more than we can have. And, since I can't have more... since we can't have more... Oh, David, I'm so afraid of taking what we *can* have. Because it's so likely to lead to hurting."

"Christie, I'm not sure I understand. You want more than we can have? Christie, we can have it all. I... Christie, I'm absolutely crazy in love with you." He watched her face, afraid to breathe.

She slowly smiled. A smile was a good sign, wasn't it?

"David, that makes me so happy and so sad at the same time. Because we have to be sensible. The odds on the two of us managing to have it all are so darn low—"

"Low? How can you even say that?"

"Because I'm realistic, David. And logical. Because your life is here and mine's in New York. And I don't want to delude myself—don't want to walk into something with my eyes shut against the future."

David merely stared at her. He'd told her he loved her. And she'd told him to be sensible. He suddenly realized there was another thing hearts could do that he'd never really believed possible. They could break.

"David, I don't want *just* an affair with you. And I can't manage to convince myself that there's any possible future for us. But, David...I'm absolutely crazy in love with you, too."

"You are?" *Absolutely crazy!* Those just might be the two most beautiful words in the English language. She wasn't merely in love with him. She'd fallen just as absolutely crazy in love as he had.

Then why was his heart breaking? She loved him. But she was so damn concerned about the future that—

"Yes," she murmured. "I am."

She was *what*? God! She had him so confused he didn't know whether he was coming or going.

"I'm absolutely crazy in love with you," she whispered once more.

"I...I wasn't certain you were," he offered inanely.

She smiled the sexiest smile he'd ever seen. "Well, I am. And no matter how sensible I try to be or how logically I try to think, I just can't turn my back on the way I feel about you. It makes fighting the odds seem worthwhile, David. So I guess what I'm saying is I want to be with you for whatever time we can have together. I'll...I'll just have to worry about the future later. Right now I only want to make love to you."

As if in a trance, he watched Christie reach up to his face, felt her trail her fingers slowly, tantalizingly, along his jaw, then slide them around the back of his neck and draw his mouth to hers.

Her lips were lushly soft against his. He encircled her in his arms, and she began kissing him more deeply, her tongue seducing him with its provocative searching, her mouth mesmerizing him with the sweetness of her taste.

She slid her hands up his back, drawing him so near that her breasts were crushed against his chest, her nipples telling him of her arousal.

The way she snuggled against him, so that her body heat was spreading through him like wildfire, made him hard with desire. He wanted to keep kissing her...but he wanted so much more than that.

He drew back a little and looked at her. She was the most beautiful, desirable woman he'd ever met. No one before had even come close. And she was here with him...telling him she loved him. Well, to hell with the future. They'd sort it out somehow. Right now he could afford to shrug his shoulders at the future because he was holding the present in his arms.

She smiled at him again. "Wasn't the way I feel obvious, David? I told you the other night—I don't go around kissing just any old Eskimo I meet. And I've certainly never kissed any old Eskimo the way I kiss you...or any young Eskimo for that matter...or any non-Eskimo, either..."

He simply stood staring down at her, feeling happier than he could remember ever feeling. "Christie," he finally murmured, "if we're absolutely crazy in love with each other...if you want to make love to me...what are we doing in the living room with our clothes on?"

"Beats me, David. I was beginning to think it had something to do with an old Eskimo trick."

He grinned a grin that felt a mile wide, wrapped his arm around her shoulders and started for the bedroom.

CHRISTIE STARED at the large bed, at its elaborately carved headboard, once more aware of twinges of nervousness...but far more aware of David's arm resting on her shoulders...far more aware of how much she wanted him. She glanced around the dim room with its closed verticals, telling herself to relax.

"Don't be anxious, Christie," David murmured. "When two people are absolutely crazy in love with each other, making love is perfectly right."

He left her for a moment to pull the quilt and top sheet back, then turned to her again and tentatively slipped his hand down the V of her neckline, past the top couple of buttons that were already undone. He began toying with the third one, his fingers brushing against her skin, sending hot little rushes of desire through her body.

"I think this must be the sexiest dress ever produced in the fashion capital of western Canada, Christie. Since the first moment I saw you this morning I've been wanting to undo these buttons."

He bent and kissed her, gently caressing her back with one hand, unbuttoning her dress with the other. Smoothing her hands up his chest, she began undoing his shirt, needing to touch his naked skin. At last she pushed his shirt open and slid her palms across his chest, delighted by the mass of chest hair her fingers discovered, wondering if she'd ever discover anything about David that didn't delight her.

At her caress David's kisses grew hungrier, so hungry that they made her shiver in delicious anticipation and started a dull throbbing deep within her. He stopped kissing her for long enough to shrug out of his shirt. Then he stepped closer once more and slipped her dress slowly off her shoulders.

She felt herself trembling slightly when he eased it down over her hips.

"I love you, Christie," he whispered as her dress slithered onto the carpet. He brushed the straps of her slip to either side and it quickly fluttered down to join her dress. His gaze slowly swept her. When it reached her legs, a smile began playing on his lips. "Garters? My God, Christie, I've never in my life seen anything that looked as sexy as your legs wearing those lace garters."

"I'm glad. I only bought them this morning," she murmured, a little embarrassed, "just for you."

"Just for me," he repeated quietly, the expression on his face making her glad she'd told him.

He knelt and slowly removed the whimsical garters...then carefully rolled down her stockings...one by one...his touch almost melting her bones.

And then he kissed his way back up her legs, nuzzling her inner thighs until she thought she might die with wanting him. "David," she murmured. "David, please...I..." She reached down to his shoulders and drew him up.

But then he began kissing her throat, making her wanting deliciously worse. He released the catch on her bra, freeing her breasts, and gently stroked them for a moment, making her moan at the delight of his caress. Then his flattened palms teased her nipples into impossibly firm arousal, turning her entire body liquid with desire.

The throbbing between her legs had become a painful ache. "David," she whispered, "David, I love you...and I want you so much."

Still kissing her, he scooped her up into his arms and placed her on the bed. Finally he slipped her panties off, leaving her fully naked to his gaze, making her feel suddenly shy and yet still so incredibly eager.

"You're beautiful, Christie and I'm absolutely crazy in love with you," he murmured once more.

She could listen to him tell her that forever. And her shyness vanished at his words, leaving only her desire.

David quickly removed the rest of his own clothes, then stood beside the bed for a moment, looking down at her. He was fully aroused and his naked body was every bit as beautiful as she'd imagined it would be.

When he finally slid into bed beside her and pressed the length of his body against hers, fitting his hardness against her softness, it felt as if they'd been born to lie together, as if he was the only man in the world who could possibly ease the aching need consuming her—the aching need he'd set on fire with his touch.

"Christie, do I need to...?"

"No. It's all right. I—"

David silenced her with a kiss...a deep, probing kiss. His tongue possessed her mouth the way she desperately wanted him to possess the rest of her. Her body began moving rhythmically against his, telling him of her need.

He started kissing her throat once more...trailing kisses down to her breasts...kissing her nipples until she clutched his head tightly against her, unable to bear the sensual teasing of his tongue any longer.

And then his hand slipped to her hips...between her legs, and every nerve ending in her body came alive. She arched against him, moving rhythmically, as ready as he was, wanting more of him, needing all of him.

"Oh, Christie, this is...I..." He stopped speaking as he covered her with his body and quickly entered her.

She wrapped her arms and legs around him, loving the feel of him inside her, loving his body so closely that he was part of her. He began thrusting, each hard stroke sending a delicious rush through her, making her feel complete.

"Christie...honey...Christie, I'm not going to be able to last very long... Oh, God, Christie!"

David collapsed against her; she felt his body relaxing...felt his pleasure.

As the minutes passed and he lay motionless, the ache of desire still throbbing within her dulled a little. She heard his ragged breathing gradually subside but continued to hug him closely, not wanting him to move from above her.

Eventually he shifted onto his side and began stroking her hair, one arm still around her. "I'm sorry, Christie," he murmured. "I wanted that to be wonderful for you."

"It *was* wonderful for me."

"Wonderfully quick," he offered ruefully.

"David, it was wonderful for me because I love you."

"But I wanted it to be perfect. I wanted you to—"

She covered his lips with her fingers. "I'm not going anywhere just yet, David."

"Good," he whispered, slipping his hand down over her hip, discovering the wet, tender center of her longing.

She moaned at his touch, her body instantly beginning its primordial response once more, moving as he caressed her, as he made her certain she could never have enough of his touch.

How, she wondered hazily, could this man make her respond so intensely? How could he know so well how to please her, how to arouse her so...so that she could no longer think? So that she was aware only of the incredible sensations that were carrying her nearer and nearer to total oblivion of anything but her own physical desire...her own physical pleasure.

Then suddenly that pleasure was deliriously out of control and David's touch was sending spasms of delight through her, spasms so overwhelmingly wonderful that she couldn't breathe. She could merely feel...could merely love...love the ecstasy that David was giving her...love David.

"PERFECT," Christie whispered, doubting she could manage more than one word. She was wrapped in an aura of contentment and her eyelids felt so heavy that she could barely open her eyes. She'd never felt so completely and deliciously exhausted.

"Mmm?" David cuddled her even more closely, fitting her sweat-slick body so tightly against his that not even a wisp of air could possibly come between them.

"I said that was perfect, David."

"It was from my side, too."

She could hear a smile in his voice; it made her smile in return, even though her back was against his chest and he couldn't see her face.

"The first time," she offered, stroking his arm, "was wonderful. And the second time was marvelous. But that...I don't have the words for that one, David. I'll have to make do with perfect. I love you, David. And I love making love with you."

David nuzzled the back of her neck, and his hand stole across her breast to caress her nipple. It responded instantly...and the slow, dull throbbing between her legs started again.

She turned in David's arms so that she could kiss him, knowing he couldn't possibly be ready for anything more than that but not caring. She'd never get enough of kissing him. It was a taste of heaven.

He kissed her lovingly, his tongue doing delightful things to hers. Then he moved to kiss her breast and his hand drifted down her body and began stroking her inner thigh again, making her begin to quiver once more.

She covered his hand with her own, stilling his caress, uncertain she could bear any more of the rapture he'd given her. She was already aching from his love.

"Careful," she whispered, "or you'll end up with a love slave on your hands."

"A fate worse than death," he teased quietly, propping himself on one elbow and smiling at her. "Or maybe the fate worse than death is having to get out of this bed."

"We don't have to yet, David. It's only..." She paused, realizing the room had grown almost completely dark. The sole light was a soft glow from the hallway. She glanced across at the clock radio. "Nine-thirty? It's nine-thirty? We've been making love for over three hours?"

David grinned. "I think we've just proved the truth of an old saying. Time flies when you're having fun."

"Mmm...*fun* doesn't even come close." She kissed him one more heavenly time, then forced herself to shift away from him. "I have to make those calls."

"I guess you do. And I guess we should have some dinner, too. But somewhere between the grocery store and this bed, I lost my craving for chicken cacciatore.... Well, to be honest, I'd just rather not waste our time cooking. How about ordering a pizza? Could you stand one again tonight?"

"Sure. Just remember to hold the meat—and the pineapple chunks."

David switched on his bedside light and rolled out of bed. As he headed across the room, Christie feasted her eyes on him. He'd make a perfect male centerfold. Every inch of him was hard muscle and rugged maleness. Where had she ever gotten the ridiculous idea that blond men were wimpy?

He took a gray bathrobe from the closet and shrugged it on, spoiling her feast. Then he reached in again, pulled out a red one and tossed it across to her.

"There's no point in putting your clothes on, Christie. And you can stay right where you are and use the bedside phone. As a matter of fact, I can't see any reason for you to get out of my bed at all. Is that list of numbers in your purse?"

She nodded.

"I'll go get it for you. And I'll get us some wine. And later I'll just bring the pizza in here."

"You will, will you?" she said, laughing.

"Sure. Wine and pizza would be great in bed...although not nearly as great as some other things I've had in bed recently."

"Well, I'm glad to hear I beat out pizza and wine, David."

"You'd beat out anything in the world, Christie. And you know," he went on, grinning at her, "bed's a great place to watch *Midnight Cinema* from, too." He opened a door on the wall unit, revealing a television set.

Reluctantly she shook her head. "I'm going to have to pass on *Midnight Cinema*. Kay's going to wonder what's going on if I'm out too late."

David ignored her comment and began leafing through a TV guide.

Actually, Christie reflected, watching him, Kay probably wouldn't wonder one bit what was going on. She'd probably figure it out perfectly, the old matchmaker.

David looked across the room again, tapping his finger on the guide. "I really think you should phone Kay and tell her not to expect you till about three. Tonight's feature is *The Curse of the Murdered Vampire Mummies*. You can't possibly miss that."

"I can't, huh? Why? What's its rating? Half a star?"

"Certainly not. I have high standards. It's got a whole star."

"A *whole* star? Well..."

A whole star and being in bed with David to boot.

"Well...maybe I'll think about calling Kay. I wanted to check in with her and see how Dad's doing, anyway—make sure his session with Marchman didn't get him too excited. Or too exerted, either."

David grinned, handed her the phone, then rattled off Kay's number. "Call away."

Christie fumbled and mumbled her way through the telephone conversation, feeling as if she were thirteen years old and telling her mother a whopper. "So don't wait up for me, Kay. David will drive me home once the movie's over. I know I probably shouldn't stay up so late, but he says it's a classic."

David rolled his eyes. She made a face at him.

"Thanks, Kay. Night." Christie groaned as she hung up.

"Well?" David prompted.

"My father was fine when she left Mercy. In fact, he's apparently in seventh heaven because Marchman spent so long talking to him."

"And what did she say about you staying here to watch the *classic* movie?"

"She said..." Christie paused, unable to suppress a giggle. "She said, and I quote, 'That sounds nice, dear. I'll leave the front light on and you tell David to drive carefully.' "

David laughed. "Kay's always been a neat lady."

"She probably thinks I'm a tramp."

"She doesn't think anything of the sort. She thinks you're a darling. That's what she called you when she told me not to bring a date to the wedding."

"Well, I hope she hasn't decided I'm a darling tramp."

"Christie, there isn't a trampy bone in your body. No one could ever think there was."

"Not unless they checked the TV guide and saw that the *classic* film is *The Curse of the Murdered Vampire Mummies*."

"No problem. Kay won't check. And if she does, you can tell her I meant it was a *cult* classic. Now make your other calls. Then I'll phone for the pizza."

Barely an hour later they were fresh from the shower and back in bed, a half-eaten pizza in front of them and a half-empty bottle of Beaujolais on the bedside table next to David.

"I doubt there's anything in the world that could make me any happier than I am right now, Christie."

"You love pizza that much, do you?" she teased.

David shot her an exaggerated frown. "No. I love being in bed with you. And I loved showering with you. And you just blew your line because you were supposed to say that nothing in the world could make you any happier right now, either."

"Well, that's almost true."

"Almost?"

"I could be a little bit happier," she managed between bites, "if one of Jenny's friends had known where she was."

"Yeah. You're right." David refilled their wine-glasses, draining the bottle.

"But let's not worry about Jenny any more to-night, hon. I think your father being concerned about her made Marchman take her disappearance seriously. And I got the impression he's going to check around for her."

Christie nodded. "I did, too. I'll call him first thing in the morning—let him know I didn't have any luck with her friends.

"You know," she added guiltily, "I think I made a mistake when I phoned Brent."

"Yeah?"

"Yeah. He sounded so glum that nobody I'd talked to knew anything that I told him about Marchman being worried. I thought knowing the police were going to do something might make him feel better. But it didn't. In fact, he sounded as if that just upset him more—the idea that they were taking her disappear-ance seriously now, I mean. I felt so badly talking to him, David. When I called, he answered on the first ring. And I got the impression he'd just been sitting beside his phone, hoping to hear from Jenny."

David brushed her cheek with a kiss. "There's nothing you can do to help him. So try to put it out of your mind, okay?"

"Okay. I'll concentrate on thinking happy thoughts."

They finished the pizza and wine in silence. Finally Christie sighed contentedly.

"Thinking happy thoughts worked?" David asked.

"That and the wine, I guess. It went straight to my head. I'm so sleepy I'm going to have a terrible time making it through a movie."

"Don't worry. I'm sure Kay won't quiz you on the plot. And I don't care whether you actually watch the silly thing or not. I just wanted to have you here beside me for a few more hours."

David put the empty pizza box onto the floor and wrapped one arm around Christie's shoulders, snuggling her against him. "The movie doesn't start for a while yet. Why don't you try to sleep for half an hour or so?"

"Mmm...what a fine suggestion. But what will you do?"

"Just sit here and hold you."

Christie smiled tiredly. "Sounds awfully boring."

"Not to me it doesn't."

"Well, I guess you can watch away, then. But be sure to wake me before the first vampire mummy appears."

CHRISTIE WOKE gradually, the blackness behind her closed eyelids fading first to gray, then to a pale yellow that told her it was morning.

Morning!

She jolted to full wakefulness, her eyes flashing open. Simultaneously she felt and saw David's arm sprawled across her waist—her naked waist. Oh, Lord! Neither of them had made it until *Midnight Cinema*.

She struggled to sit up, trying to see the clock radio across David's chest. His bedside lamp was still on, but its light was dissipating into the daylight that was seeping through the fabric verticals.

"Mrrmmph," David mumbled, drawing her down on top of him before she could see the time.

"Never mind 'mrrmmph'" she cried, pushing herself away from him and struggling into a sitting position. "It's morning. We missed the vampire mummies. I missed going back to Kay's. David, she's going to think I'm awful."

David finally opened his eyes, then grinned an infuriating grin. "Just tell her I'm absolutely crazy in love with you."

"David, this isn't funny. It's embarrassing as hell."

David didn't stop grinning. "Christie, you're twenty-seven years old, not seventeen."

"That's not the point! The point is what Kay's going to think about me. I mean, I don't care if she doesn't believe I'm straight out of a convent. But I've only known you for a few days. And Kay's prim and proper and I'll bet she didn't sleep with my father before they were married, and they knew each other for months."

"You win."

"What?"

"You win the bet. She didn't sleep with him before they were married. She still hasn't, in fact. We've had him in the hospital since Saturday night, remember? And not having had a chance to consummate his marriage was one of the main reasons he was kicking up such a fuss. He told me that."

Christie groaned. "Terrific. That's one bet it would have made me feel better to lose. What on earth am I going to tell her, David?"

"Tell her the truth."

"What?"

"The truth. Tell her we were both tired and fell asleep."

She looked over at the clock radio again and groaned a second time. "It's almost eight. Kay will be up already. She's probably worried sick about me, David. I'm going to have to phone and . . . and tell her we were both tired and fell asleep, I guess. Lord," she muttered, grabbing the phone, "I feel like little Suzy in that old Everly Brothers' song. Remember? The girl who fell asleep on her date? As I recall, the bottom line was that her reputation was shot."

David gave her a quick kiss. "Well, little Suzy of shot-reputation fame, I don't have to be at Mercy very early, so—now that your reputation's already shot— I've got a wonderful idea about how to fill in the time."

He shoved the phone aside and kissed her again . . . not nearly as quickly this time . . . and far more passionately.

She struggled free of his grasp. "I really do have to call Kay, David."

"All right. I can wait. But not for long, so don't move from this bed after you've finished. While you're talking to her I'm going to make you some breakfast."

"I don't eat breakfast. Why does everyone in this town insist on forcing breakfast on me?"

"Because love slaves have to keep their strength up, Christie. And I'm talking about breakfast in bed. Nobody can resist that."

Before she could protest again, David had grabbed his robe from the floor and was halfway out of the room. He paused in the doorway, reminded her what Kay's number was, then thudded off down the hall.

Wishing she could die rather than have to make the call, Christie dialed. Her alibi sounded pathetically transparent to her ears, but Kay simply listened quietly.

"Of course, dear," she finally murmured. "I knew it must have been something like that. Now, are you going to come home this morning, or will I just see you at Mercy?"

"I... I guess, that even though I hate wearing the same clothes two days in a row, I might as well go straight to the hospital with David."

"Fine, dear. I'll see you later, then. Oh, and, Christie?"

"Yes."

"Perhaps we shouldn't mention your falling asleep at David's to your father. You know how men are. He might read it the wrong way."

"Yes. Yes, I guess he might. Well... thanks, Kay. I... I appreciate *your* not reading it the wrong way. Kay," Christie murmured to herself as she hung up, "you're an absolute living doll."

Ignoring David's order not to get out of bed, she grabbed her purse and the red bathrobe and raced into the en suite bath. When she looked into the mirror, she wished she hadn't. The mirror wasn't her friend. Not this morning, at any rate.

Her face and neck were red with whisker burns, so red that she almost couldn't tell where her skin stopped and the bathrobe started. And her lips were still swollen from David's kisses. One look at her and anyone over the age of consent would know what she'd been doing last night.

She quickly washed her face, then threw on some moisturizer and a pound and a half of powder. She couldn't decide whether that made her look better or made her look sickly pale. But it was too late to wash it off because she could hear David coming back along the hall.

She dashed for the bed, dived in and propped herself up just as he made it to the room, carrying a white wicker breakfast tray. He looked totally domesticated and totally desirable. But how could she possibly want him again? The idea was positively indecent.

He glanced at her robe and grinned. "I didn't realize we were dressing for breakfast. Guess it's a good idea, though. There's probably something unsanitary about eating without any clothes on."

"Unless it's pizza in bed," she teased.

"Right. But I think that only vegetarian pizzas qualify."

Carefully David put the tray down beside her. "Well," he asked, climbing into bed, "did Kay call you a scarlet woman?"

"No. Kay was terrific," Christie said, eyeing the food—delicious-smelling coffee, toast and several tiny jars of imported jams. "You know, David, I could probably get used to eating breakfasts if the service was always this good." *And,* she added silently, *if you were always in bed beside me.*

David smiled. "The service always will be this good, Christie. I promise."

Always? she wondered, silently munching a slice of toast. Always wasn't going to be possible once she'd gone home.

And the future she'd decided not to think about until it became the present was coming closer with every passing minute.

CHAPTER TWELVE

"WE'RE OFF THE CASE," Christie announced, hanging up from calling Marchman and looking across David's office at him.

"Just like that?"

"Just like that. Amateurs no longer welcome. He thanked me for what we'd done and told me politely but firmly to butt out—said they still figure Jenny will turn up on her own but that they're going to do a little checking around, anyway."

"What kind of checking around?"

"He didn't elaborate—doesn't seem to be a man of many words."

"No. I noticed when I was talking with him yesterday that I seemed to be the only one talking. It's strange that he and your father hit it off so well when they're so unalike."

"It's probably just that they've had so much in common—all those years as detectives. But they *are* awfully different, aren't they? Dad's always so gung-ho about things and Marchman's that tall, thin, gray sort of man who quietly fades into a crowd. Daddy's never even tried for that image—guess he knew he'd never manage it."

"Well, I like your father's image better. I like your father better, in fact. He lets us in on what he's thinking."

"Maybe we should wander down and see what he's thinking right now, David. He'll know what the police are up to."

David rose. "Good idea. I'm curious. I was starting to get into the swing of this detective game. You know," he added, sauntering across to where Christie was sitting, "I'm a bit put out that Marchman's dumped us. Here it is, barely ten-thirty in the morning, and I'm left with all this time I freed up today. *Now* what am I supposed to do with it?"

"Well, you could call New York again and see how they're coming with Dad's medical records," she teased as he took her hands and drew her up into the circle of his arms.

"Pierre LeBlanc's already done that. They promised him they'd have what I want by tomorrow at the latest. And they'll fax it to us right away."

"Oh, that's great, David. Dad will be so relieved to get out of here." She paused, wondering when she'd stopped doubting that those records would bring anything other than good news. Her father seemed so well that she was almost certain he must have had his irregular heartbeat for ages, that it meant nothing.

But if he hadn't had a heart attack, he'd be discharged . . . and she'd be flying home. She'd have to leave by tomorrow night and go into work on Thursday. The clinic was short-staffed enough without her being away longer than necessary.

Gazing at David, she wished with all her heart...but she'd known when she'd first decided to stay over that it would only be for a few days. She just hadn't expected them to pass in an instant.

She forced a smile. Letting herself be unhappy during the last of their time together would be foolish.

"Getting back to today, David, to all that time you freed up, doesn't anything come to mind that you could be doing with it?"

"Well . . . not unless you happen to have some free time, too."

"David Lawrence, that leer on your face is downright obscene. I'm beginning to think you're insatiable."

"Yeah. Ain't it great?"

Yeah, she silently admitted. It was. As long as he was insatiable only for her. But once she was two thousand miles away . . .

David was bending to kiss her when someone knocked on the door.

"Do you think that if I don't say anything, they'll go away?" he murmured.

"I think," Christie whispered, "that when you're acting chief of service, unwanted interruptions go with the territory."

Clearly reluctant, David released her, strode across the room and opened the door. Brent Wakefield stood in the hallway, hand raised, about to knock again. He glanced from David to Christie. "Have you called that detective yet?"

"Yes, just now," she replied.

"And what did he say?"

"Not much. Now that the police are investigating, you, David and I are supposed to keep our noses completely out of things. But he did tell me they're talking to people in the hospital—trying to track down Raspy Voice."

"I know. There was a fellow asking questions on the unit when I got in this morning."

"If they figure out who the guy is," David continued, "they're going to charge him with attempted extortion. And they *are* going to see if they can learn where Jenny's gone."

"How?"

"We were just heading down to ask Dad about that. Marchman wasn't giving away any police secrets."

"You don't mind if I tag along, do you?"

"Of course not."

"Ah, good. Company," Sid greeted them a minute later when they trooped into his room. "Kay's gone for a walk and I was getting lonely. But I thought the three musketeers would have been officially disbanded by now."

"We have been," David admitted. "But we want an inside scoop on what the police are going to do to find Jenny."

Sid looked as if he wasn't certain he should volunteer anything.

"Come on, Daddy. After everything we've done, we deserve more than the pat on the head Marchman gave us."

"Well . . . yeah, I guess you do, baby. Of course I can't say for sure how they'll proceed, but if I was handling this, I'd have someone calling the local hospitals, to see if there's been an accident of some sort or, well," he added more gently, looking at Brent, "an abortion."

Christie glanced at the intern; his expression had grown even more strained.

"And," her father continued, "if checking with the hospitals didn't bring any results, I'd poke around Jenny's apartment to see what I could find as far as suitcases go—or spaces where there might have been a suitcase or two stored. Then I'd find out whether she's withdrawn money from the bank in the past few days."

"And then?" Brent prompted.

"That would depend on what I'd already found. But I might put out an alert for her car and—" Sid stopped speaking and looked over at the opening door.

A nurse peered in. "Dr. Lawrence?"

"Yes, Millie?"

"May I speak to you for a minute?"

David joined the woman in the hall. As the door closed again, both Christie and Sid gazed expectantly at Brent.

"Millie's our head nurse," he explained. "She could want anything."

David was only gone for a minute. When he returned, he took one glance at the others and grinned.

"You three look as if you're waiting for me to drop a bombshell. That was nothing. Millie just wanted me to know there's going to be a problem with the lunch service today. You know how she is," he added, directing his remark to Brent. "If there's a screwup on her shift, she doesn't want to be blamed. And Walt Lesco didn't show up this morning."

"Walt's that orderly who's been bringing me the god-awful food?" Sid asked.

"*Specials*, Sid. Not god-awful food. With that attitude, I'm glad I put you in a private room. Otherwise you'd probably cause a food riot."

"You people deserve one. But forget about that and get back to this Walt. He's the fellow with the...the specials?"

David nodded.

"Does he often not show up?"

"Not according to Millie."

"Did someone phone to see why he wasn't here?"

"Yes, but there was no answer at his apartment."

Christie looked from David to her father, wondering about his interest in the orderly.

"I think," Sid suggested, "you should give Marchman a call, David. Tell him Walt's address. If this was my case, I'd be interested enough to take a trip to that apartment."

"Just because the guy didn't show up for work?" Brent asked.

"No. Because he's the second person on this unit—within the space of a few days—to suddenly not be where he's expected to be."

David eyed Sid skeptically. "I'll go back to my office and phone," he finally said.

Christie hesitated for a moment, then hurried after David. The more convoluted this situation became, the more curious she was getting.

"Well?" she demanded when he hung up. "Did Marchman sound interested? Is he going to go to Walt's apartment?"

"He's sending a patrol car."

"Do you think he'll tell you if he finds out anything?"

"Who knows? I . . . I'm starting to think I'd better stick around here for a bit, though."

Christie nodded, wondering if that darn mysterious power was rolling out its obstacles once more. It seemed she and David were never going to have an opportunity to be alone again. "Things are getting stranger and stranger, aren't they?" she murmured.

"Could be. Or could be your father's way off base on this one."

"I told you before, Daddy's never wrong. I've always wished I'd inherited his intuition."

"Then I guess I'm definitely stuck here for a while. And," David added ruefully, "I was having such wonderful thoughts about what we'd be doing today."

Christie didn't admit that she'd been having wonderful thoughts, too, but she seemed to have become every bit as insatiable as David was. "There's always tonight," she offered. "We've even got groceries at your apartment."

David grinned at her. "What? You want to waste time cooking? You can't handle pizza three evenings in a row?"

"David, you're a doctor. I let you off the hook about pheromones," she teased, "but you're definitely supposed to know about nutrition. The olives on a pizza hardly count as green vegetables. And there's all that cholesterol in cheese. And—"

The phone began ringing, interrupting her.

"Hell," David muttered, reaching for the receiver, "I'm not cut out for administration. I'm far happier seeing patients and doing my research than sitting in an office taking calls."

Christie watched him as he answered the phone. Research. That was the first time he'd mentioned being involved in research. There was so much they didn't know about each other.

"Okay," David said, "I'll be right down."

He hung up and shrugged. "Someone's waiting to see me in the security office."

"Who?"

"The fellow didn't say—just said it was important. I'll come back to your father's room when I'm done.

I didn't have a chance to tell him that his records are practically on their way from New York."

"Would it be all right if I told him, David?"

"Sure. But I'll still drop by in a few minutes."

"COME IN," a deep voice answered David's knock.

He opened the door, and the large man behind the security office desk rose and extended his hand. "Remember me, Dr. Lawrence?"

Even in these surroundings, it took an instant for David to match a name to the fiftyish face. He hadn't seen the man who owned the security firm for several years. "Of course. Austin Allison," he finally said, reaching across the desk to shake the man's hand.

Austin gestured David to one of the office chairs and moved from behind the desk to sit beside him. "Thanks for coming down. I didn't want to go up to your unit. With my luck I'd have run smack into Ruth."

David nodded, waiting curiously for Austin to continue. The man was clearly upset.

"Dr. Lawrence..."

"David. It's David."

"David, then. David, what do you know about what's happened to Jenny?"

"I..." he paused uncertainly. Marchman had said they were off the case. And even if they weren't...

Austin shook his head impatiently. "Look, David, her disappearance isn't a secret. There's a damn investigation going on in this hospital. Do you think the police didn't have the courtesy to tell my security head about it? And he called me immediately and filled me in. But there are some other things I need to know."

"Such as?"

"Such as what time the extortionist phoned you yesterday, what time you told him the hospital wasn't going to play *Let's Make a Deal*."

David shrugged, not seeing any harm in answering the question. "He called in the morning, around ten. And then he phoned back a little after four to see if I had the money."

"And exactly what did he say?"

"I...look, Austin, I'd like to cooperate with you, but you're putting me in a difficult position. I've been officially told to butt out of this. And I imagine butting out includes not discussing those phone calls with anyone."

"Damn it, David! I'm not just anyone. Jenny and I are old friends. And I'm already involved in this. I simply need to compare notes with you."

"What do you mean, you're already involved?"

"I got a ransom demand, too."

"What?"

"Late yesterday afternoon."

"But why would the guy call you?" David tried to remember everything Brent had said about Austin and Jenny. He was still carrying a torch for her. But surely not many people could know that.

"I...I guess he phoned me because Jenny and I are old friends, David. The call still took me completely aback, though. I couldn't figure out why anyone would decide *I* should be the one to try. But this morning, when I heard he'd tried to hit the hospital, things started making sense. And now that you've told me what time you talked to him, they're making a lot more sense."

David shook his head. "Not to me they aren't. Mind filling me in?"

"Well, it was close to five before he phoned me the first time—I was just about to leave my office. So he only tried me because you hadn't come through. He was probably grasping at straws. But I still need to know what he said to you, David. And the police sure as hell aren't going to tell me that."

"Have you talked to them?"

"Not yet. I will. But I need some answers from you before I do."

"Why before?"

"Damn it, David! Because I know how the police work. They work at a snail's pace. And there might not be much time. Maybe I can do something fast. Once I've talked to them, though, I'm going to be ordered to butt out, too."

David shook his head. "There's nothing to do. The police don't figure the guy's for real. They want to get him for making extortion threats, but they don't believe he actually knows anything about where Jenny is."

"He does."

"What makes you think so?"

"I don't think so. I know so."

"How do you know?"

"Because he told me where her car is. I saw it last night. It's in an underground garage, a hotel parking garage. And Jenny isn't registered in the hotel. Nor, as far as I could establish, is anyone matching her description. I talked to the desk staff about the guests."

David stared at Austin, starting to feel sick. "But the police..."

He stopped himself from adding *and Sid*. If Austin learned about their in-house detective, he was liable to want to talk to him. And talking to Austin—hearing this latest development—just might get Sid's adrenaline pumping to beat the band.

"Austin, I asked the guy to let me speak to Jenny and he said no way. I was sure he didn't have her to put on the phone."

"That's why I need to know what he told you, David. Because he gave us two different stories. He didn't tell me he had her at all. He told me he knows who does and where she is."

David swore. "So, after I'd insisted on speaking to her, he must have realized that you would, as well. And he changed his story. But if he actually knows where her car is, then he must know more."

"That's the way I figure it. But the cops could take forever to get their act into gear. That's why I didn't call them last night. Instead, I went and checked that her car was where the guy said it was. And, when he called me back, I told him I'd pay his damn ransom and agreed to meet him this morning."

"You met him? You paid him twenty-five grand?"

Austin shook his head slowly. "He only asked me for ten. Guess he thought the hospital was good for more than I was, eh? Or maybe he realized that his initial story—about actually having Jenny—was worth more than just knowing where she was. But, to answer your question, no, I didn't pay him. I said I'd meet him at nine-thirty and we'd go to my bank together. But I never intended to pay him. I only intended to meet with him . . . just him and me and my gun. If he'd showed, I'd have found out everything he knew without paying him a cent."

David didn't doubt that for a minute. Austin might be graying and a little overweight, but he looked as if he belonged in a wrestling ring. Put a gun in his hand

and he could probably find out everything that just about anybody knew.

"But the S.O.B. didn't show, David. I waited half an hour for him and then came here. Now I have to figure out who he is. And that's why you've got to tell me what he said. Maybe that'll help me. He has to be someone who knows that I know Jenny. And there can't be many people who do."

David stared at Austin, trying to recall the details of those thoughts Sid had been tossing around yesterday. What if Austin was somehow involved in Jenny's disappearance? If there was a chance of that . . .

But if Austin *was* involved, what was he doing here, asking for help? That made no sense at all. Did it?

Damn! Where were those Sherlock Holmes instincts Sid had complimented him on when he really needed them?

"David . . . Jenny could be in serious trouble. To the police she's just a name, but to me . . ."

Decision time. David eyed Austin for another moment and went with his gut feeling. "All right, Austin. I'll tell you what the guy said to me and you tell me what he said to you. He's got to be someone on staff here, so I probably know him. Maybe, between the two of us, we can figure this out."

They couldn't.

They went over the telephone conversations half a dozen times but couldn't come up with a single suspect.

"What about that guy Jenny's been seeing the past few months?" Austin finally asked.

"Wakefield?"

"Yeah. Could he have anything to do with this? I . . . I call Jenny the odd time and he's answered the phone once or twice. She might have told him we were friends."

"No, Wakefield isn't involved, Austin. He was sitting in my office when I got the second call. And he's worried sick about Jenny. But..."

David paused, uncertain he should raise the unasked question that was bothering him. Well, what the hell? Austin had started this. "What about Ruth, Austin?"

"Ruth? My ex?"

David nodded.

"What about her?"

"Well... someone I spoke to mentioned that when it comes to disguised voices...well, it's apparently not always easy to tell the caller's sex."

"That's true. But Ruth? I was married to the woman for twenty years. Surely I'd have recognized her voice—no matter what she did to disguise it. And what on earth could she have to do with this?"

David cleared his throat. "To answer that, we're going to have to stop pussyfooting around about you and Jenny. I know more of the details than you probably think I do. She told Wakefield the two of you had an affair."

"I... I wouldn't have thought she'd tell anyone."

"Well, she did. And she also told him Ruth's learning about it was what broke up your marriage. But did Ruth ever find out that it was Jenny you were seeing?"

Austin pursed his lips, then finally nodded. "Yeah. Someone let it slip—a year or so ago."

"But she never confronted Jenny?"

"No. At least Jenny never mentioned it. And I'm sure she would have. I was the one who took all the heat from Ruth. I was here for an early meeting one morning and she came roaring into the office—must have seen my car in the lot when she was coming on shift. At any rate, she screamed and yelled and called both me and Jenny every name under the sun. I tried to reason with her—told her Jenny hadn't known that I was married, told her the whole thing was my fault, told her she'd be crazy to start a feud on the unit when it wouldn't do either of them any good. She must have finally decided I was right because, as I said, Jenny never mentioned Ruth saying anything.''

"And you never told Jenny that Ruth had found out." A statement, not a question. Wakefield had already said that Jenny believed Ruth was still in the dark.

"No. I didn't tell Jenny. It would only have upset her. Like I said, though, Ruth found out a year or so ago and I can't imagine that after all this time . . . it wouldn't make sense."

After all this time, Jenny had suddenly disappeared and Ruth had taken to eavesdropping in the hallway. Or had Christie simply imagined that the nurse she saw was Ruth? If it had been, though, was there any significance to the fact? David shook his head. He had a million questions and not a single answer.

"I can't imagine anything that makes sense, either," he said at last. I think we'd better talk to Marchman. Better tell him about your calls, about Jenny's car . . . and about you and Jenny . . . and Ruth.'' So much, David thought as he dialed Marchman's number again, for butting out.

DAVID WALKED into Sid's room and slumped down on a chair without speaking. Christie, Kay and Sid were all gazing at him expectantly, but he wasn't certain he was up to a run-through of the past few hours. His brain was still spinning. And his stomach felt as if he'd been kicked—repeatedly.

"I was beginning to think you were never coming back," Christie murmured.

"I...it was Austin Allison who was waiting in Security for me."

Sid sat up straighter in his bed. "And?"

Briefly David recounted their conversation.

"So Jenny's in trouble after all," Christie offered quietly when he'd finished.

"It seems that way."

Kay made a distressed little sound in her throat.

"Kay," David said, glancing at her, "if this is upsetting you, you'd better leave...because there's more."

She shook her head and reached out to take Sid's hand. "I'll be all right."

"What else?" Sid demanded. "What did Marchman say when you called him?"

"He told Austin and me to sit tight—said he wanted to talk to both of us himself. And, when he arrived...well, he'd been by Walt Lesco's apartment."

"I thought he was sending a patrol car," Christie said.

"He did." David glanced uncomfortably at Kay once more.

She smiled. It was clearly an artificial smile, but she was apparently determined to stay.

"He sent a patrol car and then he went over himself...after his men had discovered Walt's body."

"Body?" The word seemed to practically strangle Christie on its way out.

Kay's face turned gray. She visibly tightened her grip on Sid's hand.

"Cause of death?" Sid asked matter-of-factly.

"A drug overdose."

"Accidental?"

"They aren't sure, Sid. There were needle tracks on Walt's arms. He was clearly a regular user, so it could have been an accident. Or suicide. But the police haven't ruled out foul play."

"Foul play?" Kay asked, her voice quavering.

"He means murder, love," Sid said quietly, patting her arm. "What was the time of death, David?"

"Sometime between midnight and two this morning."

"And does this," Christie asked, her voice no more steady than Kay's, "have anything to do with Jenny?"

David shook his head. "I have no idea. I asked Marchman what he thought, but it didn't get me anywhere. Basically he got to ask all the questions and Austin and I got to give all the answers. He only told me what he did about Walt because I'm acting chief."

"Daddy? What do you think?"

"I don't know, baby. I just don't know. How well did Walt and Jenny know each other, David?"

"Not well at all, not that I'm aware of at least. Jenny works nights. Walt works days...worked days," David corrected himself, swallowing over the lump in his throat.

"I'm not close enough to the case to have any answers," Sid muttered. "Don't know enough of what the police have seen or heard. Damn, but I wish I did! The only connection that occurred to me was the coincidence of them not being here when they should have been. But if they didn't know each other well...and a drug overdose...it doesn't tie in. Not on the surface, anyway. Not unless . . . you don't suppose Jenny does drugs, do you, David?"

"No. I can't believe that for a minute. But..." Hell, he didn't know what he could believe any longer. "I don't know, Sid. I can't believe it of Jenny. Then again, I never noticed any signs that Walt was shooting up. I'll talk to Wakefield. If Jenny was on anything, he might know about it. That might even explain," he added, speaking the words as he thought of the possibility, "why Wakefield's so damn worried about her."

Sid shook his head. "Don't talk to Wakefield about anything more. The musketeers are disbanded, remember? Let Marchman ask his own questions."

"All right." David checked his watch. "I've got a couple of things to do. Marchman wants Walt's personnel file and he asked me to get it rather than make an official police request. They're trying to keep the death quiet until they've finished nosing around the hospital."

"Good luck to them," Sid muttered. "There probably isn't a person on staff who hasn't heard about it already."

"Well . . . I'll be back after Marchman comes by to pick up the file. Do you want to catch a little lunch then?" he asked, turning to Christie.

"I couldn't eat, David. I feel as if . . . I don't even know how I feel, but it sure isn't good. I'm starting to wish the world would just go away."

David nodded. He knew exactly how she was feeling. He wished the world would go away, too—the entire world except for Christie Lambert.

Numbly he rode the elevator down to Personnel, collected Walt's file and took it back up to his office. He sat glancing absently through the folder, noting that Walt had been thirty, that he'd worked at Mercy for the past eight years, that his performance appraisals were excellent, his work attendance good. What the hell made a guy like that get into drugs? How could he be dead when—?

Someone knocked on the door.

"Come in," David called, closing the file and mentally gearing himself up for another session with Marchman. But it was Ruth Allison who opened the door—her face pale and drawn. Looking at her, David had a horrible premonition that this visit was only going to add to the enigma of what was going on. "Come in," he repeated more quietly. "Have a seat."

Ruth closed the door and sat down in the chair beside his desk.

"What can I do for you," he prompted when she didn't speak.

"I . . . Dr. Lawrence, that detective just talked to me."

"Marchman?"

"Yes. He . . . he was asking me questions about Walt Lesco . . . everyone's so upset about him . . . no one can . . ."

"I know, Ruth. It's difficult to believe."

"But not just Walt. Marchman was asking me about Jenny Doyle . . . and . . ."

"And?"

"And...Dr. Lawrence, I have to back this story up or it won't make any sense. This is awfully embarrassing." Ruth swallowed hard, then rushed on. "I don't know who else to talk to with Dr. Rothman away. And I need someone to tell me what I should do."

David sat staring at Ruth, hating administration more than ever. This woman wasn't the no-nonsense rule-bound nurse he was used to seeing—the dragon lady, as Sid had dubbed her. At the moment Ruth looked like an anxious, middle-aged woman who was about to burst into tears.

"Take it easy, Ruth. I'll do whatever I can to help."

"Just before Marchman talked to me," she managed, "I had a call from downstairs...from Austin."

"Oh?" Brilliant response! Absolutely brilliant. But what was he supposed to say when he didn't know what the hell was going on? What had Austin been up to after Marchman had told them to keep quiet?

"Austin said he talked to you...that you know about him and Jenny."

David nodded uneasily.

"And that he told Marchman," Ruth went on, her voice cracking a little. "He called me because he said he just had to know..."

Oh, God! Ruth's tears were spilling over. David fumbled in the drawer for his box of Kleenex and held it out to her.

She grabbed a handful and continued speaking between sniffs. "Austin asked me whether I had anything to do with Jenny's disappearance. How could he even think that? What did he imagine I'd done? Why did he tell Marchman I hated Jenny? I don't. Not anymore. Deep down I always knew it wasn't her fault. It was Austin's. She wasn't the first. And it was always Austin who was to blame. So why would he think...?" Ruth gave in to a series of loud sobs.

"I...I'm sure he didn't really believe you'd done anything, Ruth," David tried once she'd calmed down somewhat. "We're all just trying to figure out what's been going on."

"Nothing's been going on. At least not with me. But then, after what Austin implied...and when Marchman seemed so suspicious of me, I decided I'd better not tell him. Since he knew about Austin and Jenny, I didn't want him to think..."

"Think what?"

Ruth shrugged and wiped her eyes. "I didn't even know what he'd think. But he got me so upset I was afraid that if I told him, he might figure I was lying...trying to get back at Jenny by getting her into trouble."

"Getting her into trouble by telling Marchman what?" David asked, trying to keep his voice calm but silently swearing at himself. Sid would undoubtedly have had Ruth's entire story straight five minutes ago.

"By telling him about Jenny and the drugs," Ruth blurted out.

David simply stared at her, his mind reeling. His premonition about this enigma getting more confusing had been right.

"What about Jenny and drugs, Ruth?"

"The past few weeks...over the past few weeks I've seen her at the drug cupboard after she'd gone off shift...several times...rearranging things...doing...I don't know what she was doing. But I could never think of any reason she should have the cupboard unlocked when she wasn't on duty. I didn't say anything to her. I mean, she *is* a supervisor. But what she was doing didn't make any sense. I didn't tell Marchman about it. But as soon as he finished with me, I started thinking that maybe I should have.''

David ran his finger's through his hair. Jenny and Walt and drugs and...and what the hell had been happening on the CCU?

Or had Ruth just given an Academy Award performance? He considered asking her about being in the hall outside Sid's room, then decided against it. He'd already told Marchman that Christie had seen Ruth there, and Sid had said to let Marchman ask his own questions.

Besides, the more he heard, the more confused he was becoming. He couldn't believe that Jenny...but it didn't matter what he could or couldn't believe. And maybe things he'd always believed about Jenny weren't true.

"I think," he finally said, "you'd better have another talk with Marchman."

CHAPTER THIRTEEN

DAVID SAT at his desk for a long while after Ruth Allison had left, and long after Marchman had stopped by to pick up Walt Lesco's personnel file.

What had originally seemed a few worrisome loose threads had turned out to be a tangled web of uncertainties and unknowns. And no matter how hard he tried, he couldn't seem to untangle even one strand of that web...and who knew how far it might stretch.

There had to be something more he could do. But he couldn't imagine what.

"You're off the case," Marchman had told them. "Let Marchman ask his own questions," Sid had advised.

If only he wasn't left wondering and worrying.

Footsteps in the hallway stopped outside his office...a quick tap on his door made his stomach knot. Every time the phone rang or someone appeared...

Pierre LeBlanc burst into the office without waiting for a reply to his knock, a huge grin on his face, an ECG tape trailing over one arm and a length of fax paper looped over the other.

"New York came through, David. I've got Lambert's old medical records."

David felt himself breaking into a grin of his own. Pierre's expression was shouting "Good news," and that was something they all could use.

"I only brought along the earliest ECG reading they faxed. It was taken years ago."

Certain what he was going to see, David spread the fax across his desk and quickly lined up the ECG on it against the one they'd done when Sid was admitted. And sure enough, there it was, plain as day—exactly the same regular, repetitious rhythm disturbance on the ECG faxed from New York as on the other. He breathed a sigh of relief. Strange how he'd been almost certain Sid hadn't had a heart attack, yet was still so grateful for this final confirmation.

"Thanks, Pierre. And thanks for taking so much of the work load off my shoulders since Sunday."

"No problem, David. I owed you. And if I'd admitted a patient with a daughter who looked like Lambert's, I'd have come crawling on my knees asking you to take up my slack."

David laughed. "Well, as long as you're being so understanding, would you mind writing the order for Sid's discharge? I'm going to head down to his room and brighten his day. Hell, this'll brighten his entire year. He'll want to break out champagne. No, I guess he won't," he corrected himself, grinning again. "Not when it was drinking too much champagne that landed him in here."

David strode down the hall, ordering himself to forget about Jenny and Walt for the moment. There was no point in telling Sid about Ruth's visit...about Jenny and the drug cupboard...no point in throwing a shroud over the good news.

He rapped a single time, then shoved Sid's door open. "Your records arrived from New York, Sid. And we're ready to discharge you now."

"You mean you're actually going to let me out of this bed?" Sid threw back the sheet, looking as if he was simply waiting for David's okay to leap to his feet and dance a jig.

"Yes. You're fine. You've had that irregular heartbeat for years—maybe forever. I'll want to run a few out-patient tests on you, but there's no hurry."

"You're sure there's no hurry, David?" Kay asked.

"Positive. I doubt there's a thing to worry about. Some people's heartbeats simply aren't perfectly regular."

Kay let out a delighted little squeal and kissed her husband.

"That's wonderful, Daddy," Christie said, hugging him the moment Kay released him. "Just wonderful."

"Barbados here we come, Kay!" Sid exclaimed, climbing out of the bed and modestly clutching the front of his pajama bottoms. "Although," he added thoughtfully, "I wouldn't mind waiting around Winnipeg for another day or two.... I hate to leave in the middle of a case."

"Sid Lambert!" Kay exclaimed. "This is Marchman's case, not yours. And he can catch you up on it when we get back."

"Yeah. Yeah, I guess you're right, dear. Marchman's not a bad guy, you know," he offered, looking from Christie to David.

"He was telling me there's a social club in Winnipeg for retired cops—said that as soon as I was up and around he'd take me to one of their get-togethers." He glanced back at Kay. "Why don't you phone the travel agency right now before it closes for the day and confirm that flight for tomorrow?"

"You've already booked a flight?" David asked.

"This is a honeymoon trip we're talking about, David. And it's been delayed long enough."

"Daddy's impossible sometimes," Christie said. "When I told him these results would be here by tomorrow at the latest, there was no stopping him. He had the agent holding seats for both tomorrow and the next day."

"You don't believe in taking any chances, do you, Sid?"

"David, I have to admit that, for a while there, I was worried I'd run out of chances. And now that I'm sure I haven't, Kay and I are going to make the most of every minute. I guess," Sid went on, turning to Christie, "this means you can head back to New York, huh, baby? Thanks for staying," he added quietly. "I know you must have been eager to get home. And it's not that I'm anxious to get rid of you, but you might still be able to get a flight out tonight."

David stared at Christie, his heart catching at Sid's words. In the excitement he hadn't been thinking about her father's clean bill of health meaning that she'd be leaving.

"Well...it's probably a little late to get packed up today, Dad. And...and David and I made plans for tonight."

"Plans?"

"Dinner," David said quickly.

"I...I guess," Christie went on, "if I leave tomorrow, if I'm back at the clinic on Thursday, that'll be soon enough."

Leave tomorrow. So she was giving him tonight and part of tomorrow. But that wasn't enough—not nearly enough. Eternity with Christie wouldn't be nearly enough. Suddenly that future she'd been worrying about, that future he'd shrugged his shoulders at, was staring him square in the face.

"You know, Christie," Kay offered, "you're still welcome to stay at the house for a few more days if you'd like. Actually, I feel better having someone there when I'm away."

"Thanks..."

David realized he was holding his breath, waiting for her to continue.

"Thanks, but I can't, Kay."

He exhaled slowly. Of course she could stay. And he couldn't let her leave. Somehow he had to convince her that she belonged here with him. They loved each other and they belonged together. But she was so darn cautious. He was going to have to take things step by step. Maybe step one should simply be to convince her that they needed more time together right now, time to think things through, time to plan their future. And then, by the time Sunday arrived...well, he'd just have to try his damnedest.

He edged toward the door. "Well, Sid...Kay, I guess I won't see you again until you're home from Barbados."

"Not necessarily, David," Sid said. "We may still be up later."

David stared at him blankly.

"We may still be up when you bring Christie home."

"Oh...right."

He glanced at Christie. She gave him a weak smile that said there would be no *Midnight Cinema* tonight.

Of course. She might be an adult, but as far as Sid was concerned she was his baby. So much for another entire night in her arms. Well, they still had the evening. He turned back to Sid. "Why don't you go ahead and get dressed? A pink lady will be along in a few minutes to help you make good your escape."

"A what?"

"A volunteer, dear," Kay explained. "They wear pink smocks."

"Oh." Sid headed across to the closet. "Well, I guess I'd better not let a pink lady catch me in my pajamas."

"And I guess I'd better get going and let you change," Christie murmured. "Don't feel you have to wait up for me tonight, though. I've got a key. And if I'm late getting in, I'll see you before you leave tomorrow."

"Fine, baby. You two enjoy yourselves."

"Yes...enjoy yourselves," Kay repeated, smiling the unmistakable smile of a self-satisfied matchmaker.

"I'D NEVER HAVE believed it," Sid said as the door closed behind Christie and David.

"Believed what, dear?"

"That Christie would even give a doctor the time of day, let alone spend as much time with one as she's been spending with David. Course, he's a good guy. But still..."

"I think she's well beyond giving David the time of day, Sid. I think those two are..." Kay searched for the right words—words that wouldn't prompt Sid to load a shotgun. "I think they're completely smitten with each other, dear. You never know. You might end up with your daughter living right here in Winnipeg."

"Not a chance. Christie would never leave New York. No matter how smitten she was."

"How can you say that? Especially after Holly traipsed off to Denver to be with Mac. And when you're here with me."

"Well, Kay, you can hardly compare a move from Winnipeg to Denver with a move from New York to Winnipeg. I mean, Winnipeg and Denver are about the same size. But leaving the Big Apple for a place this small would give Christie culture shock."

"You left New York, Sid."

"That wasn't the same. I didn't use the city the way Christie does. I stuck pretty well to the Bronx. But not Christie. As soon as she left home, she headed straight for the bright lights. You were in her apartment. She's right in the center of Manhattan, right down where all the action is. And she's always going to the theater or galleries or the Met or jazz clubs. She wouldn't be happy in a small city."

"She might be, Sid. With David."

Sid grinned. "Haven't I convinced you yet that I'm never wrong?"

"Oh? Aren't you the same man who didn't think Christie would even give a doctor the time of day?"

"That wasn't being wrong. That was simply a slight exaggeration. But there's a big difference between the time of day and an entire lifetime. "Look," he continued, "why don't you call about those plane tickets while I get dressed?"

Kay nodded, searched through her purse for the travel agency's number and absently dialed. How could Sid think he knew what Christie would do? When it came to love, men didn't understand a darn thing. Women were so willing to compromise for men they loved that . . . Of course, Holly was always going on about that being an old-fashioned attitude, but—

The agent answered and Kay confirmed the flight.

When she hung up, she watched Sid button his shirt. Women—at least women of her generation—were so willing to compromise for men they loved. And she loved Sid . . . so much.

He put on his jacket and smiled at her. "Now what? Do we really have to wait for that pink lady to show up, or can we just sneak out on our own?"

"I think we'd better wait, dear. It seems to me that patients need a discharge slip to get out of the building."

"You know, Kay, Mercy's like a damn prison. First they dragged me in here against my will. Then they strapped me down. Then they wouldn't even let me out of bed, let alone out of this cell of a room. And now I need a pass to get out the damn building."

"Don't fuss, Sid. A few more minutes won't make any difference. Come and sit beside me."

"Sit," Sid muttered, slumping down in the chair next to her. "All I've been doing for days is lying down and sitting. I really hate that, Kay. I like to be on the go."

"I realize that, dear," she murmured, taking his hand. "You know, when we first met, when we were on the cruise, I thought you were keeping us so busy because you didn't want to miss anything on the islands. But now I realize you need adventure in your life. I . . . I only hope you don't find that living with me isn't exciting enough for you."

Sid patted her hand. "Don't be silly, Kay. We'll be on the go together. Look at how much we did and saw on that cruise. And how much we did when you visited New York. We could hardly have packed anything more into the days."

"Well...that's true. But when we were in the Caribbean and when I was in New York...well, I wasn't exactly me, Sid."

"You weren't you?" he teased. "Then just exactly who were you?"

"Oh, Sid. I mean I was away from home and everything was different. And I wanted to be with you and you were always planning things to do, so I...Sid...I'm almost afraid to admit this, but before Holly and I went on the cruise, she told me I'd become a couch potato."

"But that," Sid offered quietly, "was before you met me."

"Yes...that's true. Sid?"

"Uh-huh?"

"That social club for retired policemen Marchman told you about. Do wives go to the events?"

"I don't know, dear. I didn't ask. Why?"

"Oh, I've been thinking about you being the one to pull up your roots and leave New York...and about you saying you'd give the symphony a try...and that you'd even have a shot at bridge. And I know that after you retired you still spent a lot of time with your police buddies. And, well, it seems to me the least I can do is taken an interest in police...police *things*."

"Really?" The smile Sid gave her made the thought of kidnappings and drugs and foul play and whatever other gruesome things he was interested in seem marginally less horrific. "That would be great, Kay. You...well, you've been so upset about what's been going on around here that it didn't occur to me you'd want anything to do with police *things*."

"I didn't. I mean, I'd never thought about it. I was going merrily along, thinking I was marrying a retired detective. But I'm beginning to wonder if such an animal exists."

"Maybe it doesn't, Kay. The way I think didn't change when I left the force."

Kay nodded slowly. "Sid, I realize that when Jenny disappeared...and with Walt being dead...well, I do find that sort of thing terribly upsetting. But maybe I've just led an awfully sheltered life and I'm too squeamish. Maybe I'm...well, regardless of what I am, the last thing I want to be is a nag or a wet blanket. And the more time I've had time to think—and to see how fascinated you've been, trying to figure out what's happened—the more I've realized that you can't simply turn your back on what you did for twenty-five years."

"I'll admit that I do need the occasional cop fix, Kay."

"Well, I don't know much about detectives. I've never been exposed to one before. I can learn, though. What if I read some detective novels? And start watching police shows on television?"

Sid laughed. "Most of those aren't very realistic."

"But you can tell me which ones are. And I'll watch them. And who knows? I might like them. I never thought I'd enjoy gambling until you dragged me into the ship's casino."

"You didn't? I never realized that. I thought you were eager to hit those tables."

"Not at first. At first I was only eager to be with you."

"And you aren't anymore?"

"Of course I am, dear. I want to spend all the time I can with you, Sid. And if that means sharing your police things with you, then I will. I want to spend every minute with you ... for the rest of my life."

"That sounds to me," Sid whispered, leaning forward to kiss her, "like precisely the right amount of time."

DAVID CLOSED his apartment door and motioned Christie toward the living room. "Why don't I light a fire? We can relax and talk for a while."

Relax and talk? She glanced at him curiously. He'd spent half the trip from Mercy devouring her with his eyes—had practically driven into another car before he'd begun concentrating on the traffic. But now that they were here he wanted to relax and talk. He certainly was a man of surprises.

She made herself comfortable on the leather couch and watched his profile as he started the fire. He looked thoughtful ... and not happy. "Are you still upset about Walt?" she asked when he finished poking the logs. "And still worried about Jenny?"

"Yes. But it's not them I want to talk about. It's us." He sat down beside her and took her hand. "I thought maybe you'd reconsider going home tomorrow, that you'd stay through the weekend. I'd like you to meet my mother."

"That sounds serious," she teased.

"Don't joke, Christie. I *am* serious. If you took Thursday and Friday off work, we could have four more days together."

The moment she began to shake her head, David realized his step-by-step plan wasn't going to work. He'd have to lay all his cards on the table. Otherwise she'd be gone. Tomorrow. Or possibly Sunday. But, regardless of which day, she'd be gone. And she'd leave him terrified that she might be gone from his life forever.

"I'd give anything to stay, David, but the clinic's chronically short-staffed. And now that I've got no reason to stay—"

"No reason? Christie—"

"I didn't mean *no* reason, David. You understand what I meant. And we knew up front that I'd be going home as soon as my father was discharged."

"Why?"

"Why what?"

He took a deep breath and plunged ahead. "Why go home? Why ever go home?"

"David, don't be silly. I told you the clinic is—"

"I'm not being silly, Christie. I've never been less silly in my life. I love you. I love you so much that I can't believe it, so much that I can't conceive of living apart from you. Christie...marry me?" He sat watching her expression. Watching and praying.

Christie stared at David, certain she wouldn't be able to speak if she tried, unable even to think of any words.

Marry him? Marry this man she'd fallen insanely in love with? That made perfect sense. And yet, given the circumstances, it made no sense at all. She loved him so incredibly much, but she couldn't ignore reality.

"I love you, Christie. I'm absolutely crazy in love with you, remember? Isn't that why people get married?"

"David...David, I love you, too. You know that. But you can't just get married on a spur-of-the-moment whim. You have to think things through."

"I've thought things through, Christie. It's just that I've thought awfully fast because we have so little time. I wouldn't have mentioned marriage this soon if you lived in Winnipeg. Well," he amended with a grin, "maybe I would have. Maybe I wouldn't have been able to help myself even then."

"But, David, people don't decide to get married when they've only known each other for a few days."

"We aren't just people, Christie. We have something special—we realized that from the start. And if you value something, you should commit to it, shouldn't you? Christie, I'm thirty-four years old, and I've never felt about anyone the way I feel about you."

"And...and I've never felt about anyone the way I feel about you, David. But a few days is still a few days."

"Christie, if I feel like this after a few days, I can't even imagine how I'm going to feel after a few weeks or a few months or a few years. Before we met, I'd practically decided I wasn't capable of falling in love. But now I feel as if I'm in a free-fall. I keep thinking I couldn't possibly love you any more than I do. Then you do or say something that makes me realize I love you more than I did a few minutes earlier."

Christie smiled nervously. How could the idea of marrying David be making her so deliriously happy? It was far too soon to seriously consider marriage. She had to make him understand that.

"David, I'm not saying no. I'm just saying I need more time—need to be certain this something special is going to last. I know so many people, people the same age as I am, who've already been married and divorced. I even have a friend who's separated from her second husband. And she was certain she'd found love that would last—twice."

"Neither of those loves could have been like ours, Christie. Nobody can ever have found a love like ours."

"Oh, David," she said gently, "do you think we're the only two people who've ever fallen deeply in love?"

"Well—" he paused, grinning at her "—I guess there was Romeo and Juliet."

"That's just a storybook romance—and don't forget how they ended up."

"Well, Antony and Cleopatra, then. Oh, and I'll give you the Duke of Windsor and Mrs. Simpson, too. But, aside from them, we just might be the only two."

"I...I almost believe we just might, David. But I can't rush into something like marriage."

"Cautious Christie," David murmured, leaning forward and kissing her lips lightly.

"Don't tease, David. With half the marriages in North America breaking up, being cautious makes sense. And, with us, there would be so many things to decide. So many difficulties to work out."

"Then we'd work them out, Christie. Just say you'll marry me and we'll work them out in no time."

He kissed her again—not lightly, but with a deep, possessive kiss that left her wishing he hadn't stopped. Maybe...just maybe...well, if they could really work things out in no time...and they had all evening...well, it couldn't hurt to explore the possibility.

"David, just for starters, where would we live?"

"Well...I assumed here."

Of course he'd assumed here. What had she expected? But no matter how desperately in love they were they'd never be each other's entire life.

"It would make perfect sense, Christie. My practice is here. My mother's here—and a sister and brother. And now your father's here. Everything would be terrific."

"Well...I'm sure *we'd* be terrific, David. I just have a few problems with the *everything* part."

"Such as?"

He began caressing the side of her neck, making it difficult to think until she captured his hand and held it firmly. "Such as...David, I know everyone loves his hometown, but...well, I have trouble picturing myself living in a city this small."

"You'd get used to it, Christie."

She shook her head. "I'm sure Winnipeg has its good points. But life here would be a drastic change for me. I'd miss my friends. And I'd miss New York. There's so much to do there."

"You'd make friends here. My sister Susan is your age—instant friend. And there are things to do. This isn't exactly a cultural wasteland. We've got the Winnipeg Art Gallery. And the Manitoba Theater Center."

The gallery. *The* theater. In Manhattan there are dozens and dozens. "I...there's *the* weather, too, David. I really abhor winter, even the mild winters New York gets. How long are Winnipeg winters? I mean, Kay told me about your weeks of forty below, but winter doesn't *really* last eight or nine months, does it?"

"Of course not. I told you, an April snowstorm's rare. And the streets are usually still bare at Halloween."

Christie mentally counted months: May, June, July, August, September, Halloween. Oh, Lord! It could be below freezing here for half the year. And she was certain she wouldn't look good in chilblains.

David smiled. "Besides, winter is why I have a fireplace. And if one isn't enough, we can move—buy a house with fireplaces in every room. If you like, you could spend the entire winter curled up beside them."

"Be serious, David. I'm not the hibernating type. And what about working? I don't even know how difficult it would be to get licensed here."

"You wouldn't have to work, Christie."

She glanced around the luxurious living room, focused on the fireplace. Outside, night was quickly falling. But the fire cast a warm glow into the expensively appointed room.

No, she wouldn't *have* to work. She could play lady of the manor until she was bored to tears. And that would certainly do a lot for their marriage.

"Actually, I *would* have to work, David. Not simply because I need to be independent. Though, there's that, too, of course. I'd feel uncomfortable being a kept woman. But mostly it's...well, I really enjoy my work. And I believe in it. Modern medicine isn't the answer to everything. I think people should have options—and naturopathy provides one of those options."

"Christie, isn't that a little—"

"No. Wait, David. I don't want to get into a philosophical discussion about conventional medicine versus naturopathy. I realize there's a place for both—that a heart bypass is going to do a lot more for a person with clogged arteries than herbal tonics would. But what I do is important, too. I help people. I know that the way you help them is more obvious—you pick up the pieces after they've been critically ill.

"Whereas I...well, I have people coming to me who want to prevent health problems. And I help them do that. And it's rewarding when someone tells you how much better they've begun feeling. Wherever I was living, I wouldn't want to give up my profession. I wouldn't be happy if I did.''

"Well...Christie...I can understand that...but...'' David looked extremely uncomfortable.

"But what? What aren't you telling me?"

"I... well, I made some calls...checked into the status of naturopathy in Manitoba.''

She eyed him closely. So much for this being a spur-of-the-moment whim. He really had been thinking things through. "So you checked into its status and...?''

"And, well, you might have a little difficulty getting licensed in Canada with your American credentials.''

"How much difficulty?"

"You might have to take a few additional courses.''

"I see. But I'd take them and then there would be no problem?''

"Right. But...well...there isn't a college in Winnipeg. The nearest one's in Toronto.''

"In Toronto? The nearest Canadian naturopathic college is in my least favorite city in the world? The city with the killer customs? A city that's a two-and-a-half-hour flight from Winnipeg? I'd have quite a commute to my classes, wouldn't I?"

"I thought...well, I thought maybe you could... I...''

"You thought maybe I could do all the compromising,'' Christie said quietly.

"I...well...yes, I guess I did. I figured if you loved me enough, you'd...''

"I do love you, David. I love you very much. But have you thought about what you're asking? You're asking me to give up the entire life I know—my city, my friends, my pastimes, my job. And if I can't even work at what I love here? David, I need time to think. We both need time to think—time to consider *all* of our options. For example, what about you compromising? What about you moving to New York?"

David stared at her as if she'd suggested he move to Mars.

"Christie, I told I think New York is too big and fast and dangerous. Hell, the last time I was there for a convention, I ended up helping a mugging victim on the street—and that was in broad daylight. I...Christie, since the first time I visited New York I've wondered why sane people live there. I don't want to live in a city that you can't walk around in after dark. I'd just...I just couldn't handle it."

Christie silently watched him, waiting for him to recognize the irony of his admission.

"Oh," she finally said, "I was assuming that if you loved me enough, you could get used to it. That you could easily adjust to a city with a size difference of seven or eight million people from where you grew up. And you wouldn't have any problem practicing in New York, David. We even have medical schools right in Manhattan...in case you had to take a couple of courses before you could be licensed."

A sheepish expression appeared on his face as she spoke. "I see what you're getting at. I...I'm sorry. I didn't think I had any chauvinistic tendencies, but I guess convention dies hard. I just assumed..."

"Remember what Dad said, David? Never assume. But at least," she added, forcing a smile, "you didn't tell me that I should be the one to move because your job's more important than mine. I'll have to admit that was pretty unchauvinistic of you."

"Well...I'll have to admit that your father warned me you weren't too impressed by doctors."

"Present company excluded, David."

"I'm glad." He kissed her gently once more. "I guess maybe it's going to take a little longer than I thought to decide how we're going to work things out. But what happens in the meantime?"

"In the meantime I have to go home."

"Christie, how the hell are we going to work things out if we're two thousand miles apart?"

"There's the phone, David. And letters. And we can see each other whenever we have the chance. And surely, if this is really a lasting kind of love, we can manage a significant relationship long-distance for a while."

"Sure. I suppose I can spend my evenings taking significant cold showers. Look, Christie, at least stay over the weekend. At least give me that. We need to talk more—need to decide—oh, hell, Christie, we just have to figure out what to do. The only thing that really matters is that we end up together. Don't you realize how lucky people are when they find something like we've found?"

"They're even luckier if they get to keep it, David. I simply want to be certain we can work things out so that keeping what we've found is the final result."

David wrapped his arm around her shoulder and drew her to him. "We'll get to keep it, Christie. What's a little geographic difficulty? And, until we sort out the future, I can handle New York for visits. If Rothman wasn't away, I'd fly back with you tomorrow—spend the weekend there. But, as it is . . ."

"As it is, I'll stay here until Sunday night," she murmured. "The clinic isn't going to fall apart if I'm not there for two more days."

David kissed the top of her head. "I love you. And we'll work this out somehow. We'll work it out just fine. But what do you want to do right now? Make chicken cacciatore . . . or make love?''

Before she could say, "Make love," a quiet buzzer sounded.

"That's the concierge," David said. "Don't move."

She watched him walk to the hallway, wanting more than anything to believe they could work things out.

He pressed an intercom button. "Dr. Lawrence."

A disembodied male voice floated into the apartment. "Dr. Lawrence, there's a Dr. Wakefield in the lobby. He'd like to come up."

"Did my choice of activities," Christie whispered across the room, "just expand to include making dinner, making love or making conversation with Brent?"

"'Fraid so," David whispered back. "Want me to have Frank give him some excuse?"

Reluctantly she shook her head. "You'd better not. Whatever he wants, it must be pretty important for him to have come here. But let's get rid of him fast."

David grinned. "You're that fond of chicken cacciatore?"

"Well . . . not really."

CHAPTER FOURTEEN

DAVID USHERED Brent into the living room and Christie caught her breath at the sight of him. He looked gray and completely wrung out. He must have heard something about Jenny. Something awful.

Afraid to ask what it was, she watched silently as the two men crossed the room. David sat down beside her once more, motioning the intern to one of the wing chairs on the other side of the fireplace. Brent slumped into the chair and silently stared across the coffee table at them, looking as if the weight of the world was on his shoulders.

"What's up?" David finally asked.

Christie glanced at him. His voice had sounded strained, as if he hadn't wanted to ask the question. And he was watching Brent with apparent concern.

Then, before her eyes, David's body stiffened and his expression of concern was replaced by one of disbelief.

Her gaze flashed back to Brent.

For a moment she was flooded by a sense that she was seeing things. Then that sense gave way to fear—a more terrifying, gut-wrenching fear than she'd ever known. Her stomach lurched and her heart stopped midbeat. She couldn't breathe or swallow. All she could do was stare at the tiny black hole...the tiny black hole at the end of the gun barrel.

This couldn't be. Simply couldn't be! There was no rhyme or reason to Brent's pointing a gun at them. It was insane.

Insane. Temporary insanity. Yes, that had to be it. Whatever had happened to Jenny must have completely unhinged him. Whatever crazy thoughts had lodged inside his head, she and David had done nothing to—

David was speaking again. But his voice sounded like a stranger's—measured, pronounced, devoid of emotion. It was only because he was sitting beside her that she knew the words had to be his.

"Wakefield...what kind of macabre joke is this?"

Brent slowly shrugged. "Sorry, David. No joke. I never meant this to happen. I never meant any of it to happen. But it did. And now the only way it'll end is if you two are dead."

Dead. Christie continued staring at the man, unable to think past that word.

He couldn't kill them. David had asked her to marry him, had promised her that they'd work everything out. They had their whole lives ahead of them, yet Brent was saying—

His glance flickered down to the gun and then across the coffee table once more, his aim wavering from Christie to David...finally coming to rest centered on her stomach.

She began trembling, then felt David's hand cover hers. But his touch did nothing to reassure her. It only enabled her to feel his fear as well as her own. And hers alone was making her physically ill.

She took a deep breath, trying to quell her nausea, trying to control her panic, and forced her gaze away from the gun, up to Brent's face once more.

His brown eyes were devoid of emotion. They looked black—every bit as black, as dull and deadly black, as that tiny hole at the end of the gun barrel.

Think, she ordered herself. She was a New Yorker. New Yorkers were tough. They could cope with threatening situations. And she'd dealt with people who were out of control before this—addicts who'd come into the clinic hoping to find drugs, schizophrenics wandering the streets.

But she'd never come face-to-face with a gun. She *had* dealt with people out of control, though. So why couldn't she remember the rules? What would her father tell her to do?

Remain calm. Oh, thank heavens! Her mind was beginning to function again. The first thing to remember was to remain calm and talk sensibly...keep talking sensibly until Brent realized the insanity of what he was doing.

But how could she talk sensibly? How could she talk at all when her throat was so tightly constricted that she felt as if she were being choked?

"Wakefield," David said quietly, "what didn't you mean to happen?"

Christie offered a silent prayer of gratitude that David's voice was still working, that he was managing to put words together coherently.

"Jenny."

"What about her? Did the police find her?"

"Not yet."

"Then what's wrong?"

The silence was deafening. Each time the fire softly crackled, it sounded like fireworks exploding.

"Then what's wrong?" David finally repeated.

"She's dead."

Impossibly, Christie's throat grew tighter; her fear seemed to have wrapped a vise around it. Brent's brain was definitely dysfunctional. Jenny couldn't be dead. If the police hadn't found her, then why would he think...?

Because he was imagining the worst. That was why. But what did even the worst have to do with that gun he was pointing at them?

"Wakefield...Jenny isn't dead. When the police turn her up—"

"When the police turn her up, she'll be dead, David. And that's why you and Christie...I'm sorry, but there's no other way."

"Look, Brent, you have to get hold of yourself. You're overtired and overwrought. Neither of us are psychiatrists, but we both know what stress can do to people."

"It's not stress, David. I...we had an argument. Jenny was going to turn me in. I was only trying to shake some sense into her, but her neck...I was...I got onto her carotid artery, and she was unconscious in only twenty or thirty seconds. But it was an accident. I didn't mean to strangle her." Christie gasped and Brent's gaze shot to her. "I didn't mean to kill her, Christie. It just happened."

"But her body," David said, his voice unsteady. "If you killed her...?"

"We put her in Mercy's morgue."

Christie's glance flickered to David. The same horror and lack of comprehension she was feeling were written on his face. Jenny was dead. Jenny was dead and her body was lying in a hospital morgue. And this man—the man Jenny had been in love with—had killed her.

"We," David murmured dully. "You said *we* put her—"

"Walt and I. He was there."

"Walt Lesco?"

"Yes."

"And he's dead, too. Wakefield, you killed Walt, too? You went to his apartment and gave him an overdose, didn't you? Because he knew you'd killed Jenny."

"No! I wouldn't have done that." Brent leaned toward them. "I'm not a killer. I told you—Jenny's death was an accident."

"If it was an accident," Christie managed, amazed to hear the words actually come out, "then the best thing you can do is tell the police what happened . . . how it happened."

"No. They'd never believe me. Not now. Not after Walt."

"I thought," David said slowly, "you just told us that you didn't kill Walt."

"I . . . I said I wouldn't have killed him simply because he knew about Jenny. But . . . I have to start at the beginning . . . have to explain. David, I was . . . I was taking drugs from the unit. If interns were better paid, I never would have started. But I did. And it was so damn easy to keep on doing it. I just passed them to Walt and he sold them on the street."

Brent's words had begun tumbling out, as if he'd had them bottled up inside for days and now felt compelled to tell someone how everything had happened.

"But on Sunday morning," he continued, "I was late coming to pick Jenny up because I had a meeting with Walt downstairs first. We always met down by the morgue where there's never anyone around. But on

Sunday Jenny came looking for me and...well...A few weeks ago she'd found out what I was doing and I promised her I'd quit. But it turned out she'd started checking the drug cupboard, matching the inventory against the med orders, checking to see if I'd really stopped."

"And you hadn't," David concluded.

Brent shook his head. "No, I hadn't. And when she caught us on Sunday, she said she was going to turn us in and...and we started fighting...and I..."

"My God!" David murmured. "My God! So that note...you wrote that note and stuck it under my door?"

"I...I thought it would be enough to keep anyone from worrying about her, that it would give me time to figure out how to get her body out of Mercy. Then when you started pressing, I made up the bit about her being pregnant, about her having a good reason for taking off."

"So she wasn't pregnant. You just...but what about Walt?"

"I...at first I figured he wouldn't say anything. After all, he'd helped me—helped me hide Jenny's body. And he drove her car away from the hospital and dumped it someplace. But later, when I told him we'd have to cool the drugs for a while, that I couldn't risk someone noticing the shortages—not when sooner or later there could be cops nosing around—he balked. Said he'd counted on the money. He owed some debts that wouldn't wait. That's why he tried his extortion game. And it was those ransom calls that made me realize I had to get rid of him. It was his own fault. He left me no choice. The police would have caught up with him and he'd have squealed like a stuck pig."

"You knew it was Walt on the phone," Christie whispered. "You knew, but you didn't let on."

"Yeah. When David told me about the first call I figured it had to be Walt. And then, when I was listening, when David insisted on talking to Jenny and Walt got flustered, he called David, 'buster.' He sometimes called me that when he was annoyed."

David leaned forward a little.

"Sit back," Brent snapped, sitting up straighter himself and waving his gun.

David cleared his throat and slowly leaned back against the couch. His hand was pressing Christie's so tightly that her fingers had grown numb, yet his voice retained its control.

"Wakefield, I'm sorry you're in trouble. If there's anything you want me to do, any way I can help you, tell me. And there's no need for that gun. I'll do what I can. But harming Christie or me isn't going to get you anywhere."

"Oh, yes, it will, David. That's why I'm here. I've got no choice but to get rid of you two. That's my ticket out of this entire mess."

"Brent...think this through for a minute. You can't get out of anything by killing us. The concierge let you in. You gave him your name. If you killed us, don't you think the police would talk to him? Don't you think he'd remember your being here?"

Brent stared blankly at David, as if that eventuality hadn't occurred to him.

Please, Christie silently begged. *Please see that David's right.* Her hopes inched upward when Brent nodded... and plunged back down as he spoke.

"We'll all have to go out, then. The concierge will see us leave and...and we'll take your car and I'll tell the police you dropped me off at my place...and that you both were fine then."

"It's not that simple, Brent. The police would figure out what happened. Look, you said Jenny's death was accidental. And Walt...well, I'm not a lawyer, but maybe—"

"No way, David. I'm not spending my life rotting in some jail. Not when I can prevent it. And you two are the only people who can tie me to either death. You've got the evidence, David. And Christie's seen it. I have to kill you both. It's the only way."

"Brent, I don't have a damn thing! I don't know what the hell you're talking about!" David's voice cracked and Christie held her breath as Brent began waving his gun again.

"I told you to sit back," he snapped at David. "I know you've got it. And maybe it's lucky for me that you do. You'll be dead and the police will find it here and they'll think...well, whatever they think, it won't be that I had anything to do with Jenny's death...with anybody's death."

"Wakefield, I've got nothing!"

"The earring. You've got Jenny's earring."

Christie stared at Brent, trying to make some sense of his statement. She couldn't.

"You grabbed it out of Christie's hand and stuck it into your pocket."

The scene in Brent's office suddenly flooded Christie's mind, as vivid as a movie flashback. Brent had pulled a Kleenex from his pocket. And with it had come that little gold sea gull. She'd picked it up and David had taken it—put it in his pocket. So it was Jenny's earring. But in his office Brent had told them it was Ruth's.

"Jenny's earring," David murmured, his words echoing her thoughts. "It's still in that pocket. I completely forgot about it. But you said—"

"I said it was Ruth's," Brent mumbled. "I had to say something. And you told me that if it wasn't hers, you'd turn it in to the nursing station. Well, it wasn't hers. But you didn't turn it in. I checked before I left Mercy tonight and it wasn't in the Lost and Found drawer. It came off when Jenny was struggling," Brent went on, his voice almost inaudible. "After...after we'd finished moving her body...after we'd come out of the morgue, I noticed the earring on the floor. I gave her those damn earrings—such a strange coincidence. But the other one...the other one must still be..."

On her body, Christie silently filled in, swallowing hard.

"And when the police find her," Brent continued, "they'll look for that missing earring. And you and Christie saw it. You and Christie know I had it. So we'll all have to go out. Out past your concierge. Out in your car...drive to someplace quiet...dark..."

And deadly. The words came unbidden to Christie, sending an icy tingle of terror up her spine. Unless they could convince Brent of how insane his plan was, she and David would never have the chance to live their lives together.

Instead, they were going to die together. They were going to die together someplace quiet...dark...and deadly.

CHRISTIE SAT RIGIDLY in the back seat of the Mercedes, staring straight ahead as David drove, intensely aware of how close—how menacingly close— Brent was sitting beside her, intensely aware of his hand holding her arm tightly captive, of the gun lodged against her side.

He was huddled by the door, as far from David as he could be, as if he thought David might suddenly let go of the steering wheel, whirl around and grab for the gun.

He wouldn't, of course. Not when he knew the gun was firmly pressed against her ribs. Brent hadn't shifted it for more than a moment since they'd left the apartment.

The barrel had poked and prodded her down into the garage...along to the Mercedes. Now it was pressing against her in the confines of the car, ensuring that David continued to follow instructions, ensuring that her fear wouldn't subside for an instant.

She gazed through the windshield, trying not to notice how the passing cars were becoming fewer and farther between, trying to ignore the deadly darkness shrouding them.

Until they'd cleared the city, she'd been telling herself there had to be a way out of this nightmare. In the movies the good guys always escaped. The villain made a mistake and the good guys escaped.

But this wasn't the movies. And Brent hadn't made a mistake.

"Turn onto River Road."

She jumped at the sound of his voice and he clutched her arm even more tightly. A few moments later the Mercedes turned right...and her heart sank even lower. They were on a narrow road now and the night seemed even blacker. Her glance flickered to the left. She couldn't see the moon. No stars were visible. The darkness was complete except for the beams from their headlights.

David switched them onto high and they began illuminating threatening shapes on the side of the road . . . bushes and trees. This was the kind of terrain where bodies could probably lie for ages without being discovered.

That thought almost made her cry. She bit her lip. Crying wouldn't help. The only thing that would help was a plan, a way of escaping from Brent. She had no plan, though. And she couldn't imagine there was anything David could do. Unless they managed a miracle they were going to die.

A single tear escaped. She didn't dare move her hand to wipe it away.

"Slow down," Brent ordered.

Slow down. Was this the beginning of the end? She glanced to her right, not wanting to see Brent but wanting to see if they were coming up to something.

No. They were in the middle of nowhere. Thick, high vegetation on the left, smaller bushes on the right, and below them a wide river.

There was a moon after all, she noticed. Barely a quarter moon, but bright enough to highlight the water's motion. Here and there the odd moonbeam detailed a bit of the riverbank's edge. But mostly there was nothing except the deadly darkness.

Their headlights picked up a grassy turnoff on the river side. She felt Brent's body tense. "There," he snapped. "Park up there on the right."

David eased off the road and stopped the car.

"Cut the ignition and give me the keys. Slowly. Very slowly. Don't forget where the gun is."

David turned off the engine. The dashboard lights vanished, leaving only pale moonglow to faintly light the car. He turned to hand over the keys. In the dimness his eyes caught Christie's for a moment.

Was he trying to tell her something? Was she simply too frightened to catch his message?

"Now get out," Brent ordered. "You get out the driver's side and we'll get out this side. And once you're out, put your hands on the hood and stay put."

"Wakefield—"

"Shut up. Just get out."

David opened his door, eased himself from the car and flattened his palms on the hood.

"Now us," Brent muttered, his breath nauseatingly hot against Christie's cheek.

He released his hold on her arm but didn't move the gun. And once he'd opened the door he grabbed her arm again. She slid out of the car after him, more conscious than ever of how hard the gun was against her ribs, more conscious than ever that she and David were going to die on this godforsaken road. Brent jerked her away from the car a few feet, then stopped.

"Wakefield," David tried again. "You can't do this."

He *could* do this, though. He *was* doing it. That was the horror she could scarcely believe. But they couldn't just let him shoot them without at least trying something.

She took a deep breath and screwed up every ounce of her courage. "David!" she screamed. "A car's coming! Run! Stop it!"

Brent whirled to his left, his grip on her arm loosening as he turned, the gun leaving her side.

She threw her entire weight in the opposite direction and broke free, stumbling with the momentum and pitching forward to the ground.

"The bank!" David shouted. "Head down the bank!"

Christie stumbled to her feet and half ran, half staggered toward the edge of the riverbank. Sound exploded. A car backfiring? No! A shot! Then another!

Just as she reached the downward slope someone grabbed her arm. She wheeled around, terrified that it was Brent.

David! It was David!

He dragged her down the bank with him, through bushes that tore at her legs and caught at her dress. One of her shoes came off and she almost fell again, but David grabbed her by both arms and propelled her forward.

A third shot rang out from above. Then a fourth. But they'd reached a flat stretch that ran along the water. Christie managed to kick off her other shoe, and they raced hand in hand through the night, running until she could scarcely breathe.

Finally David slowed the pace and stopped beside a large bush. They sank down behind it and he wrapped his arms around her. She clung to him tightly, wanting desperately to believe they'd left Brent so far behind he'd never catch them.

"I didn't know you were brave and brilliant," David whispered. "If you hadn't started yelling, we'd be dead."

"I'm afraid," she whispered, "that it wasn't either bravery or brilliance. It was pure survival instinct."

They sat huddled in the darkness, holding each other and listening. But all they heard were insects chirping, tiny waves lapping up to the shore and the sounds of their own ragged breathing.

Christie's heart was still pounding. She slid her hand across David's chest and felt his heartbeat. Heartbeats and breathing. Vital signs in order. They were definitely alive.

But Brent was still someplace nearby...still had his gun.

"Do you think he'll come after us?" she whispered.

"No, not in the dark. We'll sit here for a while, but we're going to be all right now."

"How can you sound so certain? I only heard four shots. He probably has bullets left."

David kissed her cheek. "They aren't going to do him any good in the dark and from a distance, Christie. He's likely never fired a gun before tonight. We're going to be just fine."

"You're absolutely, positively sure?"

"Absolutely and positively. Hey," he added gently. "Have I ever lied to you before?"

CHRISTIE SAT on Kay's couch beside David, holding his hand. They'd been here for more than an hour, and there had been enough hugs and kisses all around to assure both her father and Kay that despite their disheveled appearance she and David were alive and well.

Not that she didn't still feel shaky. And David looked as if he might jump at the drop of a hat. But they were definitely alive and well.

She glanced across at her father once more. He hadn't yet lost his stunned expression.

And it really took something, she reflected, to stun Sid Lambert. Of course, what she and David had been through was definitely *something*. And the fact that her father hadn't suspected Brent was a killer had really rocked the detective in him.

David hadn't even quite finished his account of the evening before Sid had interrupted. And now he had them going over every detail of "the case." She knew he was trying to determine if he'd missed something he should have caught.

"Walt phoning *you* with a ransom demand was an obvious move, David," he muttered. "He knew you were in charge of the unit. But what about Allison? Why call him? How did Walt know about Austin and Jenny?"

"Wakefield didn't say anything about that, Sid. Come to think of it, he might not even have known about Walt making a second demand. I didn't mention my conversation with Austin. And Marchman doesn't give anything away."

"But Walt figured that phoning Austin was worth a try," Sid persisted. "How did he know that?"

"I don't know. Walt worked at Mercy for years. He knew Jenny. Maybe he knew who Austin was, maybe he'd seen them together some place. Or maybe...you know, Austin mentioned that he and Ruth had a big scene at Mercy after she'd found out about Jenny. I wonder if it's possible that Walt overheard it?"

"Well, I hope Marchman gets to the bottom of that. I hate loose ends. This scene with Ruth, was it—?"

"Dear," Kay interrupted, "could you ask all your detective questions after David finishes his story? I want to hear how they got from the riverbank to the police. Weren't you afraid Brent would be waiting at the car, David?"

He nodded. "That's why we didn't go back to the car. As it turned out, though, it wouldn't have mattered if we had. When the police checked for my car later, it was gone. While we were sitting, listening to be certain Wakefield hadn't followed us, he and the

Mercedes were probably halfway back to the city. At any rate, after we'd caught our breath, we started walking. Of course, it was strictly against my medical advice for Christie to do any walking without her shoes," he added, glancing pointedly at the basin she was soaking her cut feet in. "I wanted her to wait where she was."

"Fat chance I was going to do that. I'd have been sitting there all alone, certain that Brent would come leaping out of the bushes at me."

"Well, anyway, the two of us started walking. Your daughter seems to have a stubborn streak a mile wide," David added, grinning at Sid.

Sid laughed. "I can't imagine where she got a fault like that."

"Can't you, dear?" Kay asked, smiling innocently.

"Well, wherever she got it, we started walking. I knew there was the odd house along River Road, so we just kept going until we saw one with lights on. We called the police from there and...well, the rest is pretty routine. We gave them Brent's description, answered about a trillion questions and they finally drove us here."

Kay shook her head. "I still can't believe that a nice young man like Brent...well, of course he's not a nice young man at all, is he, Sid? What on earth makes a person do such awful things?"

"He's a psychopath, Kay. I ran across a lot of them in Homicide. They never really love anyone but themselves and they have no consciences. When Jenny threatened to turn him in, his only concern was that she didn't, regardless of what he had to do to ensure that. I should have spotted him for what he was."

"Daddy, how could you have? You only saw him a couple of times. And he had all of us completely fooled—including Marchman, I'll bet."

"Yeah. Yeah, psychopaths are good at fooling people."

"But he seemed so concerned about Jenny," Kay murmured. "I never doubted that he loved her. Yet all the time he'd killed her."

Sid nodded. "He had to play the worried lover. That way he not only threw us off track but succeeding in keeping himself involved in the investigation. He got to know what Christie and David turned up and what the police were doing. He would have known if they'd picked up any clues that pointed to him."

"But the one clue we did pick up," David muttered, "we didn't even recognize as a clue. His cover story about that earring was so damn believable."

"As I said, David. Psychopaths are good at fooling people."

"You know, Daddy, Brent kept insisting that he didn't mean to kill Jenny, that it was an accident. Do you think that's possible?"

"Anything's possible. But the fact remains that he murdered Walt because he was causing him problems . . . and almost murdered you two, as well."

Sid eyed Christie for a long moment, then stood up and crossed the room. He sat down beside her and David and hugged her so tightly that she could barely breathe. "It's just a miracle you weren't killed, baby. Don't you know enough not to wear a white dress if you're going to be a nighttime shooting target?"

"Oh, Daddy!" Suddenly the tears she'd held back all evening began to flow. She squeezed her eyes tightly shut, but it didn't help.

"There, there," her father murmured, patting her back, making her feel like a little girl again. "Everything will be all right. You're safe here. You know the police are watching the house. And they'll track Wakefield down in no time flat. They might even have him already. Why don't I phone Marchman and see what's happening?" he suggested when she regained control.

The moment her father released her, David put his arm around her shoulder and drew her to him.

"Is there anything you'd like, Christie?" Kay asked. "Anything either of you would like?"

Christie managed what she hoped looked like a smile. "A new dress? I was awfully hard on this one."

"And it was such a pretty dress," Kay said, laughing. "Once Sid's finished talking to Marchman, why don't you go upstairs and take a shower. You'll feel better."

"That's probably a good idea. And then..." She paused, glancing at the mantel clock. "I guess there won't be a then. I hadn't realized it was past midnight. And you and Dad have to get up first thing, don't you? To catch your flight."

"We won't leave tomorrow, Christie. Not unless the police have picked up Brent by morning. I know your father isn't going to want to let you out of his sight until he's sure you're safe—whether it means your staying here or him flying back to New York with you. I'll just go and hurry him along," she added, rising. "He's liable to be giving Marchman the benefit of twenty-five years experience."

"I don't want to let you out of my sight, either," David whispered as Kay left the room. "And I could use a shower every bit as much as you."

"With neither you nor my father letting me out of your sights," Christie whispered back, "that shower could get awfully crowded."

"Lord, that's another reason for hoping they find Brent quickly. When I asked you to stay for a few more days, I sure wasn't thinking about sharing you with your father."

"What about your father?" Sid asked, bursting back into the room with Kay on his arm and a grin plastered across his face.

"Ah...David was just saying..." Christie paused. Her father clearly wasn't listening. Just as well. She didn't have a believable explanation.

"So, Daddy, what did Marchman say?"

"He said that they got Wakefield! He was just about to call and let us know."

Christie felt herself sagging with relief—sagging into David's arms as he hugged her. She'd known she was safe. She'd been certain Wakefield wouldn't try anything further. But the fact that he wouldn't have the opportunity to made a world of difference.

"That's wonderful, Daddy. What else did he say?"

"Well, they only nailed Brent a few minutes ago—put out an APB based on David's description and picked him up at the airport. Got your car, too, David. He left it in the lot. Ten minutes longer and he'd have been on his way out of town. Instead, he's on his way to jail. I'll get all the rest of the details once Kay and I are back. The important thing is that we don't have to worry about you two." Sid paused, staring at them on the couch...at the way David's arms were wrapped around Christie.

She cleared her throat and tried to look nonchalant. "That means you and Kay will feel okay about leaving for Barbados tomorrow."

"Right. We'll be heading south and you'll be heading back to New York. What time's your flight, baby? Maybe the three of us can go to the airport together."

"Well . . . actually, I decided to take Kay up on her offer and stay at the house for a few more days. Not go home until Sunday."

"But why would you—?"

"Oh, I'm glad about that, Christie," Kay said, cutting Sid off. "You need a few days to relax after all this terrible trouble. Now, would anyone like some hot chocolate? You, Sid?"

"No. No thanks."

"You're probably right, dear. Maybe I won't have any, either. We should get to bed, so we won't be starting our honeymoon tired."

Sid eyed David uncertainly.

"I'm too keyed up to sleep yet," Christie said quickly. "David and I will just sit here and talk for a bit before he calls a cab."

"That's fine, Christie," Kay offered. "We'll see you in the morning, dear. Good night, David."

"Night, Kay. Night, Sid."

Christie watched her father being led meekly away, trying to recall whether she'd really once been worried that Kay might have trouble coping with him.

"As I've said before," David murmured, "Kay's a terrific lady. And she makes a terrific exit, doesn't she?"

"And," Christie whispered as David leaned closer, "her timing's impeccable. I couldn't have lasted without a kiss for one more minute."

CHAPTER FIFTEEN

THE PUBLIC ADDRESS SYSTEM crackled to life once more. "Air Canada flight 823 to Chicago is now boarding at gate D. All passengers should proceed to the boarding area at this time."

David tightened his arm around Christie's shoulders. "Having to waste an hour or two transferring midway is going to mean just that much less time together when we visit."

"I know." *Visit.* She hated that word. It reeked of impermanence. And how, she wondered for the thousandth time, could she be going home without their having arrived at a solution to their geographic standoff? How could they not have come up with a better plan than visiting back and forth for the next few months?

Some *plan.* Of course, it was always possible that David would gradually decide New York wasn't quite as awful as he believed. Or that she'd decide Winnipeg might be an okay place to live. But there was a gigantic difference between *possible* and *likely.* And she doubted the odds on either of them doing an about-face were very high.

She told herself again that one of them would. If only she could truly believe herself. If only she wasn't so terribly afraid that their visits would gradually taper off. That, in the end, she'd lose David.

"I wish you weren't changing planes at O'Hare," he muttered. "That airport's too darn busy to be safe. How can there be no direct flights between Winnipeg and New York?"

Christie merely shrugged. She'd given up wondering how any place in North America—at least any place that called itself a city—couldn't have direct flights to New York. But she had an uneasy suspicion that it was another example of their old nemesis, the mysterious power, throwing obstacles in their course.

She stared at the sign reading Passengers Only Beyond This Point. In twenty minutes she'd be on her way to Chicago. In a few hours she'd be back in New York. And David would still be here.

"I can't believe," he murmured, taking her into his arms and hugging her, "that the days have passed so quickly."

"I can't, either." She rested her cheek against the secure warmth of his shoulder, thinking how awfully much she'd miss not being with him.

Aside from the hours the police had spent questioning them individually, and the time David had put in at Mercy, they'd been together every moment of the past few days—and nights. And that had been heaven. Except for the nagging worry about not being able to sort out their plans for the future.

Every minute with David made her more certain that she wanted to spend forever with him. But despite how incredibly much she loved him, the stardust clouding her vision hadn't blinded her completely.

She didn't want to find, some years down the road, that she'd been transformed from David's wife into a divorce statistic. She'd seen too many marriages disintegrate to believe that love could actually conquer all. And living in a city that one of them didn't want to live in would be a pretty big obstacle to conquer.

"You'd better get going," David murmured.

"Not yet…just stand here and keep hugging me for another minute."

Another minute. If only in that minute they could come up with the solution that was eluding them. There had to be one. How could there not be when being with David felt so right?

The PA system interrupted her thoughts: "This is the final boarding call for Air Canada flight 823 to Chicago. Would all passengers please proceed to gate D immediately."

For a moment David hugged her even more tightly, then kissed her—a long, lingering kiss that made her wish Air Canada flight 823 didn't exist.

"Come on." He picked up her hand luggage and started forward. "Missing your plane isn't going to help anything. But just be careful once you get back to the Big Bad Apple. I don't want anything awful happening to you."

She forced a smile. "You're worried about something awful happening to me back home after I was almost murdered here?"

"Don't remind me of that. Every time I think about it I practically start shaking. Even while we were at Jenny's funeral I kept looking at you, making certain you were beside me, thinking about how you might have been dead, as well. Christie, the thought of anything happening to you…" They paused outside the security check. "I'll call you tonight, Christie. I want to know that you got home safely. And I'll arrange for the first free weekend I can."

"It might be quite a while, though, mightn't it, David? I mean, things have been more hectic than you'd hoped they'd be over the past few days."

"Well...losing our intern is certainly going to have the staff men putting in extra hours for the next while."

"And Rothman's still away," she pointed out. But why was she telling David something he was perfectly aware of? What was the point of rehashing these facts they'd already discussed? Did she think David was going to tell her that he'd miraculously arranged to import a couple of extra cardiologists to fill in on Mercy's CCU?

"Rothman will be back in another week, Christie. So maybe I'll be able to make it to New York the weekend after next ... or the one after that ... it'll be as soon as I can get away."

She nodded, determined not to cry but afraid that trying to say anything more would do her in. She'd see David again the weekend after next ... or the one after that ... or sometime even farther into the future.

She'd see him again, assuming, of course that the lyrics, "Absence makes the heart grow fonder—for somebody else," were just words from an old song and not an old truism. But what had her father said?

Never assume.

She tried to shut that advice out of her mind. The prospect of David finding someone else was too much to bear.

He handed over her carryon, and she kissed him a final time.

"I love you, Christie," he murmured. "I'm absolutely crazy in love with you."

"I love you, too, David." Her voice broke, thick with tears. She'd been right. Speaking again had done her in.

She turned and fled into the security check area, blindly flashing her boarding pass, shoving her case and purse onto the conveyer and passing through the metal detector.

"Gate D?" she managed once she'd been cleared.

A uniformed woman motioned to her right.

Christie started quickly down the corridor, resisting the urge to look back through the doorway, not wanting to leave David with a memory of the tears that were streaming down her face.

CHRISTIE SAT watching her phone, waiting for it to ring. David had called her every evening for the past three weeks. He must fast be becoming one of the telephone company's best customers. But April had already turned into May, and talking to David on the phone couldn't hold a candle to being with him.

Every night after his calls, once they'd hung up, she was left staring at the walls, wishing he was with her, wishing time really could fly—at least until they were together again.

This was only Monday. She had four more days to get through before the weekend. And she had no guarantee that David would be here even then. But it had been three weeks since she'd left Winnipeg. Surely he'd be able to get away this weekend. Surely they'd have two days together.

Two days. The longer she spent without him, the more certain she was that visiting back and forth for a while simply wasn't going to work.

Two days, now and then, wasn't going to be enough, not nearly enough. Not if the remainder of her time was as miserable as the past three weeks had been. She'd been walking around like one of *Midnight Cinema*'s murdered vampire mummies, forcing herself to get up every morning and go to the clinic but barely able to function once she arrived.

Her mind constantly wandered from what she was doing as images of David floated before her eyes. She missed him so much that the missing had become a physical ache in her heart. She was beginning to doubt that she could live without him for much longer. But if she couldn't live without him, then she had to live with him. That fact was becoming clearer every day.

If only she didn't have a litany of concerns about living in Winnipeg. If only there wasn't a nagging little worry in the back of her mind that she might someday regret giving up her career and her life in New York...that the regret might turn into resentment of David.

Of course, resenting David seemed almost inconceivable. But what if in ten years or so...? And yet, at the moment, she couldn't see how anything but being with him would make her happy.

And if giving up the life she loved was the only way she could have the man she loved, shouldn't she pack her woollies and learn to enjoy making snowmen? Shouldn't she?

The prospect filled her with a mixture of excitement and anxiety.

Should she or shouldn't she? She was about to begin a game of "eenie, meenie, minie, moe" with herself when the phone rang. She grabbed for it. "Hello?"

"Hi, darling."

Her pulse began racing at the sound of David's voice. "Hi, darling yourself. How's my favorite doctor?"

David laughed. "Given your dim view of doctors, I'm not sure that being your favorite one is much of a compliment. But to answer your question, I'm beat. I'm starting to think I should have specialized in dermatology. People never have acne attacks in the middle of the night."

"And I'll bet dermatologists get every single weekend off, too." Christie bit her lip as the sentence escaped. She knew David was busy. She didn't want to make him feel guilty about not having made it to New York before this.

"Speaking of weekends, Christie..."

She held her breath in anticipation—for at least three seconds—until she couldn't stand the suspense any longer. "You're coming, David? You're coming on Friday?"

"Well...no."

No? Her spirits plummeted to her toes. What if...what if he'd been having second thoughts about her, about them? What if—?

"I don't mean no, exactly, Christie."

He didn't mean no, exactly? Well, what the hell did he mean?

"I...I want you to meet me somewhere."

Her spirits made it all the way back up to her knees before she got her voice working again. "Where?"

Where? Why had she even bothered to ask? She'd meet him in Timbuktu if he wanted her to.

"Well, I don't want to tell you where. I want it to be a surprise."

"David, if you don't tell me where, I'm going to have a devil of a time getting there, aren't I?"

"You can come then? You haven't made any plans for the weekend?"

"David! Do you really think I'd have made any plans as long as I thought there might be a chance of seeing you?"

"Well . . . just checking."

She could hear a smile in his voice, could feel a silly smile on her own face. "So where do you want me to meet you?"

"I told you. I want it to be a surprise. Can you get off work early on Friday?"

"I . . . yes, of course." If it meant getting down on her knees and begging, she'd get off early.

"Good. Then be at the American desk at La Guardia by four. There'll be a ticket waiting for you."

Her smile turned into a grin. David was the most wonderful man she'd ever met. "All right. The American desk by four on Friday. And what should I pack?"

"Oh . . . we'll be going out for dinner, so you'll need a dress or two. And the weather will be warm—bring a bathing suit. And walking shoes for sight-seeing."

"Okay. Anything else?"

"Let's see . . . don't bring very many of your vitamins or any of that crazy white powder. You're going to have to go through customs."

Customs? Christie's thoughts began to race. Customs and warm weather? Good grief, was David taking her to Spain or Portugal?

"I guess," she offered, trying to sound far more calm than she felt, "that if we're going through customs, I'll need my passport, huh?"

"Uh . . . no. No passport. You'll only need your birth certificate."

No passport. Not Europe, then. No...of course not Europe. He'd said La Guardia, and flights to Europe left from JFK. But warm weather...well, planes heading for the Caribbean took off out of La Guardia. And she didn't need a passport for the Caribbean. David must be taking her to a glamorous sun spot!

"I'll call you tomorrow, darling. I love you."

"I love you, too." Christie hung up and hugged herself. She'd be with David at four o'clock on Friday. He wasn't fooling her a bit. A ticket wasn't the only thing that would be waiting at the American desk. David wouldn't fly alone to wherever they were going and have her do the same. Not when they could spend those hours with each other. She'd bet her last dime that his surprise was going to include meeting her at La Guardia.

Of course...of course this crazy idea of his was actually cheating. Whisking her off to a vacation paradise wasn't exactly living up to his agreement to spend some time in New York. But...well, just for this one weekend it didn't really matter because she and David were going to be together on Friday!

She danced out of the living room, into her bedroom and threw open the closet door. Clothes for dinner...her black bikini for the beach...walking shoes for sight-seeing.

And, she silently added, glancing at the Sak's box that had been sitting on her dresser for the past two weeks, that gorgeous new negligee she'd been cutting down on cabs to pay for.

"YOU'RE HOLDING a ticket for Christie Lambert?" she asked the woman behind the American desk.

"I'll just check."

Christie surreptitiously glanced around once more. Still no sign of David. She'd expected to find him waiting for her at the counter. But maybe he was going to join her in the departure lounge.

He was certainly playing his cards close to the vest. Every night when he'd called, she'd waited for him to drop a clue about their destination. But he hadn't.

And every night she'd bitten her tongue, determined not to try to wheedle it out of him like a curious child. Wherever they were heading, she'd play the game every bit as coolly as David was—act as if flying south for a weekend was something she did regularly.

"Here we are, Ms Lambert. And you just have that one case?"

Christie nodded and passed it over. The agent took about two hours putting a destination tag on it.

YYZ. Christie read the tag as her suitcase started along the conveyer. The letters looked vaguely familiar but—

"And would you like a window seat, Ms Lambert?"

She paused uncertainly. If David was going to be flying with her, why hadn't he preselected two seats together? But maybe he'd set something up with this woman. Maybe her question about the seat was simply part of a game to keep Ms Lambert guessing.

"Would you like a window seat?" the agent repeated.

"Thanks. That would be fine." But what she'd really like was to know which airport YYZ was the code for. Which city was she going to?

Her ticket was lying open. She stared at it, trying to read the destination while the woman typed away at her computer keys. Not only was the print too small to see clearly, it was also upside down.

"All set, then," the agent offered, tucking a boarding pass into the ticket folder. "The plane will be boarding at gate C in...oh, forty-five minutes. Enjoy your flight with American."

"Thank you." Christie took the folder, her fingers itching to open it, her brain reminding her that she was going to play this cool.

"Oh, Ms Lambert?"

She looked back at the agent.

"Sorry. I almost forgot to give you this. Whoever made up your ticket left a message for you."

"Thanks." She reached for the envelope and glanced around a final time, still not seeing David. But he just might be lurking nearby, watching for her reaction when she checked the ticket.

Be cool, she reminded herself, putting on her best poker face. She walked over to a wall, opened the folder...and stared in disbelief at the ticket.

Toronto? A ticket to Toronto? Not a trip to some romantic Caribbean island, but a jaunt to the city with the killer customs?

She tore the envelope open and read the message:

I'm in Toronto already. I'll meet your flight.

Love, David

Damn it! Damn it to hell! Of all the presumptuous gall!

It was one thing for David to cheat on their deal and not come to Manhattan if he had a fantastic alternative in mind. But not coming here and expecting her to go to Toronto wasn't fair at all.

She wasn't going. She darn well wasn't going. Let him meet the plane without her on it. And when he phoned to find out why she wasn't there, she'd remind him of their bargain, suggest he catch the next flight to New York—where he was supposed to be.

Well...well, on second thought, maybe that wasn't the best idea in the world. What if he couldn't get a flight tonight? Then she wouldn't see him until to-morrow....

Maybe she'd better go. But when she got there, she'd give him a major piece of her mind.

CHRISTIE WAITED anxiously on line, staring ahead at the sign reading, Please Wait at the Red Line/Veuil-lez Attendre a la Ligne Rouge. She felt a distinct sense of déjà vu, certain of what was going to happen next.

She'd wait at the red line until the young man standing in the little checkpoint box waved her for-ward. He'd look at her birth certificate, ask her a few questions, then hand her a card.

Everyone else's card would let them sail merrily on out once they'd collected their luggage. But her card would have an evil code on it that would mean she and her suitcase were in for another round with Canada Customs.

She gritted her teeth as the last person in front of her proceeded forward. And then she saw someone wav-ing at her from a glassed-in office on the far side of the checkpoint.

David! David was right there! But how could she be overjoyed to see him when she was so angry at him?

The young man motioned her forward and asked her the routine questions. She mumbled her way through the answers, her eyes flickering back to Da-vid as she spoke. He was coming out of the of-fice...was walking toward her, a giant grin on his face.

"Have a nice day, ma'am."

The young man's words drew her attention back to him. *Have a nice day.* Right. She'd heard that one the last time through.

Then, suddenly, David was folding her into his arms and kissing her...and she could scarcely even remember her name let alone why she was angry at him.

"Come on," he murmured, leading her along a corridor. "Let's find your luggage and get the hell out of here so I can kiss you properly."

"But what are you doing here, David? I mean, how did you get on this side of the customs area? How did you get to wait in that office?"

He grinned at her again. "I said I was a doctor and was meeting a woman who had a terrible phobia about flying. And they...well, I think they somehow got the impression I was a psychiatrist and that they might be wise to let me stick around."

"David, I don't have a terrible phobia about flying. I have a terrible phobia about Toronto." Aha! She remembered why she was angry at him. "Which brings me to the question of what the hell we're doing here instead of being in New York. Well?" she demanded when he didn't answer.

"We're looking at a compromise."

"We're what?"

"Your luggage will be coming down here," David offered, stopping in front of a carousel.

"We're looking at what?"

"A compromise. After you left Winnipeg, I realized I have trouble thinking when you're around, Christie. There we were, debating the merits of New York versus Winnipeg until we were blue in the face. But we'd fallen into the trap of linear thinking—we were so focused on A and B that we weren't even considering living in C or D or XYZ."

"Or YYZ, you mean."

":Pardon?"

"Never mind. David, you don't seem to think very straight when I'm *not* around, either. I don't want to consider living in Toronto. I hate Toronto."

"No, you don't, Christie. You've never seen an inch of it beyond this airport. All you hate is the customs check. And you probably only hate one particular customs officer, at that."

"But I don't—"

":That your case?" David interrupted, pointing at the carousel.

:"Yes."

"Good. Then let's get going," he suggested, grabbing it with one hand and her arm with the other.

"David, this is damn high-handed of you! I don't—"

"Your card, ma'am?"

Christie stared at the customs officer. Here she went again.

The man took her card and barely glanced at it before he focused on the people behind them. David propelled her through the exit into the main area of the terminal.

"I wouldn't have been so damn high-handed if you weren't so damn stubborn," he muttered as they walked.

"I'm not stubborn. It's my father who's stubborn, not me."

"Oh? Well, if I'd told you I wanted you to meet me in Toronto, you wouldn't have come. Right?"

"Well . . ."

"Right. You know I'm right. You'd have fussed and fumed and told me that Toronto was your least favorite city in the world and I'd have ended up in New York for the weekend."

"But you deliberately misled me, David. That really makes me angry. The weather will be warm, you said. Bring your bathing suit, you told me."

"The weather *is* warm. Toronto's climate is every bit as mild as Manhattan's. And my brother has a house with a heated pool—which he's opening a little early this year, in your honor. Look, Christie, all I want you to do is have a look around. Toronto isn't New York, but it isn't Winnipeg, either. It's kind of halfway between—both size-wise and geographically."

"But, David, Toronto would make less sense than either Winnipeg *or* New York. There's your job and my job and our families and friends and instead of only one of us giving up things we'd both be and—"

"Christie, let's just set all those considerations aside for the moment and look at Toronto, okay?"

"Well...okay," she agreed. She could hardly not agree. Despite what David thought, she wasn't a stubborn woman.

He bundled her into an airport limousine, told the driver they were going to the King Edward, then wrapped his arm around her shoulder and kissed her gently on the cheek. "I want you to concentrate on the city on our way downtown. Then, when we get to the hotel, I want you to concentrate on me."

She couldn't help smiling. There was nothing she liked better than concentrating on David Lawrence.

Obediently she stared through the window as the limo pulled onto a highway—a serious, multilane freeway with heavy traffic.

"How big is Toronto, David?"

"Three million or so."

"Oh." Well, yes. It would have to be. Beyond the freeway, buildings stretched as far as she could see.

The driver turned onto an exit that led to another highway.

"This is the 427," David offered. "We're heading south now, toward the lake."

The lake. Right. Geography wasn't her specialty, but she did know that Toronto was on Lake Ontario. Well . . . living by one of the Great Lakes had to be a bonus. In New York people practically killed for apartments that afforded even a glimpse of river.

She continued to stare out. Three million. That . . . that sounded like a reasonable size.

"Look over there," David told her, pointing to the left. "That's downtown in the distance. See the CN Tower? It's the tall, needlelike structure sticking up above the skyscrapers."

She nodded. Skyscrapers. A whole lot of skyscrapers . . . just like home.

They raced along until the 427 curved into another highway—this one running east and west. The city center lay ahead of them now. A few miles farther the highway became a raised expressway and the lake appeared below them on their right—dotted with sailboats, Windsurfers and catamarans skimming across the water, their brightly colored sails taut against the wind. Ahead, the CN Tower had grown taller than the Empire State Building.

"What's that?" she asked, pointing at an immense, shiny white, circular structure at the base of the tower.

"That's the SkyDome. The Blue Jays play there."

"It's . . . it's certainly more impressive than Yankee Stadium."

David grinned. "Christie, this is going to work. I promise you. This is our solution. Toronto has restaurants and galleries galore—really good ones. And all kinds of theater. A lot of plays come here either right before or right after they're on Broadway. And the winters are mild, Christie. Honest. And with my brother here we wouldn't be starting out not knowing a soul. And we'd only be ninety minutes from New York. You could easily visit your friends there. We could go down any weekend we liked. And we'd only be a couple of hours from Winnipeg—from your father and my mother. And the naturopathy college is here. You could take whatever courses you'd need for licensing. And—"

"And what about you, David?" Christie held her breath, waiting for his answer. Maybe this city really was a possibility. Of course, maybe it wasn't. All she'd seen so far were highways and the exteriors of buildings. But if David wasn't exaggerating, if there actually were good galleries and theaters and restaurants . . . and if he'd be happy here . . .

But what if she hated Toronto? Or what if she liked it and David couldn't find a position he wanted here? Or what if there was a catch he hadn't mentioned yet?

She was so excited about the possibility that the two of them just might be able to be together in a place they both liked that she was terrified the old mysterious power was about to zap them with an insurmountable obstacle. She wasn't certain, but she thought she could even hear it—and it was chuckling evilly.

"Well . . . I didn't just fly here today, Christie. I've been in Toronto since Tuesday night."

"You were phoning me from here and you didn't tell me?"

"And give you a chance to argue about coming? No way. But, at any rate, I've been talking to people that I met at a medical conference last year. They're doing the most fantastic research. They wrap an electrode-studded sock around the heart's exterior and insert an electrode-studded balloon into the heart and shock abnormalities out of action."

"David...David, socks and balloons? I don't quite understand what you're talking about but...but is that something that appeals to you?"

"Very much. It's a giant leap beyond the research I've been involved with in Winnipeg. It's as exciting as hell, Christie. Ever since I first talked with the fellows who are into it I've had the idea in the back of my mind that I'd like to join their team. But it would have meant moving to Toronto. And there was no other incentive to do that—not until now, that is."

Christie's excitement level had climbed so high that she could barely sit still. "And do you think you might be able to work with these fellows and—"

"There's no think about it, Christie. I've been offered a position at their hospital. I'd be doing research and patient care—and no administration. It sounds too good to be true."

"Oh, David! This entire idea sounds too good to be true." Oh, she *had* to like Toronto. She simply had to!

They pulled to a halt and she stared out. They had stopped in front of an extremely elegant-looking old hotel. On the other side of the limo a streetcar rumbled by. A streetcar...and this elegant old building. At first glance Toronto did seem to have style.

She looked back at David. "I got so carried away listening to you that I missed seeing half of the city."

"That doesn't matter. If you want to, you can spend the rest of your life seeing the city."

"Oh, David...let's start with the weekend...let me have a little taste before I say yes or no. But I have a feeling—woman's intuition, I guess—that I'm going to like it here."

"I thought you once told me," David teased, "that you were pretty weak in the intuition department."

"Well...well, I've always assumed I was. But this feeling I have now...well, you know my father's saying. Maybe I should never have assumed."

David drew her closer and kissed her the delicious way that only he could.

Her excitement level soared higher than the CN Tower. And the mysterious power's chuckle faded to nothingness.

Harlequin Superromance®

A June title
not to be missed....

Superromance author Judith Duncan has created her
most powerfully emotional novel yet, a book about
love too strong to forget and hate too painful to
remember....

Risen from the ashes of her past like a phoenix,
Sydney Foster knew too well the price of wisdom,
especially that gained in the underbelly of the city.
She'd sworn she'd never go back, but in order to
embrace a future with the man she loved, she had to
return to the streets...and settle an old score.

Once in a long while, you read a book that affects you
so strongly, you're never the same again. Harlequin is
proud to present such a book, STREETS OF FIRE by
Judith Duncan (Superromance #407). Her book merits
Harlequin's AWARD OF EXCELLENCE for June 1990,
conferred each month to one specially selected title.

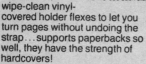

HARLEQUIN
American Romance®

THE LOVES OF A CENTURY...

Join American Romance in a nostalgic look back at the Twentieth Century—at the lives and loves of American men and women from the turn-of-the-century to the dawn of the year 2000.

Journey through the decades from the dance halls of the 1900s to the discos of the seventies ... from Glenn Miller to the Beatles ... from Valentino to Newman ... from corset to miniskirt ... from beau to Significant Other.

Relive the moments ... recapture the memories.

Look now for the CENTURY OF AMERICAN ROMANCE series in Harlequin American Romance. In one of the four American Romance titles appearing each month, for the next twelve months, we'll take you back to a decade of the Twentieth Century, where you'll relive the years and rekindle the romance of days gone by.

Don't miss a day of the CENTURY OF AMERICAN ROMANCE.

A CENTURY OF
AMERICAN ROMANCE
1900's

The women...the men...the passions...
the memories....

CAR-1